UNHOLY SANCTUARY

AN ELA OF SALISBURY MEDIEVAL MYSTERY

J. G. LEWIS

For the incredibly talented Madeleine Brolly, who has brought Ela and her circle to life so vividly and brilliantly in the audiobooks for the series.

ACKNOWLEDGMENTS

Many thanks to Madeleine Brolly, Betsy van der Hoek and Judith Tilden for their careful readings of the story and their helpful suggestions.

CHAPTER 1

S*alisbury, Wiltshire, July 1232*

"He dropped dead at the altar?" Ela Longespée, Countess of Salisbury, urged her horse Freya into a trot. She'd barely had time to break her fast this morning.

"At Matins service very early this morning. The lay brother hastened here in the dark to find me." Coroner Giles Haughton rode beside her on his bay palfrey. Wildflowers bloomed along the roadside and white clouds skittered across a pale blue sky. How did death stalk even the most perfect summer day?

"Was the deceased very old?"

"Not even two score years, from the sound of it," said Haughton. "A man in his prime, with no known illnesses."

Ela glanced back at the lay brother, who rode silently behind them on a heavy horse more suited to pulling a cart. He'd pulled his cowl over his head as if he wished to disappear into it. "Brother Michael," she called. "Who sent you to fetch the coroner?"

"Our abbot, Father Augustine, my lady." The brother

sounded tired, as well he might after riding a long way at such an early hour. "He's sure it was murder."

"Any unexpected death suggests foul play," agreed Haughton. "Were there any physical signs to suggest how he was killed?"

"I don't know, Sir. I didn't see him. But the anchoress cried out a warning right before he fell."

"What did she say?"

The lay brother hesitated, heaving his black-clad bulk in his saddle. "I was in my bed when it happened. But I'm told she said 'Beware, Father Gilbert, beware!'" He cried it out with some emphasis. "As if she knew he was going to die."

~

THE CHURCH TOWER of Bradenstoke Priory rose above the treetops as they approached from the lane. Ela had been here on several occasions. The monastery had been founded by her great-grandfather, Walter of Salisbury, who had chosen life as a canon there after his wife's death. He and his wife were both buried there, as was Ela's father. She'd not visited recently, though, and didn't know the current prior.

They dismounted under the arch that led into the cloister and more lay brothers took their horses to the stables to rest. Father Augustine descended from his rooms directly over the gate and greeted them. He was a tall, pale man of about three score years, with wispy gray hair combed across the narrow, shiny pate in front of his tonsure.

"What exactly happened?" asked Ela.

"Dear Father Gilbert was in the middle of reciting the usual psalm, and had just finished uttering the line, "*Quoniam magnus Dominus, et laudabilis nimis; terribilis est super omnes deos,*" when he suddenly collapsed. Naturally, we all rushed toward him at once. I felt his pulse myself, and he was found to be quite dead."

"May we see the body?" asked Ela, after initial introductions. "Coroner Giles Haughton would like to examine it as soon as possible to determine the cause of death."

He ushered them into the cloister, but instead of turning right into the chapel, he took them into a small antechamber off the cloister, where the body lay wrapped in a linen winding sheet.

Ela's heart sank. "Why did you move the body? That greatly impedes our investigation."

Father Augustine looked shocked. "Should I have left him dead on the floor of our Lord's house?"

"Yes," said Haughton without hesitation. "It would help me greatly to know exactly how he fell. Now I'll have to rely on eyewitness accounts."

Father Augustine looked utterly uncontrite. "It seems a sacrilege to leave a brother in Christ lying sprawled on the floor in such a manner as angels are bearing him into the arms of our Lord."

"No doubt his soul has taken flight to Heaven," said Ela crisply, "But his body is now the subject of a possible murder investigation. We must undress him so the coroner can examine the body."

Nonplussed, Augustine stared at her as if she'd asked for the corpse to serve her a cup of ale.

Haughton stepped forward and plucked at the edge of the sheet. Without looking up, he muttered, "Countess Ela is the High Sheriff of Wiltshire and will naturally wish to see the body for herself."

"I see." Father Augustine viewed her down the considerable length of his nose. Ela already disliked the man. Did he have some reason to obfuscate the circumstances of the death?

"Tell us what you know about the dead man while the coroner examines him."

The tall priest winced slightly as Haughton pulled the linen sheet back to reveal the dead man's stark white face. "The deceased is Father Gilbert Berwick. I believe he is thirty-three years of age and has been at Bradenstoke for most of his adult life. I'm not sure what else there is to say about him."

"Has he been taken ill before?" asked Ela. Giles Haughton eased the winding sheet down over his shoulders and past his torso.

"Nothing beyond the usual ailments. He had an upset stomach two days ago, with vomiting and..." he glanced sideways at Ela.

"Diarrhea?" suggested Haughton, helpfully.

"Yes," said the prior, "So I covered for him during Matins and Prime, but he recovered without incident."

Father Gilbert had fine light brown hair that stuck out from his head in tufts now that the sheet was pulled away. Haughton lifted his eyelids to peer into his eyes, which were a watery blue. Ela crossed herself as a wave of sadness swept over her. The priest's kind face with its small features and youthful aspect filled her with a sense of lost promise.

"His pupils look normal for a dead man," muttered Haughton. Ela knew that dilated pupils were a common sign of belladonna poisoning.

The coroner lifted Father Gilbert's hands and studied the nails. They were the pale, unblemished hands of a man who handled the sacred host rather than a hoe or a plow. Haughton did keep a discreet fold of cloth over the man's private parts as he explored his lower limbs. His legs were almost hairless, with knobby knees that bore a darker, discolored area under the kneecap, suggesting he spent large amounts of time on his knees in prayer.

"He was a pious man?" asked Ela, hoping to stimulate Father Augustine into further revelations.

"He was a priest, my lady," said Augustine primly.

"It may surprise you to learn that not all men of the cloth follow the commandments of our Lord," said Ela. "But I have the impression that Father Gilbert was a man of true faith."

"Quite so, my lady," said Father Augustine.

Haughton looked at his feet, including their soles and between his toes. "He appears to have been in excellent health, my lady. I see no signs of an unnoticed heart defect or lingering traces of disease."

"What, then, made him fall dead at the altar this morning?" asked Ela.

"He was bewitched," said Father Augustine suddenly. "Cursed! We all heard the witch's prophecy ring in the air."

Ela tried to hide her surprise at his strange response. "Who is this witch you speak of?"

"The anchoress. Sister Alisande."

"And what exactly did she say?"

Father Augustine puffed up his chest, "You will die!" he exclaimed.

Ela frowned. "Those are not the words that the lay brother used to relate the incident to me."

"The lay brother was not in the chapel this morning."

"I'll need to speak to other witnesses who were there in the chapel." *And before you coach them on what to say.* "Please take me to another man or woman who was present when this happened."

"I'll go fetch one." He turned to leave, but Ela touched his arm to stop him. He snatched it back as if the very Whore of Babylon had seized him.

"I'll come with you," said Ela coldly. "Lead the way."

~

Father Augustine led her out into the cloister, where a young monk in a black robe was listlessly sweeping the stone walkway. "Brother Oswin, you were in the chapel for Matins this morning, were you not?"

The monk looked at him with sad brown eyes set in a flat face. "I was indeed, to my distress." He noticed Ela for the first time and stood up straighter. "My lady, I apologize. I was lost in my grief."

"I understand," said Ela softly. "I've come to ask what, if anything, you saw or heard before Father Gilbert collapsed at the altar."

"I already told her—" started Father Augustine.

Ela held up her hand to silence him. "Don't say another word unless I ask you to, Father Augustine. This is a murder investigation."

Brother Oswin blinked. "Father Gilbert had prepared the Host and was just about to raise it high when Sister Alisande cried out…." He frowned as if trying to remember. Had someone told him what to say?

"Cried out what?" asked Ela, trying to hide her impatience.

"'Oh no!' That's what I think she said. 'Oh no! Father Gilbert, have a care!'"

Ela glanced at Father Augustine. "Your accounts differ."

Father Augustine looked furious. "She said 'You will die!'"

Brother Oswin looked at him, visibly nervous.

"Which is it?" asked Haughton, who had followed them into the cloister. "Did he say 'have a care' or 'you will die'? The meaning is quite different."

Brother Oswin looked reluctant to argue with his superior. If they were both to spend the rest of their lives in this monastery, a difference of that sort could cast a shadow over the next few decades of his life.

"It was such a shock, my lady," said Brother Oswin. "Both

the anchoress crying out and then Father Gilbert dropping to the floor. My mind is all addled by it."

"Try to recreate the moment in your mind," said Haughton softly. "Visualize the scene, and try to remember the exact words she said."

Brother Oswin squeezed his eyes shut and drew in a breath. "Beware!" He opened his eyes. "She said 'Beware'. She let out a shriek as he fell."

"Father Augustine," said Ela. "Could you please fetch Sister Alisande? I wish to speak with her."

Father Augustine hesitated for a moment. Ela wondered if he was unwilling to leave Brother Oswin to exchange unguarded words with her and Haughton. "The anchoress does not leave her cell."

"What do you mean?"

"She's an anchoress. Do you know what that is?"

"I have some understanding, but perhaps not enough." As far as Ela knew, an anchoress was like a nun, but not attached to any particular order—rather attached to a particular spiritual place.

"She lives in a cell that's attached directly to the chapel. I'm sure you've noticed it."

"I can't say I have."

"It was built for her, decades ago, when she first committed her life to worshipping God here at Bradenstoke Abbey."

"But Bradenstoke is an order of Augustinian canons. Male canons. How is a woman here at all?"

"I'm not entirely sure, my lady. Her occupancy of the cell predates the memory of every man here. From my understanding, she was given last rites before being walled up in her little room. An anchoress does not leave it for any reason. Which is why it might be difficult to bring her to you."

"Do you mean she hasn't left her cell in decades?"

He licked his lips awkwardly. "She has left it at least once. She was ill and in the infirmary last year. She was given last rites again as we thought she would die of her illness, but she recovered and returned to her cell. Still, she won't leave it lightly."

"Then I shall go to her in it."

~

FATHER AUGUSTINE LED her into the chapel and directly across the nave. They passed through a colonnade on the far side and approached a small unglazed window in the stone wall.

"We speak to her through this window," said Father Augustine.

Ela moved close to the window so she could see in. The cell was tiny, perhaps eight feet by eight feet, with stone walls, a stone floor, and a plaster ceiling. Inside, she could see a tiny woman kneeling at a crude prie-dieu. Her dark habit almost swallowed her. The thin skin stretched over her pale face suggested great age.

The old woman turned and her light-blue eyes gazed calmly at Ela.

Father Augustine cleared his throat. "Here's the witch, my lady. Have a care."

Ela found it odd that he parroted Brother Oswin's original account of her speech. "I'd like to speak to Sister Alisande alone."

"I don't think that's advisable, my lady," said Father Augustine with stern authority.

"Oh, and why is that?" she said, deliberately obtuse.

"She has hexed and murdered a dearly loved member of our order!" the priest's eyes bulged.

"Father Augustine, witches are the stuff of folklore and ignorant suspicion. Do you believe in fairies and goblins as well? Please leave us."

Father Augustine made a harrumphing noise and shuffled off back through across the collonade and into the main part of the nave. Once he was out of earshot, Ela looked back at the anchoress, who appeared to have resumed her prayers.

"I need to talk to you," she said. "About the matter of Father Gilbert's death. Please tell me your full name, age, and anything else I should know about you."

"I'm Sister Alisande," she said in a tiny voice that barely stirred the air. "Sir Robert Marshal was my father's name. I came here to Bradenstoke when I was sixteen and I've been here ever since."

"How old are you now?"

"I'm not sure, my lady. I've lost count of all the winters and springs I've seen."

"Was your father related to the Earls of Pembroke? To Sir William Marshal, who served Henry II, Richard and King John as well as our current king?"

"Yes."

This pleased Ela. Being a member of such a distinguished noble family would provide a measure of protection for Sister Alisande. "Why would Father Augustine have formed the idea that you are a witch?"

"It's because I have the sight," said Sister Alisande in her tiny, reedy voice.

"What do you mean?"

"I can see things that others don't. Sometimes I see things that happened in the past, and in this case I saw something that was about to happen."

Ela's heart sank. "You had a premonition that something was about to happen to Father Gilbert?"

"I saw that he would drop dead, yes." Her bright eyes

looked at Ela with a childlike simplicity. Obviously, the poor old woman's mind was addled by her great age.

"Such a thing is impossible. You must have imagined it."

Sister Alisande smiled a placid smile. "That's what they all say. I don't know how I knew that he would die, just that I did."

"You don't seem very disturbed by it." The elderly nun's beatific expression was jarring under the circumstances.

"Dear Father Gilbert is with our Lord now. If envy wasn't a sin I would envy him."

"I see. So you have experienced instances like this before, where you have seen into the future?"

"Yes, but usually I have the good sense to keep the visions to myself. I spend my time alone in my cell, with my prayer-book. I can watch all the holy services and take communion during Mass. I always pay close attention during services, so naturally, I was watching when Father Gilbert raised the host into the air. I was caught by surprise and cried out in alarm when I saw poor Father Gilbert collapse."

"When you saw him collapse in your mind?" Ela frowned, trying to puzzle this out. "But before he collapsed in body, before the assembled worshipers?"

"Yes, my lady."

"Father Augustine seems to think that you put a curse on Father Gilbert." She felt guilty for even putting such nonsense into words.

"I did no such thing."

"Why would he suspect that you did?"

"Fear of the unknown, I suspect." Her soft voice made her hard to hear. Her whole person weightless as a dandelion puff. She still knelt at her prie-dieu, her body swallowed in her black robe.

"Why would he be afraid of you?"

"Perhaps he thinks I know too much." Sister Alisande's pale eyes took on a faraway look.

"And do you?"

Sister Alisande's birdlike chest rose and fell beneath her habit. "Too much for some."

"Do you have any reason to wish Father Gilbert dead?"

"Oh dear me, no. Father Gilbert was a good and kind man. I shall miss his benedictions."

Ela's eyes had adjusted to the dim light of the cell, and lighted upon a bird's nest high up near the small opening. "Do you know of anyone else who might wish harm to Father Gilbert?"

"I should hope not. I've learned to mind my own business." She pressed her thin lips together, wrinkling her upper lip.

This response struck Ela as evasive. "I am the sheriff of Wiltshire and I must ask you not to conceal any information from me that might help explain Father Gilbert's mysterious death."

"If I knew anything I would be sure to tell you," said Sister Alisande, sweetly. "I shall pray for his soul."

Father Augustine returned with four lay brothers who would apparently guard Sister Alisande to prevent her from killing again. Once they were out of earshot of the anchoress, the prior persisted with his suspicions.

"How would Sister Alisande know that Father Gilbert was about to drop dead unless she'd witched him?"

"Do you mean, unless she poisoned him?" asked Ela. "It seems likely that he was poisoned since he bears no wounds and suffered no known ailments. Since Sister Alisande never leaves her cell, she has no access to poison or the means to administer it."

"A witch has no need of poison," spat Father Augustine. "She probably cast a spell on him. She's always muttering nonsense. I should have paid more attention but until now I saw it as the harmless babbling of one in her dotage."

"That is exactly how I see it," said Ela. "I don't suspect her of any involvement in Father Gilbert's death."

"She must be tried, my lady," said another man. A squat friar with a shiny bald dome atop a thick fringe of brown hair. "Tried by a jury."

"I don't think that's necessary," said Ela. "Is there anyone else here who might have enmity toward Father Gilbert?"

"No one," said Father Augustine.

"And why would you suspect Sister Alisande of harming him?"

"Because she's a witch! She showed her powers. Powers granted by the devil himself, I'm sure."

Ela glanced at Haughton, who stood quietly nearby. "Perhaps we should bring Sister Alisande back to the castle with us." Father Augustine's hostility made her fear for the elderly nun's safety. If nothing else they might try to perform an exorcism and frighten or hurt her.

"I see no harm in that," said Haughton gruffly. "And it will give her a chance to tell us everything she knows about the people here."

Ela half expected the prior to protest that an anchoress cannot be removed from her spiritual home, but instead he said, "As you wish," with a rather cheerful expression.

"I do wish," said Ela. "I'm sure she has a lot of tales to tell. But first I would like to see Father Gilbert's private chamber."

CHAPTER 2

Father Gilbert's cell in the presbytery was barely large enough to hold a narrow bed and a prie-dieu. The only window was high in the wall and revealed a sliver of pale blue sky. Ela peered under the bed looking for a chest with his possessions or a folded robe or some parchment and ink, but found only a small spiderweb, with a busy spider trimming its hem.

"Where are his things?" asked Ela.

"Residents to the monastery part with all worldly goods," said Michael, the tired lay brother who'd led them from Salisbury to Bradenstoke and now to Father Gilbert's room.

"He has no spare robe, or a cloak?"

"According to the rule of the order they are kept in a shared store and distributed among us at the start of each season." Ela knew this was normal for monks and nuns as a way to chastise vanity and maintain humility, but priests often enjoyed a few more small luxuries.

"He has no drinking cup for water or comb for his hair?"

"Those items are shared, my lady." Michael wore a robe worn almost to the point of raggedness. "Now, Father

Augustine is not quite so austere and does keep a few small personal items, but Father Gilbert was unflinching in his adherence to the rule of the order. The only item he kept from his former life was this prayer book that his parents gave him when he joined us. He showed it to me on occasion. It was copied and illustrated in France and is a book of surprising beauty. I wonder what will happen to it now that he has died."

Ela's eyes rested on the small prayer book. She approached the prie-dieu and turned a few of the pages with a fingertip. Delicate black and red script covered each page, along with small drawings that ornamented the margins on some pages.

"It's very dusty. It looks like he didn't use it much."

"Oh, he used it daily, my lady," said the lay brother. "Sometimes several times a day. I apologize for the dust. It was my duty to keep his room clean and perhaps my efforts have been lacking."

Ela decided not to mention the spider under the bed. "I don't see anything else in here to examine. I suppose the book might be returned to his family as a memento to remember him by."

The lay brother's face creased into a grimace. "I'm not sure Father Augustine will agree with that. He's collecting quite a library."

"I am aware of the book collection here. My own family has contributed to building it. I would appreciate the book remaining here until Father Gilbert's family can be contacted about his death. Do they live very far away?"

"I believe they are from somewhere north of here, my lady."

"Then I'll take it with me for safekeeping. I shall write to ask them if they wish to make a gift of it to the monastery."

She looked at Giles Haughton. "Would it fit in your scrip, do you think?"

"Yes, my lady." He stepped forward and closed the book, then tucked it into the leather bag that sat at his hip. He looked up at Michael, the lay brother. "And please don't touch anything in this room. We may need to examine it further. For now, we shall return to Salisbury."

"It's a long ride to make twice in one day," said Brother Michael, "speaking from experience. Do let me bring you a cup of ale and some sweet cakes before you leave."

Thinking more of Giles Haughton than herself, Ela agreed, and they ate the hasty repast before retrieving sister Alisande from her cell next to the chapel.

ALISANDE'S modest hermitage had no door for a person to pass through. There was a window to the outside, and a path leading to a back door into the presbytery. Below the window was a wooden door large enough to admit a chamberpot, which was apparently passed through it daily, along with her bowls of porridge and cups of small ale and any necessary clothing.

It was lucky sister Alisande's person was so slight, as this door was the only means for her to exit the room without removing stones from the wall. Ela could hardly believe she'd fit through it, but she eased herself out with surprising agility for one so old. Ela was forced to reflect that if she wanted to, Sister Alisande was quite capable of quitting her tiny cell and wandering around the abbey in the dark hours when the rest of the clerics and lay brothers were asleep.

Alisande sat atop one of the guard's horses while he led it from the ground. She stared in amazement at the scenery along the roads on the ride back to the castle. Dog roses still bloomed in the hedgerows, filling the air with their sweet scent. Sheep grazed peacefully on the hillsides and a string of red and white cows passed them on their way to their evening milking.

"I haven't left the walls of Bradenstoke since I entered them," she said. "I feel as if I've ascended to the Kingdom of Heaven!"

Rays of late afternoon sun brushed the castle walls with gold as they approached. Sister Alisande crossed herself as if she might indeed be about to pass the threshold into God's kingdom.

"I'm afraid you might be in for a shock," said Ela. "My castle houses the king's garrison and is thus full of rowdy soldiers."

"My father's castle was much the same," said Alisande, with a look of eager anticipation. Her tiny voice seemed to be growing louder. "Though I hope I shall not be much in the way. All I need is a small corner where I can kneel and pray."

"We shall find a private chamber for you," assured Ela. "And you may attend Mass and all the Hours in our chapel if you choose to."

"I'm not sure I shall dare leave my room. We all suffered such a terrible shock this morning when Father Gilbert fell dead."

"Indeed. We shall make you as safe and secure as can be."

In the castle courtyard, a guard helped Sister Alisande down from her horse. She watched the bustle of servants and tradespeople and garrison soldiers with wide-eyed wonder. Her tiny frame seemed to shrink from the throng of people rushing into and out of the castle.

Ela sent a servant to fetch Petronella, whom she would

appoint as Sister Alisande's guide and guardian. Her daughter dreamed of little but becoming a nun herself and could both give and receive comfort from this elderly nun who'd spent her whole life in a cloister.

After Petronella had spirited Alisande away, Ela turned to Giles Haughton. They stood in the great archway right outside the castle doors. "She will have to appear before the jury."

"Yes, but not until after I examine the body in the mortuary."

"What kind of poison was used, in your opinion?"

"I saw no signs of poisoning. The eyes, the gums, the mucous membranes all looked normal."

Ela frowned. "Then what killed him, in your estimation?"

He shrugged. "I pray that I'll uncover a clue tomorrow in the light. Otherwise, a hex from a witch might seem the most likely scenario."

"You can't be serious." It could sometimes be difficult to tell when Haughton was joking.

"Indeed I am not. But there are no clear signs of trauma or illness or asphyxiation, either. As of this moment, only the Lord knows why he called Father Gilbert to his side."

"I'll attend you in the mortuary after Prime tomorrow."

ELA MADE her rounds of the castle, then attended Prime service. She sent her maid Elsie to Alisande's room with a light breakfast of fruit and oatcakes and partook of the same herself. Thus she was relatively fortified by the time she arrived in the mortuary—which was lucky as Giles Haughton had taken the opportunity to flay poor Father Gilbert's chest quite open.

Ela's hand rushed to her mouth at the sight despite her best efforts to act like a sheriff, not a startled child.

"Good day, my lady," said Haughton cheerfully, up to his wrists in the dead man's torso. "I'm afraid I can find no signs of mechanical dysfunction or disease. Nor yet of injury, accidental or otherwise. His heart is the plump organ of a young man in good health. His humors appear balanced and his intestines functional."

"The contents of his stomach?" inquired Ela, praying that the contents of her own stomach would remain where they were.

"Ah." Haughton now plunged his hands and arms into a copper bowl of water and wiped them on a clean square of linen. "His stomach was quite empty, as one might expect it to be at the hour of Matins—in the dead of night—but his lower intestines show traces of a meal that I'll attempt to examine for traces of poison. I have yet to examine his liver and kidneys."

"I confess that I hope you find a cause for his death, or Sister Alisande's life may well be in jeopardy." The nun was already a great age, but losing her life wouldn't be the worst part of her fate if she were to be hanged as a murderer. Since she hailed from a distinguished noble family, her accusal and conviction of witchcraft could bring shame to their name and hers for many generations to come.

"In the meantime, we've learned that he didn't die of any observable natural cause. If Sister Alisande didn't kill him, then someone else did," said Haughton, tossing the soiled cloth in a basket.

"Let's talk to her in private before I call for a jury. She's so meek and soft-spoken that I fear for her at the hands of the men of the hundred."

"She's an elderly nun, surely they'll be gentle with her." Haughton drew a thick linen cloth over the body.

Ela let out a breath she didn't realize she'd been holding. "I wish I could believe that. You'd think that sensible farmers and men of business would know better than to believe in such nonsense as witchcraft, but mystery and the unknown bring out the worst in people."

HAUGHTON AND ELA climbed up the tower stairs to the highest level, where Alisande had been installed in a small chamber away from the bustle of the hall. A guard stood watch outside the door since she was ostensibly a prisoner of sorts, being at least nominally under suspicion of having killed Father Gilbert by some mysterious means.

Ela knocked softly on the door. "Sister Alisande, it's Countess Ela." She heard some rustling behind the door, then it opened slowly to reveal the diminutive nun. "Giles Haughton and I would like to interview you in your room."

Sister Alisande stepped aside to let them enter. The small room, with its plastered walls, narrow bed, and plain wood prie-dieu, looked like a nun's cell, and Ela hoped she felt at home here under these trying circumstances. "Were you able to sleep?"

"Yes, thank you, my lady. I slept like a babe in its mother's arms." The nun's peaceful demeanor and kind gaze looked entirely genuine. How could anyone think that this woman was doing the devil's work?

"Has such a thing ever happened before?" she asked. "Where someone fell sick or dead and you were blamed?"

"Not for a very long time, my lady." Sister Alisande regarded her with a serene expression.

"What happened the last time?"

"Goodness, it's so long ago I hardly recall." Ela waited for her to remember, but Sister Alisande just stood there with her peaceful gaze beaming on Ela and Haughton.

"Try your best to think back to that time. Did someone die?"

"Brother Paulinus, it was. He fell dead in the vegetable patch while he was pulling a fistful of beets from the ground."

"And you were blamed for this?"

"Not blamed, exactly, but I saw his death in my mind before he fell and cried out right before it happened, even though I was in my cell by the chapel, and he was in the vegetable rows on the other side of the cloister. The priests did find that unsettling."

"I think almost anyone would find that disturbing. Did it worry you?"

"I took it as a vision from God."

Ela glanced at Haughton, then back at Sister Alisande. "That is a dreadful vision, to be sure. Have there been others?"

"Oh yes." Again, Sister Alisande stood quietly as if her affirmation was answer enough. "I've seen the Kingdom of Heaven."

"What did it look like?" asked Ela, out of curiosity as much as scientific inquiry.

"There were angels everywhere, my lady. Hordes of angels."

"With wings?"

A smile creased her face. "Of course, my lady! They wouldn't be angels without wings, now, would they?"

The woman's wits are departing her. Sister Alisande's apparent lack of concern about her own unnatural second sight suggested that all by itself.

"Was Brother Paulinus murdered?"

"I don't think so, my lady. He was old and rather fat and they said his heart probably gave out."

"So why would you escape blame for that death, but now everyone thinks you were somehow involved in Father Gilbert's demise?"

"I think it might be because of what happened with Sister Ermentrude."

Again, Ela glanced at Haughton.

He jumped in. "What did happen to Sister Ermentrude?"

"Well," Alisande wove her gnarled hands together. "Sister Ermentrude was a widowed lady who came to live in a cottage at Bradenstoke when her son took over the family estates. Her son paid a sum to the abbey that she would be provided with her daily bread and ale. She wasn't used to a quiet life and liked to stir up gossip and intrigue. One day she visited my cell to complain as usual and I warned her that wagging her tongue would invite censure from the Lord. She wouldn't listen! The very next day she was haranguing the cook over the contents of a stew…and she was struck dumb."

"She may have been seized with apoplexy," said Haughton. "That can deprive one of speech with sudden force and no outward sign of injury."

"I don't know what caused her to be deprived of words, sir. And I didn't see it happen. I do know that people in the monastery began to believe I had hidden powers that I had used for ill."

"That sounds like bad luck," said Haughton." And I can't imagine that there's much to gossip about in a monastery."

"You would think, my lady, but some great lords and ladies come to Bradenstoke to make their peace with the Lord and perhaps the priests' ears are burning with the confessions they hear."

Ela's ears pricked up. "Would Father Gilbert have been privy to these confessions?"

"Oh, yes, my lady. And Father Augustine and Father Sebastian."

"Have any of these great lords and ladies—whose exploits might cause a priest to blanch—been to Bradenstoke recently?"

"It's not my business to spread gossip. The Lord frowns on loose tongues."

"He does, Sister Alisande," said Ela, "but the jury of the hundred relies on eyewitness accounts and inside information to find and convict criminals so they don't go unpunished."

"My mind is quite addled by so much upset. I shall pray upon your question."

~

ELA AND HAUGHTON walked back downstairs together. "Is there any way to tell whether someone has died of apoplexy?" she asked. "If you examine their brain?"

"If it produces bleeding in the brain, that might be visible on examination."

"Is there any age limit on who can suffer such an injury?"

"While it can, in theory, happen at any age, it would be highly unusual in a man so young and healthy as Father Gilbert. Still, I shall endeavor to saw into his skull and do a thorough investigation of its structures."

Ela shuddered. "Your expertise and erudition are a blessing to us. Let me know what you learn. I fear for Sister Alisande's safety if even those who've known her for her whole life are prone to suspect her of evil powers that cause harm."

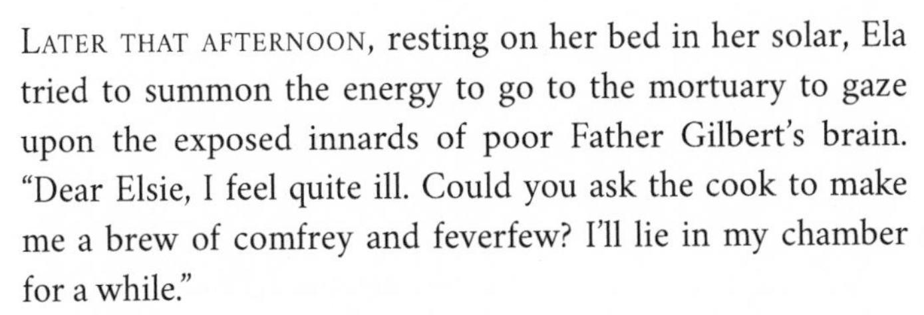

Later that afternoon, resting on her bed in her solar, Ela tried to summon the energy to go to the mortuary to gaze upon the exposed innards of poor Father Gilbert's brain. "Dear Elsie, I feel quite ill. Could you ask the cook to make me a brew of comfrey and feverfew? I'll lie in my chamber for a while."

She wanted to send the girl to the mortuary to tell Haughton that she wouldn't be coming, but she didn't want Elsie to be forced to lay eyes on the horrors within. "And could you fetch the guard from outside my door? I have a small errand for him."

Ela dispatched the guard to ask Haughton to visit her with any news he'd discovered from his examination of the body. She felt quite queasy and began to wonder if she'd be unable to eat her meal.

She had to be roused from a fitful sleep when the guard returned a short while later. "Begging your pardon, my lady, but the mortuary was locked and there was no sign of Sir Giles. Would you like me to take a message to his house?"

"Yes, please. Tell him I've been taken ill and for him to come see me to share any important findings."

She attempted—unsuccessfully—a sip of her tea and had just finished retching when the guard returned. "Sir Giles is taken ill as well, my lady. His wife came to the door and said he was sick in bed and couldn't come down."

"Oh dear. I suppose we must have both contracted the same ailment since we spent most of yesterday and today in each other's company. God willing it shall be a mild one." She turned to Elsie. "Could you please check on Sister Alisande? At her great age, even a small ailment can be quite serious, so I fear for her health."

"Yes, my lady. Shall I take her some tea?"

"That's a very good idea."

~

ELA FOUND herself unable to go down to dine that evening and also grateful for the proximity and privacy of the garderobe adjoining her chamber. She hadn't felt this ill in quite some time and hoped she hadn't passed the ailment on to any of her children.

"Sister Alisande is well," said Petronella cheerily, when she came in with a hand-sewn sachet filled with lavender to soothe Ela's senses. "And everyone else is as well. It's just you and Sir Giles that have been taken ill."

"That's a mercy, I suppose, partly because it will delay Sister Alisande's appearance before the jury."

"I can't believe anyone would think Sister Alisande a witch," exclaimed Petronella. "She's the gentlest soul I've ever met."

"She told me that there have been occasions—including Father Gilbert's death—where she saw a premonition of the event before it happened."

"Surely such a gift of prophecy could be seen as a blessing from God?"

"I suppose that depends on the circumstances. One man's blessing is another man's curse." Ela held the lavender sachet up to her nose. The loose woven fabric allowed the calming scent of the dried lavender to fill her senses and lift her spirits. "It was very thoughtful of you to bring this, Petronella. I'll have Elsie keep it among my linens when I recover."

"You're most welcome, mother. Should I make one for Sister Alisande as well, or do you suppose she would prefer to mortify her flesh?"

"I suggest that you ask her yourself."

Ela felt ill all night and most of the next day. She

attempted to rally for Compline service, but soon realized the error of her efforts and returned to her chamber without reaching the chapel. She sent Elsie to inquire after Giles Haughton and give him a bottle of Cook's freshly made tonic.

Elsie returned red-faced and panting. "He's very ill, my lady." She fussed over rearranging Ela's coverlet. "His wife wouldn't let me lay eyes on him but said she'd give him the tonic herself."

"His wife is well?"

"Yes, my lady. Though she seems quite worried. She says she's never seen him too sick to attend to his duties. He's quite eaten up that there's a body in the mortuary needing further attention and he's unable to finish his work on it."

"And his symptoms are the same as mine?"

"Yes, my lady. He's retching something awful, she says."

"Poor Giles. Oddly, no one else has been afflicted. Can you please send a messenger to Bradenstoke to see if anyone there has been taken ill? I don't mean to frighten you, but I'm not sure I've ever felt this sick before, absent a high fever."

"And you don't have a fever, my lady, do you?" Elsie cupped Ela's forehead in her hand.

"No, that's just it. I don't. It's odd."

"Should I send for the doctor?"

"If there's no improvement by tomorrow, you shall send for Doctor Goodwin, but until then I shall attempt to bear this ailment bravely."

CHAPTER 3

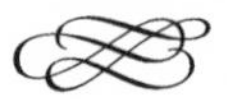

By the next morning, Ela felt well enough to rise for Prime service and take a tiny bit of breakfast in the hall. After resting for half the morning, she rose for Mass and consulted with her co-sheriff, John Dacus, who'd taken over her duties for the day.

She was just about to retreat to her solar for another rest when Giles Haughton entered the hall.

"What a sight for sore eyes," exclaimed Ela. He looked a little green around the gills—as she no doubt did herself—but at least he was upright.

But instead of his usual smile and cheery greeting, he strode over to her with a grim look on his face. "I fear I've discovered what made us so ill, my lady."

"Well, praise be to God we both seem to have recovered."

"But that's just it…" He rubbed a hand over his mouth, then lowered his voice. "If the affliction is the one I suspect, I'm afraid this may be a brief reprieve and we may both soon find ourselves on our way to join Father Gilbert in Heaven."

~

"Let us speak in the armory," said Ela. She didn't want her imminent death announced prematurely in the hall. They walked in silence past the throng of petitioners waiting to assail John Dacus with their petty grievances. The guard opened the door to the armory and she led him in.

The array of polished weapons shining on the walls could seem either reassuring or menacing, and today it was the latter. "Whatever do you mean by saying that we might join Father Gilbert?"

"Do you remember the dust in his prayerbook?"

"Yes, of course. It was enough dust that it spilled from the pages and left a pale shadow on the prie-dieu after you picked up the book."

"I suspect that dust is what killed Father Gilbert." He rubbed his mouth again. "And I picked up that book, put it in my bag, and brought it home."

"How would dust kill anyone?"

"When it's the dried and ground flesh of the deadly death cap mushroom." His dark eyes, usually filled with humor, were deadly serious. "I believe that someone deliberately sprinkled the powdered mushroom on Father Gilbert's prayerbook, knowing that he would leaf through the pages and be exposed to a fatal amount of the toxin."

"Even touching it can kill you?"

"As far as I know, you need to consume it, but eating even a very small amount can be dangerous. If he got it on his fingers and then ate a piece of bread with those same fingers, that could be enough to sicken him." He shook his head as if he wished he could shake off the idea. "You touched that book."

"I only turned a few pages."

"I picked it up and put it in my scrip. Then we both ate cake with our unwashed fingers."

Ela gasped. "Even that tiny amount could sicken us?"

"It's one of the deadliest poisons in the world. And hard to trace since its actions are delayed. It's been used as a murder weapon since ancient times."

Ela crossed herself. "But we are both recovered, praise God."

Haughton hesitated as if he didn't want to utter the words about to leave his lips. "The toxin in Death Cap mushroom has a strange quality in that it acts cruelly upon the liver and kidneys, destroying their natural function. Then, for reasons unknown to our doctors, the patient appears to rally and recover—only to be suddenly struck down, just as Father Gilbert was that fatal morning in the chapel at Bradenstoke."

"So you're saying that by this time tomorrow we may both be dead?"

"I would be remiss in my duties if I didn't warn you of that possibility, my lady."

"Dear God." Ela crossed herself again. "I'm not sure whether to call for last rites or to gather my children to my bosom. But I confess that I can't believe this entirely. I feel so much recovered as to be nearly normal."

"Your exposure was slight enough that your recovery is entirely possible. However, since you are a woman, and thus of smaller stature than Father Gilbert, it's also possible that you could succumb to a smaller amount."

"You are a strapping specimen of mankind, Sir Giles." She attempted to reassure him. "If anyone could recover from a brief exposure, it would be you."

"That is kind of you to say, my lady, and if your words were to reach God's ears I'd be most grateful for the reprieve."

"So Father Gilbert was poisoned."

"Most certainly. I took the risk of examining the mysterious dust and confirmed that—without any doubt—it is composed of dried and ground powder of Death Cap mushroom."

"How did you avoid further sickening yourself in the act of examining it?"

"I wore gloves to handle the book and washed my hands very carefully afterward. I also tied one of my wife's veils over my mouth and nose so I wouldn't breathe it in. I trust that while I did risk further exposure, it was very minimal. I've since sealed the contaminated book in a lead-lined box."

"So someone collected a mushroom from the wild, dried it and ground it with a pestle and mortar, then sprinkled it liberally in Father Gilbert's prayerbook."

"Then sat back and waited for him to sustain enough exposure to sicken and die."

"How would the killer handle the mushroom powder without injury to himself?"

"Since he knew the powder was fatal I presume he took precautions similar to my own."

"Now we need to discover who had access to Father Gilbert's prayerbook, or even to his chamber. Bradenstoke is a closed community."

"It may well be someone within the community," said Haughton. "Or a trusted visitor. We must warn them at once not to enter or disturb Father Gilbert's chamber. It must be cleaned with great care by someone who is very scrupulous in washing himself afterward."

"You did tell lay brother Michael to leave the room alone. Still, that might not prevent him from dusting it. I'll send a messenger at once to tell them to seal the room. I shall also visit Alisande and see what insights she has to share." Ela drew in a shaky breath. "And in the meantime, I suppose we should set our affairs in order in case this is but a brief respite from our illness. If the poison were to have done its worst…" She paused, unable to wrap her mind around the possibility that she could be dead within days.

"If it has wreaked havoc upon our liver and kidneys, I fear we have but two days left to make our peace with God."

Ela felt faint at the prospect. Blackness even gathered at the corner of her eyes and she realized she'd forgotten to breathe. Was the poison already working its cruel destruction on her internal organs?"

"Should I warn my children?"

"I can't tell you what to do in such a situation. I already told my wife there was a possibility she'd be a widow by Sunday but I don't think she believed me." The mischievous twinkle returned to his eyes. "Perhaps she's afraid to taste such freedom and the prospect of being a merry widow, only to have it cruelly snatched away."

"It cheers me to see you joking again. I don't think I've ever seen you so deadly serious."

"Unfortunately the poison of the death cap mushroom is deadly indeed. May God have mercy on us both."

Ela didn't want to frighten her youngest children with the prospect of her imminent death, and she worried the news would send her teenage sons into a panic. But she decided to confide in Petronella.

She called her daughter into her solar, sent Elsie to the market on a complex errand, and closed the door. "Petronella, I've called you here because you are my most trusted confidante and I know you to be strong and steady to an unusual degree for one so young."

Petronella looked rather taken aback at the compliment. "I strive to do my duty to God, mother, and not be a nuisance."

"Indeed. And I know you have a close relationship with our Lord and no fear of his Heavenly Kingdom."

Petronella now started to look alarmed. "I pray for the souls of the departed that they may rest in grace. I chastise myself daily for my sins of thought, word and deed—"

"Giles Haughton tells me that he and I have inadvertently partaken of poison and that it may yet kill us both."

Petronella stared at her for a moment, then crossed herself. "God forbid, Mother. You had but a brief illness! It was nothing. You'll live many years, yet."

"God willing, I shall, but the course of this poison allows its sufferers a brief reprieve before their death, so it's also possible that I might not wake up tomorrow. Naturally, I'll hope and pray that this is not the case, but I felt the need to tell someone in the household so that my demise will not be an utter shock to all and a mystery as well."

Her daughter's expression hardened. "Who fed you poison? I'll see that they hang."

"The poison was intended for Father Gilbert and did indeed kill him. He ingested a deadly mushroom powder that was sprinkled on the pages of his prayer book. I touched the book myself only briefly, so my exposure was very small."

"But that's what made you so ill yesterday?"

"I believe so. I had no fever, which you would normally expect in such a swift and intense illness. I'm torn on whether to tell Richard and Stephen."

"Don't tell them, mother. If you are to die, they will be crushed by grief soon enough. Let them not suffer the not-knowing as well. I'll tell them everything should the need arise. And I shall pray constantly and fervently for your full recovery."

"And that of Giles Haughton, whom I treasure as a friend as well as a trusted coroner."

"Indeed, yes." Petronella's lip almost quivered, but she held it steady.

"I'm sorry to lay such a heavy burden on you, but I don't want the news to spread abroad until it can no longer be contained. My will was revised on your father's death, so I need not call urgently for a lawyer. I do hope that you'll endeavor to help your brother William navigate the role of Earl before you retreat to the peace of the cloister."

"I promise you, Mother, I shall." Her earnest expression touched Ela's heart. Her daughter's craving for monastic seclusion had been a point of contention between them, but in recent years Petronella had shown maturity and patience that warmed Ela's heart.

On instinct, Ela clutched Petronella to her bosom. Her daughter stiffened slightly in her clutches but patiently submitted to her embrace. Ela pulled back, with tears in her eyes. "We're not a family given to displays of affection, but I do love you with all my heart and I trust that we will meet again in Heaven one day."

"Mother! You're not dead yet." Petronella's face had turned pale and Ela could see emotions roiling beneath its surface. "I quite understand if you're not averse to hurrying to the halls of Heaven, but we need you here on Earth for a few more decades. The nunnery at Lacock will soon be finished and God may yet want you to serve him as a nun or even an abbess before you escape this earthly plane."

Ela laughed and wiped the tears from her eyes. "My sensible Petronella, you are so right. I shall endeavor to tuck my emotions back where they belong and demonstrate the fortitude that you are showing in this trying circumstance. In the meantime, I must speak with Sister Alisande about who might have had access to Father Gilbert's prayerbook."

~

Ela dispatched a guard to Bradenstoke, with strict instructions that Father Gilbert's chamber must be locked and left exactly as it was, with no cleaning or rearranging—by order of the sheriff.

She then climbed to Sister Alisande's chamber and found her on her knees in prayer. "I'm sorry to disturb you but I must speak to you urgently. We've learned that Father Gilbert was poisoned by a substance sprinkled in his prayer book."

Sister Alisande rose creakily to her feet. "I suspected as much."

"You knew it was his prayerbook?"

"No, but I thought he was poisoned."

"From your..." she hesitated to give credence to unearthly powers. "From your second sight?"

"No, because he was young and healthy. What else could have killed him but poison?"

"Why are the men of Bradenstoke so quick to suggest that he was felled by a spell that you put on him?"

Sister Alisande looked at her calmly. "Some of them will not countenance ideas that their minds are too small to understand."

"Are you capable of...of magic?" Ela felt embarrassed to even ask such a foolish question.

Sister Alisande regarded her with a level gaze. "Even you think I am a witch."

"I truly don't, but you must admit that it is eerie that you can see into the future."

"It's not as if I keep a scrying stone I can gaze into at will. I'm blessed—or cursed—with flashes of knowledge that I can't explain."

"I see. Does this unwelcome knowledge give you any insight into who might have poisoned Father Gilbert?"

Sister Alisande hesitated and a bouquet of wrinkles arranged themselves around her mouth. "I'm not sure."

Ela's heart started to beat faster. "I won't take what you say as the gospel truth, but if you have any idea....any idea at all, I'd be grateful if you'd share it with me so I can investigate."

Sister Alisande drew in a long, slow breath. "I hesitate to utter damning words when I have no proof..." She did hesitate, and for so long that Ela wondered if she'd ever start speaking again. "I can't be sure, but I believe Father Gilbert was murdered by the same man who murdered your husband, Sir William Longespée."

Ela felt her knees give way and she reached for the nearest wall. After she'd steadied herself on the plastered stone, she attempted to gather her thoughts. "What makes you think my husband was murdered? Most people believe that he died of a brief but severe illness."

"Do you believe that, my lady?" Sister Alisande's kind eyes softened as she asked the question.

Ela hesitated. Did she dare to trust the elderly nun with her darkest and most dangerous suspicions? No, she didn't. Sister Alisande was unpredictable and had yet to appear before the jury. Ela had no idea what she might say if pressed. "I can't be sure. He did have enemies. I suppose there is a chance that one of them saw an opportunity to rid the world of him."

"Ah yes. And his killer also rid the world of my cousin, who was one of the most powerful men in the kingdom. Some called him the Greatest Knight."

"Sir William Marshal?" Ela didn't much like the moniker that seemed to have attached itself to the man. She remembered him well from her early years of marriage as he'd been close to the king and a fixture at court, but he was hardly the greatest man to have ever lived.

"The very same. And his namesake, too."

"Do you mean his son, William Marshal, the Earl of Pembroke, who died just last year?"

Alisande drew in another slow breath, then nodded her head gently. "There's a curse on the family."

"What?" Ela frowned. Maybe Sister Alisande was gathering wool between her ears instead of thoughts. "Who would curse them?"

"Why the Bishop of Ferns, of course."

"Where did you hear such an outrageous suggestion? I begin to wonder if your mysterious insight is the work of demons."

Sister Alisande did not flinch at this pronouncement. "I've wondered that myself, my lady. But this news did not come from a vision in my mind. It came from the lips of a visitor to the castle. Sir William's brother Richard."

"The current Earl of Pembroke?"

"The very same. I heard him in the chapel. I hesitate to repeat his words as he didn't know I was listening. I doubt he knew I was there at all. He asked Father Augustine to offer up a Mass for him as he had heard whispers of this curse. Someone had warned him that he and all his brothers would die without issue and the very name of Marshal would soon be forgotten in the land."

Ela fought the urge to cross herself. Something in Sister Alisande's tone made her feel as if the ghost of William Marshal the elder might be sitting on the nun's slim shoulder, whispering these secrets in her ear. She shuddered slightly. "I'm afraid that all sounds like a lot of superstition and nonsense."

"Indeed it does," said Sister Alisande, cheerfully. "And as for whether it is true, nor not, only time will tell."

"You haven't mentioned a name."

"A name?" Sister Alisande looked about the room as if a name might appear in the air.

"Of the man who killed all three Williams—your two relatives and my dear husband." Ludicrous as the accusation seemed, she burned with curiosity to know who Alisande suspected.

"Hubert de Burgh, of course."

Ela swallowed. Her heart started to pound. She made a great effort to steady her nerves and her voice. "What makes you think he killed them? Was it some vision you saw?" Suddenly she found herself willing to lend more credence to Sister Alisande's strange gifts.

"I can't say it was, my lady. Sometimes I overheard things…that I shouldn't."

"Could you hear people making their confessions in the chapel?"

"Not always, but sometimes. If the chapel was quiet and the wind was still and the voice carried a little."

"You heard someone saying that my husband was murdered—" Ela schooled herself to lower her voice. "By the king's justiciar?"

"You don't look much surprised by the news," said Sister Alisande, with a bemused expression.

No, I've mulled over it for five long years. "It is a shocking accusation." That much was true. "Why would he kill my husband?"

"Power."

Ela let the word hang in the air, hoping that Sister Alisande would expound on this theory, but she didn't. It was true that de Burgh and her husband had locked horns on several occasions, most recently right before her husband's death. It shocked her that he might have killed others as well. "Sir William Marshal the elder was regent of the kingdom until his death, and I suspect that it was only after his demise that de Burgh was able to have free reign in managing Henry's affairs." Ela was thinking aloud. "What reason would he have for killing his son and namesake?"

"I couldn't say, my lady," said Alisande mildly.

"Have you thought of any reason why he might want to kill Father Gilbert?"

"I couldn't say," said Sister Alisande.

"You can't say, or you won't say?"

"It would be a grave sin for me to repeat the secrets of the confessional."

Ela's pulse quickened. Had she overheard de Burgh confessing to Father Gilbert? Alisande had come right out and said that she suspected him of killing the priest. Unfortunately the half-imagined ramblings of an elderly woman—let alone one suspected of witchcraft—would not hold up in court. But that would not stop Ela from pursuing them as a path for investigation.

"Perhaps if you have any more mysterious visions or foresight, it would be best to keep them to yourself for now. And please don't mention our conversation to anyone."

"I shall be quiet as a church mouse," said Sister Alisande, quite seriously.

Ela still wasn't sure if she was fully in her right mind or not, but she decided not to mention the method of poison. Ela didn't suspect Alisande for one moment of gathering and drying poisonous mushrooms and scattering them inside Father Gilbert's prayerbook. And her ignorance of the nature of the poison might yet prove her innocence.

CHAPTER 4

Ela wondered if she should grant Giles Haughton the freedom to spend what might be his last hours with his wife. But she couldn't keep Sister Alisande's latest disturbing revelations to herself. She didn't want to share them with her children, since such knowledge might endanger their lives, and she didn't wish to take them to her grave. So she summoned him to meet her in the mortuary.

The dead form of Father Gilbert still lay on the mortuary table, wrapped in a stained linen winding sheet. The body had started to decompose and now gave off the distinctive odor of death. "Now that you've confirmed the nature of the poison, we can arrange for him to be buried at Bradenstoke," she said, lifting her handkerchief from her nose. "If you agree."

Haughton nodded. "They'll want to embalm him there. We shall send him there at once. I pray that Brother Michael heeded my advice not to touch anything else in Father Gilbert's cell."

He called for two men to remove the body and put it on a cart for its immediate return to the monastery. After the body was gone, he lit and swung a censer similar to the one used in the cathedral to fill the air with a pungent aroma that went at least some way to banishing the smell of death.

"Are you well, my lady?" he asked when they were finally alone.

"As well as I can be with the prospect of imminent death hanging over me. I don't feel entirely myself, but I'm not wretched, either."

"I could say the same for myself."

"Then perhaps we shall survive this strange misfortune. I called you here to share some other strange news learned." She hesitated, not sure how to share Sister Alisande's unsubstantiated ramblings. "I suppose I want to know whether this sounds like news or nonsense to you."

Haughton looked intrigued. "What is this mysterious news?"

"Sister Alisande told me that she suspects Father Gilbert was killed by the same man who killed my husband." She waited to gauge Haughton's reaction and watched his eyes widen. "And she said that he also killed Sir William Marshal the elder, and his eldest son who died last year."

"Hubert de Burgh?" said Haughton, barely above a whisper. "How would she know this?"

"Well," Ela drew in a breath. "That's just it. The part about Father Gilbert I believe is similar to her premonition of his death." She hesitated. "Does this sound like the foolish ramblings of the addled mind?"

Haughton cleared his throat. "Well, I dare say that her mystical visions might not go over very well with the jurors. I've heard similar rumors about both the elder and the younger Marshal. And, as you know, I've been very quietly spreading the rumor myself about your husband's demise."

"So you think there might be a grain of truth in her words?"

"There may be far more than a kernel of it in them, but with my decades of experience as coroner, I can assure you that they will not stand up in front of the jury of the hundred or the judge at the assizes."

Ela felt her shoulders sag. "You're right, of course."

"We would need some way to tie the poisoning to the man in question."

Ela shook her head. "A man of such power and influence would use a proxy to commit his crimes, would he not?"

"Most likely, but, again, unless we can find this proxy and confirm the chain of command, it's nothing but hearsay."

Ela found herself staring at the scarred surface of the empty wood table in the middle of the mortuary. The mingled odors of decaying flesh and frankincense stung her nostrils. "Do you not think the king himself might be interested to know that his justiciar is suspected of committing such terrible crimes?"

"I'm sure he would be if there were some way to substantiate the rumors." Haughton had a wary look. "Are you thinking of telling him? Because I feel I must warn you that crossing such a man as Hubert de Burgh could prove very dangerous."

"More dangerous even than the Death Cap mushroom?"

Haughton smiled. "I'm glad you can make light of our prospective demise."

"Perhaps the idea that I might drop dead at any moment is making me feel reckless enough to want to seek justice—regardless of the risk to myself."

"Perhaps—" Haughton's eyes narrowed as if he was searching his mind for ideas. "You could visit the king to warn him of the malicious rumors circulating about his beloved justiciar? As if you were warning him of the dangers as a potential threat to himself and his court."

Ela pursed her lips. "Henry has relied on de Burgh for his

entire reign. I wonder if he's starting to jerk against the reins of his advisor's guiding hand."

"Such a thing wouldn't surprise me. Henry was most displeased with de Burgh's handling of the recent aborted invasion of France."

"I did hear of that. What a foolish waste of men and money. And de Burgh lost his nephew in the Loire River. And I hear that his recent incursion into Wales was similarly disastrous. Perhaps now is a good time to test the king's loyalty to de Burgh and see if there isn't space enough opening up between them for me to drive a wedge into it."

"It would be a gamble, my lady."

"It would indeed. But could I go to my grave without at least sowing the seeds of doubt in the king's ear?"

"Only you can be the judge of that."

Ela mulled a few different scenarios over in her mind, under Haughton's watchful gaze. "I'm resolved to do it. I shall visit him at Clarendon and warn him of the cruel rumors about his dear justiciar, and take it from there."

"If you are still alive tomorrow morning," said Haughton softly.

"You tempt me to ride there at once!" said Ela. "But I'll spend the night in prayer, and if the Lord wills it, I'll visit the king tomorrow."

Ela awoke in the dead of night. She listened for the bells for Matins, which sometimes woke her in the dark, but heard nothing. *I'm still alive. I think.* She tested her fingers and toes: all still moved. Her mind appeared to be in reasonable working order. Her eyes allowed her to see thin rays of moonlight poking through the bed curtains.

She realized that she'd neglected to ask Haughton how

long the reprieve from illness and death could last. Could she enjoy two days of blissful ignorance before succumbing to the deadly mushroom? Or had she escaped its clutches?

Unable to lie still, she rose from her bed and knelt at her prie-dieu. She found strength for the luxury of a full rosary, by which time the moonlight had brightened into the first pale rays of dawn.

On retiring to bed, she'd wondered if she'd still have the courage—or audacity—to approach Henry III with a mouthful of dangerous speculation about his closest advisor. As the sun peeked over the castle's outer wall, she realized she very much did.

Am I driven by an unholy lust for revenge? She did yearn to avenge her husband's untimely death. Some might counsel her that the Lord would prefer for her to submit to the buffeting blows of cruel fate by turning the other cheek. But —the Lord had gifted her with a desire to see justice done here on earth, and surely her dear husband deserved it as much as any man in Wiltshire?

ELA'S MESSENGERS informed her that the king was in residence at his nearby palace at Clarendon and that Hubert de Burgh was not. Ela dressed in her finest array, and summoned a carriage to take her there at once. She didn't want to risk delay and lose the courage or opportunity to launch this covert attack on her enemy.

While she would normally bring Sir William Talbot—her sons' tutor in their knightly training and her close confidant —or one of her sons along on such a visit, she had no wish to embroil anyone else in the risky endeavor. If this visit went against her and she found herself imprisoned for treason, she would need Bill free to guide her sons. With these grim thoughts churning in her mind, she arrived at the palace to find the king and his men about to set out on a hunt in the nearby forest.

"You must join us, Ela," exclaimed Henry. He sat astride a large dapple-gray charger decked out in his royal colors. "I know you are a fine rider, and I dare say you are a fine shot, too."

Frustrated, Ela wanted to observe that she wasn't dressed or armed for such an excursion, but this was her king, so she had no choice but to submit. "Why, I'd be delighted."

Wishing she was on Freya, in her own saddle, Ela climbed aboard the shiny and elegant black palfrey the grooms brought for her. "What a beautiful horse, Your Grace." The king seemed to be watching her to see what she'd think of the beast. She hoped this wasn't to be some kind of test of her mettle or riding skill.

Ela felt strangely vulnerable leaving her guards and horses behind and venturing out into an unfamiliar woodland—the only woman in a group of lusty young men. Still, her horse proved spirited but steady and the game abundant. At the king's urging, she shot a few arrows into the bush, but she was glad not to be called on to match her skills against his. Truth be told, she didn't enjoy hunting and had rarely accompanied her husband or sons on such expeditions.

She could hear the bells for Nones sounding in the distance as they rode back to Clarendon with a bundle of limp pheasants strapped to one man's saddle and a bag of rabbits and hares tied to another.

"Nothing like a morning's hunting to clear the cobwebs," exclaimed the king. Red-faced and smiling, he looked impossibly young. Which, at least compared to her, he was. "I always eat better after some exercise."

Naturally, she had to chatter and smile through a lengthy repast during which the king drank several cups of wine. She began to despair of him having a clear enough head to comprehend her message when he finally invited her to accompany him to his private rooms.

She followed Henry and a host of attendants—young men from Poitou if she wasn't mistaken—into a comfortable sitting room where several chairs sat around a carved oak table. "No need to sit in ceremony on my dais with you, dear Ela," said the king warmly. Ela wondered how deep into his cups he'd fallen. "Do take a seat."

A foppish attendant in a bright blue tunic pulled back a seat for her. Ela looked around at the young Frenchmen with their wine-flushed faces. "May I speak to you in complete privacy, Your Grace?" She tried not to sound too deadly serious. Still, she didn't want her rumors to be heard to come out of her mouth or to enter the ears of anyone other than the king.

The king dismissed the young men and told them he'd ring his bell when he was ready for them to return. Then he sat down at the table next to Ela and peered curiously at her.

"I know you don't waste my time with nonsense, dear Ela, so my ears are pricked for the news you have to share."

Ela counseled her face to remain as smooth as possible. "How kind of you, Your Grace, but my visit today is rather intended to share a shocking rumor that appears to be making the rounds. I thought you should be aware that people are saying some very strange things about—" She steeled herself to say the name. "About your Justiciar, Sir Hubert de Burgh."

Henry's eyes widened. "Rumors, you say?"

"Yes, I can hardly countenance them as news, of course, but I thought you should know that there are some who believe him guilty of murder."

Her heart pounded as she paused to observe the effect of

her words on the king. He looked as stunned as if she'd clubbed him over the head.

"I know it sounds ludicrous, Your Grace, but I thought you should be aware that such scurrilous words are passing among your subjects."

"Who said this?"

Ela froze. For some reason, it hadn't occurred to her that he'd want to know her source. She tried to come up with something that wasn't a lie but wasn't the full truth, either. "The person who told me is a cleric who is bound by the secrecy of the confessional. I'm sure you understand. I only know because of inquiries in my role as sheriff."

The king's frown deepened. "Inquiries into a murder?"

"Yes, and, as I've said, I have no reason to believe these rumors or to countenance them in any way, but I felt you should know about them."

"Accused of killing whom?"

Here Ela tried to steady her nerves. *My husband and your uncle.* "The rumors suggest that he killed William Marshal the elder and the younger William Marshal who died last year." She didn't want the king leaping into the fray of her current investigation, so she kept quiet about Father Gilbert. She also didn't want to embroil her family in any of this, so she didn't mention her husband.

The king stared at her, open-mouthed. Then his mouth shut. His mind appeared to be working rapidly while he sat in silence. She had no desire to interrupt whatever thought process might be happening behind his shocked gaze.

"William Marshal, you say? Who died when I was but a boy?"

"That's what the rumors say, Your Grace. Of course, I have no reason to believe that any of this is true, but..." She let her "but" sit in the air, which seemed to be thickening around her, making it hard to breathe.

"I'll be frank with you, Ela. I have reason to doubt the fidelity of my justiciar and this shocking news comes at a most opportune time." He tented his fingers. "My friends are warning me that he still sees me as a mere child and seeks to rule the country as he sees fit."

Ela thought of the fresh-faced hunting companions he'd just shooed out and reflected that they would probably find the imperious old de Burgh to be a nuisance. "He did guide and lead you with a firm hand during the early years of your reign." She wanted to give the impression that she almost sided with de Burgh...but not quite. "Though I'm sure you no longer need such avuncular guidance now that you are more than capable of ruling on your own."

"Absolutely, and I admit that I find myself chafing under his constant advice. And of late I've found his advice to be less than stellar. He's supposed to manage the royal treasury. He now tells me I have scarcely the funds for food and clothing and to maintain my household when I need enough to make war in France!" Henry's eyes flashed. "I blame him for the failure of our recent expedition to France. In fact—and I speak to you in absolute faith in your discretion—that he rather wanted it to be ineffectual. He doesn't seem to understand my desire to retake the lands my father lost."

"I quite understand." Ela felt a flame of hope flicker alive in her heart. "And I can assure you of my discretion."

Henry looked directly at her. "And the recent debacle in Wales..." His brow lowered. "You are not the only one who's heard rumors about de Burgh. I was told that he gave Llywelyn a jewel that made him invincible in battle—all to assure that my armies could not defeat him. Would you countenance such a rumor?"

Ela tried to keep a straight face. This story sounded ludicrous but possibly not more than the idea that the king's trusted advisor may have poisoned three of his closest associates.

"That is quite extraordinary, Your Grace."

"They say he has his own interests in Wales and perhaps seeks an alliance with Llywelyn. He has several castles there."

"It does seem that collecting properties is quite the hobby of his."

"I made him Earl of Kent. He was not a man of high birth." Henry cocked his head. "And now I recall that was why you took such offense at his nephew's proposal of marriage to you."

Ela didn't want to be seen as having a history of resentment toward de Burgh—perhaps because she very much did. "My husband was alive—though missing overseas—at the time of this proposal, of course. Many thought him dead, but I knew he was alive, so naturally I couldn't countenance a proposal from any man."

"I shouldn't have made de Burgh an earl. I suspect the title went to his head," said Henry, frowning. "And I never should have let him marry royalty. Did you know that his wife, Margaret, the king of Scotland's daughter, was originally intended as a bride for myself, not for him? Yet somehow she became his bride and I am still without a queen." Henry seemed to be confronting a litany of poor life choices—likely orchestrated by de Burgh in his own interest.

"I'm sure Your Grace will marry the perfect queen when the time is right." Ela's only remaining unmarried daughters were Petronella—pledged as a bride of Christ—and young Ellie, who was in no way mature enough to become a king's wife—or she might have put one of them forward as his future queen.

"I have no shortage of prospective brides, of course," he said with a quick smile, as if trying to reassure himself. "But such a choice must be made with great care. A man and his wife must be of one mind about all things, or terrible chaos can result."

"Indeed. I stood at my husband's side in all things." Even when he was led astray by his feckless brother King John—though finally she had convinced William to distance himself from the man who'd managed to get the entire kingdom excommunicated by the Pope. "And Hubert de Burgh has reason to stand at your side in all matters."

"Yet he still treats me like a child. He should obey my orders since I am his king!" Ela silently pondered that Henry had never sounded more like a child. "He shouldn't try to subvert my will and promote his own interests."

"Indeed he should not, Your Grace." This entire encounter was going very well. So far it had far exceeded her wildest hopes. "But I suppose that when a man is used to having so much power, it is hard to rein him in."

"That's what he thinks." Henry leaped to his feet and rounded the table in three strides. "He shall see that I'm no child and not a man to be trifled with. "He shall be held accountable. He's taken things too far this time! Did you know that de Burgh, who rose from nothing, is now the second greatest landowner in England after myself?"

"I am not surprised, Your Grace. He is a man of considerable cunning." She hoped she wasn't overstepping. De Burgh had trodden a bold path to power, stepping on the heads of powerful men to get there, and she couldn't be so sure that he wouldn't find a way to seize and hold it yet—possibly at her expense.

"Indeed he is. He insists that he has the right to lifetime management of my finances—without giving any account of the comings and goings—because of a warrant he was granted by my father."

"Goodness. Perhaps it's time to take a close look at your

accounts." Again, this was not an outrageous suggestion, but she hoped it wouldn't backfire.

"I'll do just that. And I'll go further. I'll invite the nobles of the land to bring forth any grievances they may hold against de Burgh, that he shall be held accountable for all of them."

Ela blinked. She wondered if anyone would dare come forward. She could hardly see herself pointing at de Burgh in the king's chambers and accusing him of poisoning her husband. Others—including the twice-wronged Marshal family—might feel similar compunction.

"It may be difficult to find people to come forward and publicly accuse the king's justiciar."

"I'll remove such concern as an obstacle. Very soon he will no longer be able to call himself the king's justiciar."

CHAPTER 5

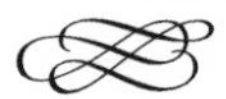

Monday of the following week began with news of a murder in the market town of Devizes.

"An apothecary, you say?" Ela sat on her dais, interrupted between petitioners by the panting messenger. "With a stall at the market?"

"Wilf the younger, they call him, though he's as old as Moses. He owns a small shop, my lady. Hard by the blacksmith on Long Street that my master owns. Found strangled on the floor of his place of business."

"Your master sent you to fetch the sheriff's men."

"He did indeed, my lady. A murderer is about."

"Can you be sure that the apothecary didn't fall dead of natural causes?" Ela wanted to know whether to summon a jury or whether Giles Haughton alone might suffice.

"Oh no, my lady. There's a bright red mark around his neck almost like a skein of thread!" The young man clutched at his own throat and his blue eyes bulged almost as if someone was trying to strangle him.

"I'll send a jury at once, and the coroner."

THE BELLS for Nones had sounded by the time Ela and Haughton reached Devizes. Two local jurors from the town, one of whom was the blacksmith whose home and shop stood next door, were already waiting.

Two broken glass jars of a brown powder had spilled on the floor, where the body of the herb seller lay stretched out on the stone, face-up. A fine red line etched the skin around his neck.

Giles Haughton knelt next to him and examined the wound. "He was strangled with a piece of twisted wire," he muttered. "The twists in it are clearly visible. And they're too deep and clean to be a piece of string."

"What might such a wire be used for?" asked Ela.

"You mean outside of strangulation?" replied Haughton. "Perhaps a gate latch, but it's not something a man would just carry on his person with no purpose in mind. This shop is filled with breakable glass and clay jars, and only two are damaged so not much of a fight took place. The scene itself suggests that someone came here armed with wire and intent on strangling the shopkeeper, and that he achieved his goal with little effort."

"Why would anyone want to kill dear old Wilf?" asked the older juror, who—he explained—owned a pie shop two doors down. "He didn't have an enemy in the world. All and sundry came here for herbs and roots to cure their aches and pains. He had a gift for healing. I swear he could tell you had a headache when you walked through the door, and he knew just the brew to cure it."

"Perhaps they wanted to rob him?" said the blacksmith, who'd introduced himself as Ned Skelton.

Ela looked at the well-stocked shelves. "Who would know if something is missing? Do any family members live here?"

"His wife died three years ago and his only daughter lives out in the country with her husband. I sent my son to find her," said Skelton. "I'm not sure if she'd know if anything in particular was amiss, unless it lay smashed on the floor, of course."

One brown powder spilled on the floor smelled strongly of cloves.

"Who found him?" asked Ela.

"Me," said Skelton. "I thought it odd that his door wasn't bolted. I get up before dawn to get my fire started and be ready for the first horse to lose a shoe or the first milkmaid with a broken bucket handle. I came outside to throw the slops in the ditch and noticed that his door wasn't shut all the way. I didn't think much of it at first, but after I'd built the fire, it started to bother me. I went out again to see if I'd imagined it, and there it was, open just wide enough for a man to put a foot in the door."

He glanced down at the body. "I called out his name, but I wasn't surprised when he didn't answer. Wilf isn't usually up and open until after first light, though he's not a man to dally abed, either."

"Did you go in?"

"Not at first. Again, I went back to my shop and set an iron to heat."

Ela was burning with a desire to search the apothecary's shop for one particular item. As she spoke with the blacksmith, she saw Haughton heading for the shelves laden with jars and boxes of herbs and powder and seeds and whatnot. He'd know what to look for.

"You thought he might just have forgotten to latch the door from the inside?" The wood door had a heavy cast-iron latch that Skelton might have forged on his anvil.

"I did. He's old, and I know my own mother can be forgetful now she's getting up in years. But I'm a man to mind my own business and not be a nuisance so I left well enough alone. I hammered out the business end of a hoe that a customer had ordered." He rubbed a hand over his face. "But then I wondered if old Wilf had a fall or other mishap and might need help. Last year he tripped on the stairs and lay crumpled in a heap on the stone floor until I came and helped him up. God be praised he was fine afterwards, but bruised and battered and—so I went and knocked on the door."

Ela wished he'd get to the point a little faster. "Then when he didn't answer, you entered the shop?"

"I did, and when I saw he wasn't standing behind the counter, or anywhere else about, I went in and called his name. I was heading for the stairs back there--" He pointed to a very narrow doorway with dark stairs just visible in the gloom. "When I turned and saw him lying here on the floor behind the counter." He pointed to the stone floor where Wilf the Younger lay stretched out on the stone.

"I take it you moved him?"

"Yes, my lady. He was quite curled up in a ball. It didn't seem right to leave him lying there like that." Normally this would be cause for consternation, at least on the part of Giles Haughton, but the ligature mark on the man's neck was as clear as if someone had drawn it there with crimson ink and a quill pen. "As you can see, he's been strangled."

"It does appear that way, though the coroner will make the final determination as to his cause of death." She glanced up at Giles Haughton, who was poring over a small canister. "What have you found?"

"This contains the powdered flesh of the death cap mushroom."

"Be very careful if you choose to open it."

"I shall do so outside in the open air, my lady. And when no breeze is blowing."

But her question was answered. Father Gilbert's killer might have bought his supplies here in this shop.

"Since he didn't rise early, and didn't lock up his shop last night, that suggests that Wilf was killed yesterday afternoon or evening. Did you happen to see anyone around who might have gained entrance to his shop?"

Skelton raised his hands. "I had an order for four buckles late in the afternoon. Decorative buckles with very specific measurements to repair a harness. He gave me one to copy and it all took me until after dark. I didn't even peep out of my shop until the next morning. I sleep upstairs, you see, much like old Wilf did."

Ela wondered if someone had deliberately busied him to keep his eyes off his neighbor's shop. "Who ordered the buckles?"

"A knight, my lady. Dressed almost like a noble. I didn't catch his name but he paid handsomely."

Ela glanced at Haughton.

"Could you describe this knight?" asked Haughton.

Skelton drew in a breath. "Well, he was tall. He wore a hood so I'm not sure of his hair color but his eyes were brown." He frowned. "Or at least I think they were. I suppose they could have looked dark in the shadow from the hood."

"Did you not find it odd that a man wore a hood on a mild summer's day?" asked Ela.

"Not really, my lady. It sprinkled off and on yesterday. I suppose he wanted to keep the rain off his head."

"What color were his cloak and tunic and hose?" asked Haughton.

"His cloak was gray," said Skelton. "Of fine wool, with a black lining. I have an eye for such details. His hose was dark green and his boots of polished black leather."

"Was he young or old?" asked Ela.

"Somewhere in between, I'd say," said the blacksmith. "I'd

guess he was a man of my age or close." Ela reckoned Skelton at about forty. "I'll be sure to take his name when he comes back with more business. I told him I'd offer a discount if he brought me more custom. I'm always happy to find a new customer."

Ela reflected that this one was unlikely to return. "Please do, and take careful note of his coloring and features. And send the information to me at once."

"Do you think he killed my neighbor?" asked Skelton, suddenly looking alarmed. "I don't know how he could have. He was stood here the whole time, watching me work."

"He may have been keeping you occupied while an accomplice did the deed. Or he may have wished to keep you inside until after dark for some reason. We must find out who he was."

THE JAR of powdered mushroom had a dust shadow on its clay interior, suggesting that it had previously contained more of the substance. Enough, certainly, to have dusted the pages of Father Gilbert's prayerbook.

"What good reason would an apothecary have for carrying such a deadly poison?" asked Ela. "Surely he would suspect anyone buying it of being capable of committing murder with their purchase?"

"Many items can be either curative or deadly depending on how they are prepared. Some use this mushroom in a poultice that can shrink a canker, though it must be done with great care. And then there is always a need for preparations to kill vermin of all kinds."

"If Father Gilbert's murderer bought the deadly substance here, why would he return several days later to kill the owner?"

"Perhaps he got wind of our investigation," said Haughton. "He may have hoped that the cause of death would remain a mystery. Then, when a very specific poison was named, he became worried that his identity might be revealed as the one who purchased it."

"That would suggest he was local, or known to the apothecary. Otherwise, he'd be just another anonymous customer."

They searched the shop for ledgers that might detail what items were purchased and on which days, but they found nothing. Ela found it extraordinary that a shop, or a business of any kind, wouldn't make careful note of all incomings and expenditures, but Haughton observed that the cost of parchment was often prohibitive and shopkeepers of the old school could keep a tally going back several years in the recesses of their brains.

The jurors followed them as they stopped men and women in the town and asked them about any strangers they'd seen. Devizes being a bustling market town with a fair amount of passing traffic, several people had noticed a tall man with a gray cloak and one said he'd had a shorter companion in a moss green cloak and a leather hat that cast a shadow over his face. No one they spoke to knew who they were.

Mid-afternoon, the apothecary's daughter Sarah arrived from their home in the countryside. Sarah was a tall middle-aged woman with ruddy cheeks, a piercing pale gaze, and a mouth that never stopped moving. She exclaimed briefly over her father's untimely death and observed that he was far too trusting and always wanted to help people when he should have been wary of them. Then she became intent on shooing onlookers out of his shop and securing it against thieves.

"The sheriff's men and the jurors need access to the shop

while we conduct our investigation," explained Haughton, as she fussed over all the foot traffic around her father's dead body. "And I'm afraid that your father must be removed to the castle mortuary for further examination."

"Can we not bury him in peace?" she protested. "It's plain as the nose on my face that he was strangled. Must you drag an old man halfway across Wiltshire when he's already dead?"

"If we are to catch his murderer, then we must," said Haughton gruffly. "Would you want your father's killer to go free?"

"Of course not! What a thing to say. Though I don't want him or anyone else to come back and help himself to the contents of his shop, either. There's a great deal of value in these jars and pots. You'd be surprised! The news of his death might attract knaves from all over to strip the place clean."

"What will happen to his shop now that he's dead?" asked Ela, suddenly curious.

"Why, I haven't had time to think about it. Perhaps my husband and I will move into town and take over his custom," she said quickly, as if the thought were already well established in her mind.

"Were you close to your father?" asked Ela, now at least somewhat suspicious of Sarah.

"Very." Sarah picked up a clay jar with pressed the cork in tighter. "I'm his only living child, you see."

"Were you worried about your father living alone here? Your neighbor said he'd taken a fall some time ago and been unable to get up."

"Of course I was! But he was stubborn and insisted on doing everything as he always had."

Ela glanced at Haughton, then back at Sarah. "You must come before the jury in Salisbury to tell them everything you can about your father."

"In Salisbury? I don't have time for that. I have this shop to run now and then there's the sheep and chickens at home that will have to be dealt with."

Ela held up her hand to silence the woman. "Tomorrow afternoon after the bells for Nones. You shall have the full morning to make arrangements and find your way to Salisbury."

"And my husband, too?"

"If you like. But it's your presence that is required."

The victim's daughter grew quieter after this, perhaps realizing that she could be considered a suspect. They certainly had precious few others. "Did your father keep account books of any kind?" asked Ela.

"Oh yes. He recorded every purchase he made and every sale. Terrible waste of materials if you ask me but he insisted on it. He has a shelf of books going back to before I was born."

"Where is it?"

Sarah pointed to a shelf behind the counter, then frowned. "They should be right there. Old leather-bound books, they are. He'd write so small that no one but him could read it, but he could remember a sale from the reign of King John and look it up in an instant if you asked about it."

"Can you think of anyone who might have taken the books?"

"Who would want a stack of old accounting ledgers?" Sarah looked at Ela as if she were mad. "Do you suppose they'd want to wash the ink off and reuse them?"

Haughton ran a finger along the shelf, which made no mark since the shelf was free of dust. "I suspect they were more anxious to remove them as a source of information about who bought the poison that killed Father Gilbert."

"A hired killer?" suggested Ela.

Haughton shrugged slightly. "It's hard to say."

Ela frowned, looking at the empty shelf. "Who would hire someone to murder Father Gilbert? Then possibly order the killing of this shopkeeper to cover his assassin's tracks?"

"Someone with a heavy purse. Murder doesn't come cheap."

~

THE FOLLOWING DAY, as she approached her dais in the hall, Ela's ears pricked up when she heard the jurors muttering amongst themselves about Hubert de Burgh.

"Can you believe it! We've seen him here in Salisbury with our own eyes, and now the king wants to prosecute him!" said Hugh Clifford, the wine seller.

"Just shows that even the mighty can fall," muttered Peter Howard, the baker, an older man who was a stalwart on the jury. "He's the type to look right over a man's head rather than look him in the eye."

"True," said Clifford. "But he is—was—the king's right-hand man for as many years as young Henry's been king. They say he's run off to Egypt!"

"I heard he fled to Paris with a boatful of whores," said Paul Dunstan, the miller. "Can't you just picture it?"

No, thought Ela. Happily, they hadn't realized she was within earshot. Hubert de Burgh was a man of many failings but she didn't suspect that debauchery was one of them. There was no money or glory in it, for one thing.

"They say his whole family has disappeared out of sight overnight," said Clifford. "Even his wife and daughter."

Ela frowned at this, straining to hear the details. De Burgh's wife Margaret was the sister of Alexander, the present king of Scotland. If she'd run for cover as well, then de Burgh's situation must be more precarious than even she had realized. And so soon after her conversation with the king! The prospect of de Burgh's sudden ruin made her almost giddy.

Petronella entered the room with Alisande on her arm. The diminutive nun looked frail and harmless as a cobweb in the corner of a chapel. Surely they could quickly dismiss her as a suspect in Father Gilbert's death.

As instructed, Petronella helped her to a chair in between the tables of jurors, where Alisande sat shakily down and turned to face the assembled men with a calm smile.

Ela stood up and said a silent prayer that Alisande wouldn't say anything to unsettle the jurors. "Men of the jury, we've had two murders in Wiltshire in the space of a week and we are here today to gather information rather than interview suspects." They tended to view everyone who appeared before them as a potential murderer. She'd contemplated keeping Sister Alisande far from their steely gaze but didn't want to draw suspicion later on by appearing to hide her. "Sister Alisande has spent her life as an anchoress at Bradenstoke, where Father Gilbert recently fell dead at the altar. We hope she can provide us with some background on the situation."

She smiled warmly—she hoped—at Sister Alisande. Petronella had been urged to warn the nun against discussing any mysterious visions or unnatural foreknowledge. The nun answered several innocuous questions about how long Father Gilbert had been there—about fifteen years—and how long she had—nearly sixty, she thought—and she had just finished expounding on what a very nice man he was when things went badly awry.

CHAPTER 6

"Did Father Gilbert have any enemies within the monastery?" asked Ela, trying to keep the conversation focused.

"I can't think of any. He was very well-liked. Always kind and understanding with the novices."

"Any from without?"

"Not that I know of."

Ela hoped that Sister Alisande would quickly be excused to return to her room. "Does anyone on the jury have questions for Sister Alisande?"

Miles Crabbet, a local farmer who was an infrequent sight on juries, asked her if Father Gilbert had suffered from any ailments that might have caused him to drop dead.

"Never, sir. He was as healthy as a horse." Then she narrowed her eyes and stared at him. "But your heart is ailing!" She pressed her hands together in a gesture of prayer. "You must take care or you may well leave your wife a widow."

"I beg your pardon?" asked Crabbet, as if he hadn't heard properly.

"Your heart, sir. It's pounding too hard. You must leave the hard work of harvesting to your son."

Crabbet's mouth fell open. "That was my intent. But my son has a twisted ankle so I've had to step in and do it myself." He turned and looked at the other jurors. "How does she know I have a son?"

Sister Alisande looked unperturbed. "Most men have sons."

"Indeed they do, but for all you know mine could be a cabinet maker in London. And how do you know I'm harvesting? My crop came in early. I wasn't expecting it for a good three weeks yet."

Sister Alisande glanced at Ela, who probably wore an expression of considerable alarm on her face. "Does anyone else have any questions?" Her voice came out higher and thinner than she'd intended.

Miles Crabbet now had a hand on his heart. "It is thudding hard." He turned to Peter Howard, who was sitting next to him. "How does she know that?"

"Is she the one that they say is a witch?" asked John the tanner. He was a younger juror with a sharp mind. Too sharp to believe in witches.

"Witches are a foolish superstition," cut in Ela, quickly.

"But she's being sheltered here in the castle, because the men at the monastery said she's a witch, isn't she?" asked John.

"She is here for protection from false accusations and to help us in our inquiries," replied Ela. "She is a woman who has devoted her life to God, not a witch."

"Then how does she know that I'm having to harvest my own crops when I haven't done it in five years?" asked Crabbet, who looked downright spooked by the whole exchange. "How does she know that my heart is beating too hard and fast—because it is! I came here today so I could shift the work onto my young grandson and take a rest. I'm not ashamed of it as I'm an old man."

"As a woman of God, perhaps Sister Alisande has special insight into the human condition," said Ela, trying to sound calm. "And it sounds as if she's quite right that you need to rest. Perhaps you could hire another lad to help your grandson do the work that your son can't do this year."

Murmuring had arisen amongst the jurors during this exchange and now spread throughout the hall. "They say she cried out that Father Gilbert was about to die," said John the tanner. "And then he crumpled to the floor. I heard it in The Bull and Bear. Some think she killed him."

"That's nonsense," said Ela quickly. "Do you suspect her of wanting to kill Miles Crabbet? I'd rather suspect she wishes to save his life by warning him of the risks of overexertion. Perhaps she wished to warn Father Gilbert so that she might save his life."

"I did," said Alisande simply. "But it was too late. It was already too late."

"Too late?" asked Giles Haughton, apparently unable to resist the inquiry.

"Something in the air about him shifted," said Alisande. "It turned dark and jagged."

"And you see the same around our juror Miles Crabbet?"

"Not to quite the same extent, but yes."

Miles Crabbet had turned quite pale and leaned back in his chair as if he might join Father Gilbert in Heaven at any moment.

"Are you ill, Master Crabbet?" asked Ela. It would certainly not help Sister Alisande's prospects if he were to drop dead in her hall.

"I'm sure I don't know. Perhaps I'd better go home and lie down." His daughter, who'd been standing nearby, rose and hurried to his side, and Crabbet left the hall amid a flurry of conversation.

Sister Alisande sat quietly in her chair with her hands in her lap. "I shall pray for him," she said quietly, amid the furor.

Ela was hoping to move on to their next witness, as Wilf's daughter Sarah stood off to one side, looking none too happy to be kept waiting. But the other jurors peppered her with questions—had this happened before? Had anyone died? Could she predict the future?—until Sister Alisande was somewhere between a murderous witch and the Oracle at Delphi.

"Why would a woman choose to be an anchoress when she could join an order of nuns?" asked John the tanner. "It's unnatural."

"I've learned that there are at least a hundred anchoresses in England today," said Ela. "I've never encountered one before, but the practice is common enough that there's even a book written to outline the rules for them to live by." She had sent a written order to her favorite bookseller in London, in the hope that he could manage to obtain a copy for her.

"Sister Alisande is not a suspect in the murder of Father Gilbert," she continued. "Giles Haughton has determined that Father Gilbert was poisoned with death cap mushroom. Since Sister Alisande does not leave her cell, let alone the abbey, for any reason, she has had no access to such a poison and has no motive to administer it to Father Gilbert. She must be tired after all your questioning. Since she's not a murder suspect, I suggest that she return to her room to rest."

There was some token protest, and the jurors asked Sister Alisande a few questions about who might have killed Father Gilbert. Ela quickly warned Alisande not to speculate but to stick with actual observations or known facts, of which she had none.

Fearing that this pointless, and potentially dangerous, questioning might continue all morning, Ela assured them that Sister Alisande was under guard in a secure room—for her protection as much as anyone else's—and that she would not be leaving the castle. Finally, the jury allowed Petronella to help the ancient nun from her chair and guide her past the assembled crowd of staring strangers.

"We are now moving on to a second and more recent murder, which may be related to the first. A herb seller, known as Wilf the Younger but of quite advanced age, was found dead yesterday morning in his shop in Devizes. The coroner has examined the body in his mortuary and will now discuss his findings."

With some relief, she turned the proceedings over to Haughton. She noted that he looked rather more haggard than usual, and wondered about lingering effects of the mushroom poisoning. She felt almost back to normal herself, but he'd likely ingested a higher dose than her due to taking the book into his home.

"The apothecary was strangled with a length of twisted wire. Since such an item is not something the average resident of Devizes would have on their person, I'm led to suspect that his killer came prepared for murder and might even have been hired to end the life of Wilf the Younger."

"But why?" asked Stephen Hale. Ela frowned.

Haughton looked less put out than she might be at being interrupted. "As your countess has observed, Father Gilbert was killed by the ingestion of deadly mushroom powder that was liberally sprinkled over his prayerbook. I myself am still suffering from the contact I had with the same prayerbook. I examined the powder and was able to confirm its origin. The mushroom had been dried and ground to a very fine powder that appeared at first glance to be ordinary dust. The substance was likely prepared by someone with experience, such as an apothecary."

"The herb seller sold this substance in his shop?" interjected Hugh Clifford.

"He did. I found a jar of it where the wax seal had been recently cut open and then resealed, perhaps so the seller could scoop out a portion for sale. Since Father Gilbert was murdered nearly a week ago, it seems possible that the killer got wind that the poison was identified, and worried that he might also be identified by his purchase of it."

"So he killed the herb seller before he could tell anyone who he sold it to," said Peter Howard with some satisfaction.

"Exactly. That's my current theory. The herb seller's daughter informed us that her father kept ledgers recording each sale and that these, too, were removed to prevent us from proving the sale."

"But how would he know we'd identified the poison?" asked Ela. "This is surely the first time it's been named in public since you learned what it is."

"I'm afraid I don't know, my lady. I never breathed a word of it to my wife, as you know."

"I wonder if they observed you removing the body—and the book—to your mortuary, or heard about it, and they assumed that once you examined them you'd know what poison it was. Your reputation for sniffing out the means of death is well known throughout Wiltshire."

"Which would mean the killer has eyes on us—or a spy among us." Haughton looked around the room as if the killer might be watching them at that very moment.

Ela called blacksmith Ned Skelton, who stood with his

leather cap folded between his scrubbed-but-still-soot-stained hands. He told the jury about the tall man with his buckles who'd kept him occupied that afternoon and evening. "Old Wilf didn't have an enemy in the world, that I know of," he said gruffly.

Ela then called Wilf's daughter Sarah, who bustled forward, a white veil pinned around her long, red-cheeked face. "It's a great inconvenience that the ledgers were stolen," she said, in a strident, high-pitched voice. "As they contained all the purchases for the shop as well as the sales. Without them, I don't know who my father bought his wares from or how to purchase more in the future."

"Did he discuss his business with you?" asked Ela.

"Never. Stubborn and independent to a fault, he was. He had trouble walking these last two years but wouldn't take on a lad or accept any help."

"So you don't know anything about his suppliers or his customers?"

"I asked him to show me and Lucas the ropes so that we'd be able to take over when he died but he'd insist he had many more years in him yet and to mind my own business. Now look at what a pickle we're in!"

"Did your father leave a will?"

Sarah frowned. "If he did I know nothing about it. Surely his goods and chattels go to his next of kin, along with the house and shop. I'm his only surviving child."

Ela glanced at Haughton. "I'll ask the clerk if a will was recorded."

Sarah blinked. "What difference would it make?"

"Well, if we discover that he had an heir, someone waiting impatiently to inherit his shop, then that might point to that person as a potential murder suspect."

Sarah's mouth dropped open. "You think I killed my father? What about this killer who murdered the priest?"

"That is only a theory. And what a convenient smoke-screen to hide a murder committed for more pedestrian reasons." Ela wasn't entirely sure why she felt compelled to needle Sarah this way. Something about the woman perturbed her—perhaps that her desire to claim her dead father's possessions superseded any sign of emotion at his death.

"I didn't kill my father."

"When did you last see him?"

Sarah hesitated. "On Tuesday, I suppose. I would visit him whenever I came into Devizes to sell my spun wool or to buy goods."

"Did he talk about you inheriting the shop when he died?"

"No," said Sarah, without much hesitation. "Much as we didn't talk about what kind of gravestone he'd like. You don't talk about those things, do you?"

Ela could see some truth to this. And while most nobles had a will of some sort, ordinary tradesmen and farmers often didn't. Perhaps the process was too intimidating, especially for the unlettered, or they felt they couldn't afford the legal assistance. If Sarah was the only surviving heir, the existing inheritance laws already made her heir to his whole estate, including the shop.

A muttering had arisen in the crowd gathered around the jury tables. Bill Talbot, sitting nearby, gave a command for silence. "What's this uproar?" he demanded.

Ned Skelton, sitting amidst the jurors, frowned. "They're saying that Mistress Willow's husband was in Devizes on the day of her father's death. And also that he was the man in green, seen in the company of the tall man in the gray cloak who gave the blacksmith work that day."

Ela looked at Sarah. "Is your husband here today?"

"No, my lady."

"Why not?"

"Someone had to stay home and tend to the animals."

"What was he doing in Devizes that day?"

"I couldn't say, my lady." Sarah's face seemed to close up.

"Did you know he was there? The subject must have come up when you told him that your father was murdered."

"He goes into the town often, my lady. He has been arranging a contract to sell the wool from this year's sheep and also for the sale of some lambs to the butcher shop."

"And such discussions take place over multiple days?" Ela's skepticism about Wilf's family was growing with every moment.

"Indeed they do, my lady."

"Master Skelton, as the neighbor of the murdered man, do you have reason to suspect that his daughter or husband were involved in his death?"

"Well, no…" his face darkened. "I have no reason to believe they'd want to kill him, but since yesterday it's become clear that the man in my shop, who kept me occupied for much of the evening, was seen in the company of her husband, who was in the locality at the time. He's the shorter man in the green cloak that was mentioned. We realized this almost as soon as you left Devizes yesterday, my lady."

"Then it must be easy to determine the identity of the mysterious tall man in the cloak who ordered the buckles. We can simply ask Farmer Willow to tell us his name. Unless someone here can identify the man?" She looked at Sarah. "Do you know who your husband met with in Devizes?"

"I asked him and he said it was a local man who trades in fleeces. I asked his name and he said it was none of my business."

Ela looked out at the crowd of strangers, who seemed to be the entourage from Devizes that had accompanied

Skelton or come along to gawp at the scandal unfolding in their midst. "Does anyone else know who this man was?"

No one moved or spoke.

"If I'd known that Farmer Willow knew the identity of this stranger, we would have summoned him here this morning. As it is, I'll have to send guards to retrieve him which will take quite some time."

Sometimes Ela wished Wiltshire was not so large a county. And this information implied something else. "Mistress Willow, did your husband visit your father on the day he died?"

"He said he popped in to say hello and exchange a few words and said that my father seemed just as normal and in good health. He was as shocked as myself to receive word in the morning that he'd been killed."

"You and your husband own a farm near Devizes?"

"We don't own it. It's rented from the abbey for a certain amount of fleeces and sacks of barley grain each year."

"From Bradenstoke Abbey?"

"Yes, my lady."

"And is the farm profitable?"

"Yes, my lady. My husband is a very good steward of his flock."

A muttering in the crowd made Ela look up. Those in attendance suddenly fell silent. Were they disagreeing with her? Ela had asked the question to see if the Willows had a motive to take ownership of a profitable apothecary shop.

"And how many years have you rented from the abbey?"

"Twelve, I believe it is, my lady."

"And your family has a good relationship with those who manage the abbey estate?"

"I daresay." Sarah's eyes darted about somewhat, as if avoiding Ela's gaze.

"You always pay the tithes on time and in full?"

Sarah Willow hesitated. "They raised the amount this year and we couldn't spare enough fleeces and ewes to meet it or we'd have had nothing left to sell to feed ourselves."

The murmuring amongst the crowd started up again.

"Had the abbey raised the amount recently?"

"Yes, my lady. Two years ago. We met the full tithe last year but it left us short of breeding ewes last spring and we couldn't raise enough lambs to meet their demands."

"Who was in charge of arranging the tithes, mistress Willow?" Ela held her breath. Was she about to solve two murders in one question?

"A man named Timothy Lissop, my lady." Ela sagged. For a second she'd be sure that Father Gilbert's name would be on her lips. The family would have a motive to kill the man whose demands were ruining their farm and also the father whose shop might support them in its stead. Still, it would be unlikely for a holy father to be involved in the grubby work of extracting tithes from tenant farmers.

"Have you found him to be unfair in his dealings?"

"I wouldn't say unfair, my lady. It's just that we told him we lost five ewes to flystrike and only had thirteen left, and he still wanted four of them."

Did she know Father Gilbert? "Did you attend Mass at Bradenstoke Abbey?"

"No, my lady. We go to Mass at St Peter's in the field. It's where my family has gone for generations." Ela knew of the tiny old church, a relic of pre-Norman times.

"And where did you make your confessions?"

Sarah looked down. Her hands fumbled in the front of her dress. "It's been some while since I've confessed, my lady."

While some might find this information damning, Ela knew many people avoided airing their sins out of fear of censure or even bribery. "If you have no sins, Mistress Willow, I must congratulate you."

Sarah's lips pressed together. "I wouldn't make that claim, my lady, but nothing to endanger my soul if that's what you mean."

Ela established that Sarah Willow was her father's sole surviving heir. She planned to adjourn the jury to wait for Sarah Willow's husband to appear and explain what he was doing in Devizes on the night of the killing—and to identify his tall friend with the buckles—but first she asked the jurors if they had any questions for Sarah.

Peter Howard cleared his throat. "Is it true that, since your father didn't share the details of his trade, that it will be difficult for you to operate his business in his absence?"

"He kept several old books with recipes for various tinctures and powders and such like. Those weren't down in the shop but were upstairs in his sitting room, so they weren't taken."

"So you think you could learn enough to run his shop from reading these books?" asked Howard.

"I already know how to make a poultice for a wound, a tincture for a headache or a posset for a fever, and such. As many of us do. I dare say I could learn as I go."

"If the shelves are stocked with deadly poisons, the like of which can kill a man who touches them and then eats from his poisoned fingers, you might find the work more challenging."

Sarah nodded. "Indeed, the prospect of selling such items frightens me."

"The truth is," said Ela. "You don't know enough about the substances in his shop to know which could kill you?"

Sarah sniffed. "That is true, I suppose."

"Perhaps Giles Haughton, who is an expert in such matters, might be persuaded to supply some advice in exchange for an appropriate trade in substances that he has a use for." Ela looked at Haughton, who nodded in agreement.

"I'd be happy to help, Mistress Willow. And rest assured I won't cheat you but I will save you from accidentally killing someone if I can." Which would allow him to delve further into her motives.

CHAPTER 7

"Have you heard the curious news about Hubert de Burgh?" Ela asked Bill at dinner in the hall that evening. "The jurors were saying that he's vanished."

"Gone into hiding, is what I heard." Bill mopped up the spiced almond sauce with a piece of bread. "The garrison commander filled me in on some details. The king summoned de Burgh to his palace and said he's to be held accountable for various misdeeds."

Ela sipped her wine. "Like what?" She looked around the hall to see if anyone could overhear their conversation. Everyone around them seemed to be engaged in some other business and—as usual—her older sons were locked in a contentious game of chess.

"No one seems to know. From what I hear, a laundry list of charges are being compiled against him and the king intends to invite every man in the land who might have a word to say against him to come speak his piece at Westminster."

Again, Ela felt a swell of satisfaction. "Does de Burgh have no allies rushing to defend his reputation?"

"Not that I've heard."

"De Burgh is a man of unusual cunning. He may yet find a way to twist this situation to his advantage."

"He does have a keen intelligence." Bill rarely said a harsh word about anyone. "But I fear that by holding power so long, and with such confidence in his authority, he's made a lot of enemies."

"And it seems the king is offering his enemies a chance to seek revenge. It is a curious situation. One that I couldn't possibly have imagined. How do you feel about the man?" Ela had always been cautious about revealing her true feelings for de Burgh to Bill. She'd hinted that he might have killed her husband, but it was not a subject of frequent discussion. She didn't want him to share the suspicion with her sons.

"He's been a fighter and a strategist for most of my life. His warlike cunning is probably unrivaled," said Bill.

"True."

"He's known to defend his friends with the ferocity of a bulldog."

Ela nodded. "Yes, such as when he took sides with King John against my husband."

"But he does have an uncommon desire to gather other people's properties to his bosom. Those who used to hold those properties—and their heirs—likely feel very ill-disposed towards him."

"I'm sure they do. And they may come forward with a host of grievances in an effort to reclaim their lost lands."

Bill glanced around the hall, then leaned in. "Much as I admire the man as a fighter and a loyal defender of the realm, part of me is glad to see him knocked off his high horse."

"Me too," mouthed Ela.

~

The following day, around noon, the jury gathered again in Ela's hall to question Sarah's husband, Lucas Willow. Once again, a good-sized crowd of curious onlookers had traveled from Devizes to listen to the proceedings.

Sarah Willow had fussed and fumed about leaving the shop completely unattended, so Ela had sent a guard to stand in front of it. She certainly didn't need anyone else breaking in there and helping themselves to the deadly poisons. Especially since the killer of both the apothecary and the priest was still at large.

Lucas Willow was a suntanned, taciturn fellow who was clearly accustomed to letting his wife do the talking for him. She introduced him to Ela and Haughton as her husband and pushed him around gently with her hands as if he were a toddler needing guidance. "Stand in the middle, then, and they'll ask you questions."

Ela wondered if Sarah had told him exactly what to say in answer to their questions. She nodded to Haughton, indicating that he should lead the charge.

"Do you happen to be in possession of a length of twisted wire?" asked the coroner.

Lucas's mouth dropped open. He glanced at his wife. She shot him a furious look that said "Use your brain and think of the right answer, you dolt!"

"I'm a farmer," mumbled Willow. "Copper wire has a variety of uses on the farm."

"Where do you buy your wire?"

"I'd buy it from the blacksmith if I needed to. And get it mended there as well."

"From your father-in-law's neighbor, Ned Skelton?"

Willow shot another panicked look at his wife—who glared at him again. "There's a blacksmith local to our farm, Harry Crutch, and I go to him for most things."

"When did you last buy a length of wire?" asked Haughton.

"I couldn't say. You'd have to ask him." Willow glanced at his wife as if looking for approval. Her face looked like a boiling cauldron. "But it was a good three years ago, I'd say."

"And what were you doing in Devizes on the night of your father-in-law's murder?"

"I went into town to discuss selling some lambs to the butcher," he said.

"You did this at night?" asked Haughton, lifting a brow.

"Well, it was evening, to be sure, but it's light until well into the evening at this time of year. I sometimes go into town after the day's work is done."

"Did you visit your father-in-law, Wilf the Younger?"

"Yes, I always pop my head into his shop when I'm in Devizes."

"You entered the shop and spoke with him?"

"It'd seem rude if I just yelled at him from the doorway, wouldn't it?" Lucas seemed very confident for a man being interviewed by the coroner in a murder case. Though sometimes cocky behavior sprang from a case of nerves. "Yes, I went in and took him some eggs and some of my wife's oatcakes."

"Was there anything different about him?"

"Different? No, I'd say much the same as usual."

"And what time was this? Before or after the bells for Vespers?"

"I'm not a church-going man so I don't pay close attention to the bells." Lucas Willow blustered on. "It was still light out."

"And how long did you stay there?"

"Long enough to inquire after his health and give him the food. Wished him well and took my leave after that. I didn't stay there jawing if that's what you mean."

"Was there anyone else in the shop when you visited?"

Lucas Willow hesitated, then glanced at his wife. She continued to glare at him as if she were trying to set him on fire with her gaze. "I don't think so."

"You were seen in the company of a tall man in a gray cloak. Could you please identify that person for the jury?"

"That would have been Sir Anselm."

They all waited for him to say more.

"And who, pray, is Sir Anselm?" asked Haughton, as if it took every ounce of patience he possessed.

"He's a local man who I sell my fleeces to. He buys up a big wagonload of fleeces from us small farmers and sells them on again in London or somewhere for a profit."

"What is his surname?"

"Allsop, I think it is."

"Sir Anselm Allsop?" Haughton drew the words out in such a way that made the name sound ludicrous. "That's his name?"

"I suppose it is," said Willow, sounding a little more uncertain.

"It's an odd time of year to be selling fleeces. They're shorn off in the spring and we're well into summer."

"I wasn't selling fleeces. I was selling this spring's lambs to the butcher."

"So you didn't come into Devizes to meet with Sir Anselm Allsop?"

"No." Again Lucas hesitated. "I ran into him outside Ned Skelton's smithy since he was getting something hammered out in there."

"So it was a surprise that he was in the forge next to your father-in-law's shop?"

"A surprise? I don't know about that. I didn't expect to see him there, but it didn't seem odd or anything like that if that's what you mean."

"You lease your land from Bradenstoke Abbey, correct?"

"Aye." Lucas Willow glanced at his wife again.

"Does Sir Anselm Allsop also lease land from Bradenstoke Abbey?"

Lucas turned white. Ela sat up in her chair. She'd wondered what Haughton was up to and now she had some idea.

Haughton leaned closer. "Well, does he?"

"I wouldn't know," muttered Lucas. "We're not close friends. I sell him my fleeces and he buys me a cup of small ale from time to time. You'll have to ask him."

"Have the two of you ever negotiated any business other than the buying and selling of fleeces?"

A murder, perhaps?

"I...I can't think of any off the top of my head."

Ela looked at the top of his head, which was perspiring enough to dampen his hair.

"You were seen speaking to him the night of Wilf the Younger's murder." Haughton stopped and stared at him.

Lucas Willow fidgeted in his chair. "We exchanged words. Would be rude not to. Wouldn't it?"

"What did you talk about?"

"I said hello and he said hello back and have a nice evening and what have you." Lucas swallowed hard.

"You were seen walking down Sheep Street in Devizes, having a conversation."

"Now that I think about it I told him about the three lambs I just sold to the butcher and he asked about buying some lambs from me next year along with the fleeces." Willow glanced at his wife. Her face remained a mask of silent fury.

"Had he ever bought lambs from you before?"

"No. Only fleeces."

"Now that we've uncovered another aspect of your

conversation, are there any other facets that you'd like to share with me and the jury and the sheriff?" Haughton gestured around the room, presumably to remind Lucas Willow where he was and caution him against lying.

"Like I said, you can ask him," muttered Lucas, sullen. "I don't remember every word that comes out of my mouth of an evening."

"Did he at any point enter your father-in-law's shop?"

Willow's foot twitched. "I don't know. I can't remember."

"Nonsense. This was barely two days ago." Haughton's voice deepened to a growl. "Either he was in the shop with you, or he wasn't."

Willow drew in a breath. "He wasn't in there with me, but whether he was in there before or after me, you'll have to ask him."

Ela glanced at Sarah Willow's face and saw it relax slightly.

Haughton, who had been sitting, stood up and walked around the tables of jurors until he was standing in the middle, right where Lucas Willow sat marooned in his chair. Willow leaned back, visibly uncomfortable at the coroner's proximity.

"Had you and your wife ever discussed the possibility of taking over your father-in-law's shop when he died?"

"I suppose we had. Be odd if we hadn't, wouldn't it?"

"Please refrain from asking me any more unnecessary questions," said Haughton calmly. "Did you like the idea of becoming an apothecary?"

"Not in the least," said Willow quickly. "I like to be outdoors around my animals. I can't think of anything worse than being stuck inside a dark smelly shop all day." For once his answer seemed entirely genuine.

"So if you took the shop over, your wife would tend to the customers?"

"Yes, she liked the idea of it. We were never able to have children so she's got time on her hands and gets restless stuck at the farm. Not that the old man would even let her lift a finger to help. She offered enough times."

"So, in a way, it would be a good thing for you if your father-in-law died as then she could take over the shop."

Willow stared at him for a moment. "No, sir, it would not be a good thing. As then my wife would insist on moving into the town and living above the shop and that would be the end of my lambs and living out in the country and might as well be the end of my blessed life." For once he didn't look at his wife.

Ela sat back in her chair, blinking. If Sarah Willow wanted her father dead so she could step into his shoes, it seemed that her husband was not of the same mind. Unless he was more cunning than he seemed.

"You were likely the last person to see your father-in-law alive on the night he was killed."

"Except for the murderer," corrected Willow.

"Did Sir Anselm know your father?"

"Not that I know of, but he may well have. Devizes isn't that large and I know most people in the town in one way or another."

Ela had to admit that he had a point. Haughton turned over questioning to her and all she could think about was bringing in Sir Anselm Allsop—if such a person really existed—and questioning him to see if Lucas Willow had been telling the truth.

She asked if the jurors had questions for Lucas Willow, and they asked about his knowledge of herbs and poisons and the contents of the shop.

"So," said John the tanner. "It would have been quite easy for you to ask your father-in-law the whereabouts of one poison or another on his shelves and perhaps even give you a morsel of it to take home to....poison rats in your thatch or whatever story you would have told him."

"You don't want to poison rats in a thatch, sir. They'll die in there and make a horrible smell," said Lucas Willow. "Better to bait and trap them. Every farmer knows that."

"That's beside the point," said John, growing agitated. "You could have obtained poison from him then realized that, once the coroner identified Father Gilbert's means of death, your father-in-law would instantly know it was you who had killed the priest."

"I suppose he could have, but I didn't kill Father Gilbert and I've never touched any of the poisons in his shop."

Ela rose to her feet. "Lucas Willow, I'm afraid that enough doubt remains among us about your activities in Devizes on the evening in question that I must keep you in custody here at the castle until we can question Sir Anselm. If he corroborates your account then you shall be freed."

Lucas Willow did not look particularly reassured by this information.

Ela sent guards to find Sir Anselm and to ensure that he did not evade the summons by leaving the county. She dispatched Lucas Willow, fussing and fuming, to the dungeon and told his wife to go home and tend to their animals in his absence.

Sarah Willow, almost apoplectic, insisted that the animals were his business and she couldn't manage them.

"Lambs and sheep don't need to be milked," said Ela coolly. "Exactly what onerous tasks do you anticipate being too hard for you?"

"We do have a cow who needs milking and she's not easy to milk, either!" she spluttered. "And I have to feed the chickens and collect the eggs and make butter and..." she tailed off.

"You'll manage for a day," said Ela. If anything the wife

was just as likely to be guilty as her husband, but she wasn't seen in Devizes on the night of the murder so he would have to do for now.

~

Sir Anselm Allsop proved difficult to locate. He was finally tracked down to the Three Keys in Devizes, where he was well into his cups. He was brought to the castle on his horse, but led by a guard, due to him being in no condition to do more than sit astride it.

A man in his early thirties, he had long curls like a girl that brushed his shoulders and big mournful brown eyes. Ela was tempted to question him on arrival, on the principle of in vino veritas, but decided to wait until the jury was assembled the following morning.

The tall thin knight was not put down in the dungeon—where he might have been able to confer with Lucas Willow—but confined to a chamber near the hall, with a guard stationed at the door. In the morning he was given a modest breakfast and the attentions of a lad to help him dress himself decently, a courtesy extended due to his knightly status.

The jurors trickled in after they had attended to the morning's urgent business of removing bread loaves from ovens or grinding flour for their customers. Once they were seated at the tables and Sir Anselm's lanky form was draped languorously across the chair in between them, she sent for Lucas Willow to be brought from the dungeon.

Before Willow arrived, she had Bill Talbot call for silence and began questioning the knight. "Sir Anselm, what were you doing in Devizes on Tuesday last?

"Why I hardly remember. I suppose I came to eat and drink at the Three Keys." He spoke with a half smile as if used to winning favor with his charm. He was not a particularly handsome man, with a long horse-face and oddly high cheekbones.

"You are aware that the apothecary Wilf the Younger was found dead the following morning?"

"I heard tell of it. A sad business."

"Did you know the apothecary?"

"Never laid eyes on him as far as I know. I'm not one for potions and possets. And he didn't frequent the Three Keys." He smiled again, revealing long ivory-colored teeth.

"Do you know a man called Lucas Willow?"

"I do. I've bought fleeces off him."

"You rent your manor?" Ela knew the answer but wanted the jury to know.

"I do. Been renting it these last two years as I am now retired from fighting for king and country." He flashed another toothy smile.

"And you make a living solely from this manor?" asked Ela, doubtful.

"I've brought the neglected orchard back to life and there's grazing for my horse but not much useful land for crops and pasture. I've found a market buying fleeces from the farmers roundabouts and selling them for a profit in London or Southhampton. Reselling them is I how I earn my bread, since I am a younger son and lacking an inheritance. I'm not a rich man but I'm able to keep a decent roof over my head."

"That roof belongs to Bradenstoke Abbey?"

"It does, my lady."

"Do you find them to be a good landlord?"

"I have no complaints, my lady."

"I've heard the tithes they charge are steep," she said. "Do you find them so?"

"I suppose tithes are always steeper than one would want.

At least that's been my experience."

"How do you pay the tithes if you're not raising any animals or crops?"

"I've paid them in fleeces once or twice, but I generally prefer to pay in coin." His easy expression had tightened somewhat. "But what does this have to do with the herb seller?"

"I'll ask the questions here," said Ela sharply. Lucas Willow had appeared, being led by two guards, and was seated off to one side. This all happened behind Sir Anselm, so he was presumably unaware that Willow was now present.

"Did you meet with Lucas Willow in Devizes that night?"

"I didn't arrange to meet with him if that's what you mean. I simply bumped into him on Sheep Street. I was headed to the blacksmith for some new buckles, and he was on an errand of his own."

"You conversed?"

"We exchanged a few pleasantries." He was sitting up taller in the chair now.

"About what exactly?" asked Ela, pinning him with a stern gaze.

"This and that. I hardly remember. Nothing of consequence."

"How long would you say you were together?"

"Just the time it took to walk from Sheep Street to the blacksmith's shop. Barely time to grumble about the weather." He seemed to be relaxing again. Perhaps because the conversation had moved away from Bradenstoke Abbey and its tithes.

"Do you ever visit Bradenstoke Abbey?"

"Well, yes, I have to visit quarterly to pay my tithes."

"And who collects the tithes?"

"All those grim clerical types look the same to me. It's not even the same person each time."

"Who did you pay them to most recently?"

He frowned. "Lissop? Something like that. A very rotund man, he was."

"Did you give him money or fleeces?"

"Money. Eleven pounds of it. I tried to give five plus a horse that's grown too slow for my needs, but he wasn't having it. Strong horse it is, too. Could pull a loaded cart all day long."

"Where did you meet with him?"

"At the tithe barn. He has a counting house of sorts there and ledgers."

"Did you visit any other part of Bradenstoke or talk to anyone else while you were there paying your tithes?"

"It was back in the spring, my lady. I hardly remember."

"The spring is not so long ago. Answer my question," said Ela.

"I don't think so. I took my payment and my horse to the tithe barn and returned home with the horse. I could hardly have gone into the cloister or made my confession with a horse in my hand."

"You could have tied the horse up in their stable yard as most visitors do," said Ela.

"But I did not."

Ela found herself running out of questions. His answers lined up well enough with Lucas Willow's and were innocuous enough to shirk any appearance of guilt. Paying tithes, willingly or unwillingly, did not provide a reason for accusation. She could open questions to the jury but most likely she would soon have to let him go back to the Three Keys and release Lucas Willow from custody for lack of evidence against him.

"Did you know Father Gilbert Berwick?" she asked, for no particular reason.

"Yes," said Sir Anselm. "He was my brother."

CHAPTER 8

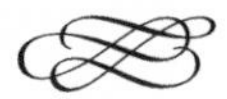

Ela tried to wrap her mind around this new fact. A sudden flurry of whispering in the hall died down to an eerie quiet. "If Father Gilbert was your brother, why do you bear different surnames?"

"I'm from my mother's second marriage and he's from her third marriage."

"You seem quite close in age."

"Not really. I'm about five years older. There are two more brothers in between us."

"So you were both younger sons." Ela struggled to think of any reason why Sir Anselm would want to kill Father Gilbert, even if they were brothers. Neither of them stood to inherit and they both seem to have found a modest but respectable place in the world. One thing was odd. "Did you not find your brother's presence to be a reason to visit Bradenstoke? You live a short ride from it according to my guards."

"Those who chose a cloistered life are not encouraged to maintain relationships with the secular world. My brother was a man of true faith and committed to the rule of the order."

Father Gilbert's austere cell, ornamented solely by the poisoned prayer book, seemed to confirm this. And Ela knew his statement to be true in many instances. It was the reason she hesitated to let her daughter Petronella take the veil at a young age.

"When did you last lay eyes on your brother?"

"Very recently. He wrote to me and begged me to make a confession as he was concerned for the state of my soul." His mouth tilted in a half smile.

"Why didn't you mention this a moment ago when you talked about paying your tithes?"

"I didn't get around to it, I suppose. I was talking about going to pay my tithes."

He's a liar, thought Ela. The kind of man who lies so easily he can barely tell the truth from a falsehood. "Did you go to Bradenstoke to make a confession?"

"I did, though as far as I'm concerned I had no sins to confess. Unlike my brother, I don't consider eating a good meal and drinking a fine wine to be a sin."

"What day was this visit to confess?"

"Looking back I suspect it was only three or four days before he died." Sir Anselm had a strange look on his face, as well he might.

Ela's nerves jangled with the realization that Father Gilbert's killer likely sat before her. "Did you visit his cell?"

"Oh dear me, no. That wouldn't be allowed at all. We met in the chapel and he led me into the confessional."

"How long were you with him?"

"Not long, my lady. As I said, I had nothing grave to confess."

His nonchalant attitude irked Ela, especially on top of his

misleading answer about visiting to pay his tithes. “At what time did this visit and confession take place?”

“It was some time shortly after morning Mass but before the bells for Nones.”

“And did you stay to make your penance in the chapel?”

He made a look of attempted contrition. “I confess I did not. As I mentioned, I did not share my brother’s conviction that I’ll be denied a place in Heaven for living a comfortable life.”

“Had you visited your brother and confessed before?”

“Once or twice. It seemed to please him. I thought it most awkward and strange to be asking my younger brother for absolution.”

“When was the last time before this one?”

“I don’t know, my lady. Some time ago.”

“Did your brother take confession from others outside the abbey?”

“I daresay he did, my lady. He was a priest after all and a good-hearted one. He found joy in helping relieve others of the burden of their sins. For myself, I can’t imagine having to go through the rest of my life carrying all those dark secrets close to my chest.” He looked up and laughed. “I’m an open book, especially after a skin of new wine. I have no secrets. You can ask anyone at the Three Keys.”

“I shall.”

Ela was still reeling from shock at the revelation that his brother was the murdered man, and that he’d visited him in the days before his death. He had to be the killer, yet he seemed so calm and confident when most men would be sweating before a jury in her hall.

“It seems a dreadful coincidence that you should pay a rare visit to him only for him to drop dead a few days later.” She let that settle in the air for a moment before continuing. “How did you learn of your brother’s death?”

"I heard the terrible news at the Three Keys, my lady. I came in for a cup of wine and the place was abuzz with news of a murdered priest at the abbey. It didn't take long before I realized that the dead man was my brother."

"Were you saddened by his death?"

Sir Anselm Allsop regarded her as if this question was too ludicrous to answer. "Of course, my lady. Why wouldn't I be? He was my brother and, even though we didn't grow up side by side, I still held affection for him. He was a good and kind man who wouldn't hurt a fly. I wept like a baby when I learned he was dead. Struck down by a witch, they said."

Ela's heart sank at this rumor that just wouldn't die. Sister Alisande spent most days on her bony knees, fingering her worn rosary and praying for the souls of everyone on earth. How could these people think her capable of evil?

"What did you think of this rumor about a witch?"

"Stuff and nonsense, of course! He might as well have been felled by a fairy. I heard a week or so later that poison was found in his room."

"Do you know anyone who might have had cause to poison him?"

"Not a soul," said Allsop. "But I don't know who his friends or enemies were, due to him being in holy orders and me being anything but."

"Did he have any rivals within the abbey?" The closed world of a cloistered community was not immune to the petty jealousies and power struggles that plagued humanity.

"If he did, I know nothing of them."

"Did he ever speak of the prior, Father Augustine, or Father Sebastian, the other priest at Bradenstoke?"

"Not to me. He spoke of little but his deep concern for the tattered state of my immortal soul." Ela expected him to smile, but he didn't. "Looking back I suppose he cared more for me than anyone else I know. It's hard to believe he's gone and I shan't hear him scold me again."

Ela did not find his mournful response in the least bit convincing. She turned to the jury. "Let me remind the jurors that the man before you not only visited Father Gilbert Berwick right before his death but spent considerable time in the smithy next to Wilf the Younger's shop on the very evening that he was killed. Do you have questions for him?"

Will Dyer, the cooper, stood and cleared his throat. "Frankly this looks very damning. Do you expect us to believe that you were within spitting distance of two murders just days apart and had nothing to do with them?"

Sir Anselm had the decency to hang his long head a little. "I'm afraid that's all I can do because it's the truth. Why would I want to kill my brother that's cloistered and no trouble to any man? Why would I want to kill a herb seller I don't even know?"

Ela hated that he had a point. Without evidence or motive, it could prove very hard to convict a man of murder. Most justices were reluctant to take a man's life—especially a man who was a noble or a knight—without solid proof or witness that he'd committed the crime.

"What did you do for a living before you came to this area?" Perhaps she could dig into his history and find a trail of mysterious deaths.

"I'm proud to say that I was in the king's service for some years. I fought in the crusades, in France, and even here at home during the Barons' War."

"Those were all some time ago," said Ela. "What have you done since?"

"For some time I enjoyed life on the spoils of war that I was lucky to bring back from my travels. I rented a manor in Hampshire and spent my days reading and hunting and enjoying good food and drink. Sadly I was not diligent in the business of running a manor and soon found myself in need of smaller and cheaper accommodations, and a means of making a living."

Ela resolved to dig into his military background. There would be records of where he served, and how he'd conducted himself. She could at least verify or challenge that part of his story. And she could write to the sheriff of Hampshire to inquire as to his conduct in that county. What else could she verify?

"You say that your brother wrote and begged to you visit Bradenstoke and make your confession shortly before his death," she said slowly. "Are you still in possession of the letter he wrote to you?"

"Sadly no, my lady. It went into the fire."

"You did not think to clean and reuse the parchment?" The work to make parchment and vellum from dried animal hides was arduous enough that reuse of the materials was the norm, rather than the exception.

"If I were a more frugal man, I would perhaps live a happier and more peaceful life."

"So you have no way to prove that your brother invited you there on that day? How do we know that you went to confession at all? Perhaps you entered Bradenstoke with a vial of deadly poison and took it straight to your brother's cell."

He didn't flinch. "I'm sure you'll find there are witnesses to the contrary. The anchoress, for one. She sees all and hears all from her perch next to the chapel."

Ela blinked. This was true. She could see the interior of the chapel from one side of her shelter, and the cloister from her outside window. Her heart sank at the thought of drawing Alisande into the proceedings. The jury had seemed so willing to believe her a witch, and she'd done nothing but compound their suspicion that she had unnatural powers during her last visit to the hall.

Still...perhaps she could provide the information needed to prove a link between Sir Anselm and his brother's untimely death. She asked a guard to bring Sister Alisande into the hall.

While they waited, the jurors peppered him with questions that he answered calmly and without revealing much information about himself that they didn't already know. He'd been injured twice while fighting and once contracted marsh fever but had recovered completely each time, by the grace of God. His straitened circumstances made it difficult to maintain friendships from his earlier years, as he could not entertain or travel beyond the immediate environs. He had a small flock of sheep but had not yet mastered the art of breeding for very fine fleece, as some of his neighbors did. He came across as modest, unassuming, and bearing his reduced circumstances with considerable grace and fortitude.

Sister Alisande shuffled slowly into the hall on Petronella's arm. She blinked at all the gathered jurors and townsfolk as if they shone too hard on her eyes.

"Good afternoon, Sister Alisande," said Ela, with fear in her heart that the old woman would again say something to incriminate herself in the eyes of the jurors. "We have disturbed your prayers in the hope that you were a witness to certain events in the days before Father Gilbert's untimely death."

Alisande moved through the hall at an agonizingly slow pace, leaning heavily on Petronella's arm. Ela was touched to see her daughter encourage and support the older woman. Finally, Sister Alisande was lowered into a chair not far from where Sir Anselm sat in between the assembled tables of jurors.

"Sister Alisande, do you recognize the man sitting next to you?"

Sister Alisande turned her head, peering past the dark veil that covered her white veil and wimple, and studied Sir Anselm.

He attempted a half smile with rather grotesque results.

"I do. He came into the chapel for confession not long ago."

"Do you remember who his confessor was?" asked Ela.

"Father Gilbert." Her thin, reedy voice had no hesitation.

"Were you able to overhear what was said in the confessional?" asked Ela, her heart beating harder.

"If I did, I would take such utterances to my grave," she said solemnly.

"Even if they provided justification for a murder?" asked Ela.

"Even then. Though in this case, I can assure you that they did not."

A murmur arose among the jurors.

"By that last statement do you mean that what you overheard was a perfectly innocuous confession of the sort that any man might make?"

Sister Alisande hesitated for a moment, looking up at one of the high windows in the opposite wall as if consulting her maker in Heaven. Then she looked at Ela. "I believe it was. At least from what I heard."

"Thank you for your frankness. Did you overhear any other conversation between these two men?"

"I did not."

"Did you see them greet each other?" Ela hoped for evidence of some enmity between them.

"I heard this man here," she indicated Sir Anselm, "approach a lay brother in the nave and say that he was here for confession with Father Gilbert. The lay brother said that

Father Gilbert was occupied in confession already and that he would have to wait. This man then approached the window of my cell and greeted me with praise for my life of prayerful solitude."

"Did you reply?"

"I blessed him with the sign of the cross. The abbot doesn't like it when I talk to people. He says it's a distraction."

"Did he say anything further?"

"He did. He asked me several questions about myself. How long I'd been there and my age and did I get lonely."

Sir Anselm sat listening to this with perfect equanimity.

"And did you reply?"

"No, my lady. It pained me greatly not to, but my duty is to the abbot and to God. I murmured a blessing so as not to be perceived as rude."

Ela turned to Sir Anselm. "Did you know that the anchoress was not allowed to speak with you?"

"I most certainly did not," said Sir Anselm. "And I now apologize for upsetting her. I've never met an anchoress before and know little of their ways. I just happened to notice her in her cell next to the chapel, and I became curious about her."

"How long did you wait before Father Gilbert finished with his previous confession."

"Not long at all," said Sir Anselm. "Just enough time to ask these questions and receive her mysterious blessing in reply. Then he emerged from the confessional box and invited me in."

"Sister Alisande, what words of greeting were exchanged between Father Gilbert and the man next to you?"

"Unless my memory fails me, I believe that he said, "God be with you, my brother."

"Who said that?"

"The man next to me said that."

"And how did Father Gilbert respond?"

"And also with you, my brother in Christ," said Alisande. "And then he beckoned him into the confessional."

"How long were they in there together?" asked Ela of Alisande.

"Perhaps enough time for me to say a few decades of the rosary."

"And they emerged together?"

"Father Gilbert emerged first, as is typical. Sometimes the penitent stays in the confessional while they make their penance, and sometimes they kneel elsewhere in the chapel. This man," she indicated Sir Anselm, "Left the confessional and came again to my window on the inside of the chapel."

Sir Anselm looked at her calmly, apparently undisturbed by her recollections.

"Did he say anything?" asked Ela.

"He thanked me for my blessings and wished me the same. Then he turned and left the chapel without making any penance at all."

"Where was Father Gilbert by this time?"

"He led another penitent into the confessional. It was a Sunday and several parishioners were waiting to unburden themselves of their sins."

"I see. Did you see where Sir Anselm went after he left the chapel?" Ela's heart surged with hope that Sister Alisande saw him cross the cloister to where the stairs ascended to Father Gilbert's chamber.

"I saw him leave the chapel by the door on the opposite side of the nave," she said. "I reflected on my sorrow at not being able to interact with him."

"Did you wonder why he didn't stay to make his penance?"

"No. It's not so unusual that men or women who make

confession are in a rush to get back to their cows or children or pot of stew and pledge to make their penance later when they have more time. I hear them say it often."

"Do you know if he left the abbey, or if he went elsewhere within the abbey walls?" Alisande's cell was off to one side, but the abbey complex was small enough that she might be able to hear activities in the area at the gates through her exterior window.

"I heard him outside the gate thanking the lay brother for watching his horse while he was within. He must have spoken very loud for me to hear this as my cell is on the opposite side of the chapel."

"Did you by any chance hear his arrival?" If he left right away, Ela now wondered if he'd visited Father Gilbert's room before making his confession.

"Now that I think of it, before he entered I heard him tell the same man to be sure his horse did not stand too close to anyone else's horse."

"Why did you make that request?" asked Ela of Sir Anselm.

"My mare has a powerful kick in her if another horse comes near her hind end. There were two other horses tied out there and I wanted to make sure they didn't place another one too near to her. I can't afford a lawsuit over another man's horse getting injured."

Ela nodded. She heard enough of these kinds of complaints in her hall all day from one petitioner after another—piglets, chickens, and lambs savaged by loose dogs, someone kicked or trampled by another man's cow or horse. "Where did you go after making your confession?"

"I headed directly to the Three Keys to enjoy a Sunday roast."

Ela sighed. She still didn't have anything but proximity to tie Sir Anselm to either murder. Still, similar to Lucas

Willow, his presence near the murder scene was enough for her to hold him while she investigated further. His knighthood, however, made it more difficult for her to put him in the dungeon, and she didn't want him talking to Willow.

"Sir Anselm, I cannot let you leave the castle. You shall be kept secure in one of our chambers while we conduct inquiries at the Three Keys and Bradenstoke."

Grateful that Sister Alisande had told her side of the story without uttering any mysterious visions or prophetic pronouncements, she wrapped up the proceedings and sent the jurors home and Sister Alisande back to the safety of her chamber. She placed Sir Anselm in a small chamber deep inside one of the thick-walled guard towers and left instructions for him to be treated as a guest but watched like a hawk day and night.

CHAPTER 9

Ela took Bill Talbot with her on her return journey to Devizes the following day. The tavern was a low, ancient-looking structure in the middle of Long Street with a heavy thatched roof hunkering over it. Smoke and the fragrance of roasting meat rose from somewhere inside, though she could not see a chimney from the street.

Ela noticed the iron rings fixed in the wood timbers of the wall outside for men to tie up their horses while they ate and drank. Even though it was only midmorning when they arrived, a gray horse stood tied outside.

Bill pulled the iron handle on the scarred oak door and opened a portal into the smoky depths. Ela always felt a tinge of apprehension on entering such a place. As her eyes adjusted to the gloom, she saw the smoke was from a piglet roasting on a spit over a great fireplace in the back of the room. Only one man sat there, hunched over a cup of ale.

"I fear we've come at the wrong time," said Ela softly, to Bill. "The regulars are either at work or still abed, nursing their hangovers from last night."

"The master and mistress of the house, or their serving wench, would overhear conversations," he replied quietly.

She nodded and lifted her skirts to walk across the dark and uneven flagstone floor, strewn with musty-looking straw, towards the fireplace, where someone sat in the shadows, turning the handle on the spit. As her eyes adjusted to the gloom, she saw it was a boy of about eight with a vacant expression on his face.

"Is your master or mistress home?"

"Aye, in the back," he said as if he was used to this question.

As he spoke, a large woman appeared through an arched doorway, wiping her hands on her apron. "Welcome, mistress. What can I serve you this fine morning?"

Ela's stomach recoiled at the prospect of taking even a cup of wine in this dingy tavern. Bill spoke up. "This is Ela, Countess of Salisbury, Sheriff of Wiltshire."

"We're here to ask some questions about one of your regular customers," said Ela. "Sir Anselm Allsop."

"He's here often enough," she said. "Is he in trouble?"

"I'll ask the questions," said Ela. "What kind of trouble might you expect him to be in?"

"Well," she hesitated and tugged at her kerchief. "He drinks an awful lot of wine which is better for my business than it is for his health. He was found laid flat out in the alley once, with his purse empty."

"He's a drunkard?"

"Yes, my lady, I'm afraid he is. Pays his bills, though, so it's none of my business what he does with his coin." Her brow furrowed. "He's not hurt or killed is he? He was in here just yesterday."

"No, he's at my castle." She'd insisted on holding him for a day so she could come to Devizes and ask about him, otherwise he'd probably be sitting in the corner sipping his wine.

"His brother was killed recently and I'm trying to discover who murdered him."

"Oh dear, what a sad thing to happen."

"You didn't know about this already?"

"I didn't even know he had a brother. He's not from these parts. He turned up about two years ago and started coming in every day, but he's not a great talker. He speaks like a gentleman but buys and sells fleeces like a tradesman."

"Do you know where he lives?" Ela thought it odd that he was such an enigma. Had he never mentioned a brother who was a priest at Bradenstoke?

"Has a manor somewhere nearby, I believe. I haven't sat jawing with him. You might get more useful information from my husband. Let me fetch him."

They waited as she disappeared into a gloomy black tunnel of a hallway, and heard her open a door to a sound of splashing water and call out to someone. After what seemed like an eternity, a harried-looking middle-aged man with strands of dark hair smoothed across a nearly-bald pate, and water splashed on the sleeves of his tunic, shuffled into the room. "My wife sent me to have words with the sheriff," he said, looking at Bill.

"I am the sheriff," said Ela, mildly annoyed. This whole expedition was starting to feel like a waste of time. "And we're here to inquire about Sir Anselm Allsop. Do you know him well?"

"I suppose I know him as well as anyone," he said. She waited for him to expand on this, but he didn't. He looked annoyed at being interrupted at his work of washing cups or whatever he was doing.

"Did he seem sad when his brother died?"

"His brother died?"

"Yes, he was the priest from Bradenstoke who was poisoned recently. Surely you've heard of it."

"I suppose I did, now that you mention it, but I didn't realize that was his brother. And you think Anselm had a hand in it?" The tavern owner looked shocked.

"We don't know who poisoned him. We're gathering information. From what you overheard, did it sound like he had poor relations with his brother?"

"Now, I didn't say that. Especially not if the man's been killed. I don't like to accuse a man of anything I didn't see with my own eyes. And Sir Anselm would hardly have brought a priest in here for a drink, now, would he?" He seemed to find this funny. "I can't see Anselm killing anyone. He's not sober long enough, for one thing."

"Does he have friends who come here who might be able to tell me more about him?"

"You can ask Edgar over there. He knows Sir Anselm as he's sold him fleeces and they've shared a cup of ale." He gestured to the sole customer, who sat at a table nursing a cup and gazing at the roasting meat. No doubt he was waiting to enjoy a meal of it.

"I thank you for your time."

Ela approached the customer and introduced herself. He was a short and compact man in late middle age with a flat nose in the middle of a square face. Somewhat flummoxed, he rose to his feet and introduced himself as Edgar Whiting, farmer. To mix things up a little, Ela asked him first about the apothecary. "Did you know Wilf the Younger?"

"Oh, aye. Good man, Wilf. Made me a paste of herbs to bandage my gout when it flares up. I daresay I'll just have to suffer with it now, more's the pity."

"Have the townspeople any theories on who might have killed him?" Ela wasn't averse to learning the gossip, even though it was often very far from the truth.

"They say his daughter and her husband have been

dragged up on charges, so maybe they decided to send him to meet his Maker and take over his shop."

Ela blinked. She knew that calling people before a jury, even for information-gathering purposes, could harm their reputation. "Do people suspect the Willows of killing him?"

"I haven't heard anyone come out and say it but Ned Skelton was on the jury recently and said that Lucas Willow visited the old man on the night of his death."

And Anselm Allsop was there too, only a few yards away in the blacksmith's forge.

"Do you know Sir Anselm Allsop?"

"Hard to come here without tripping over him. I come here for my daily meal since my wife died, but he comes for the wine and ale as well as the victuals. And he's been drinking more than ever since he came into money."

"Money? What do you mean?" Ela's mind quickened.

"Spending it like water, he is. Buying rounds and giving coins to the serving wench like he's made of it."

"When did this spending start?"

Edgar Whiting frowned. "About a fortnight ago, perhaps? The lads were asking him if he found the pot of gold at the end of the rainbow, but he said he made a good deal with a rich customer."

"What kind of a deal?"

"He wouldn't say. They asked him, of course. Chancers, some of them who'd steal a customer right out from under you. But even deep in his cups, he wouldn't breathe a word about it."

"Was it part of his usual business of trading in fleeces?"

"What else would it be? Whatever it was it left him with a heavy purse."

"Had he ever mentioned to you that he had a brother?"

"I don't think so. Never mentioned any family. He's not from around here. Blew in on the wind. I can't say I know anything about him but that he trades in fleeces and drinks like he has a hollow leg."

"Thank you, Farmer Whiting. You've been most helpful."

~

BACK AT THE CASTLE, Ela found Sir Anselm in quite a state. He was pale and shaking and pacing in the chamber where she'd ordered him confined.

She invited him to join her for the evening meal, on the assurance that he could return home the following day. She could always change her mind if he suddenly confessed to a crime or gave her reason for suspicion.

"Are you ill, Sir Anselm?"

"Thirsty, my lady. I have a great thirst."

"It shall be slaked at my table."

Ela headed down to the hall and told Bill Talbot about Anselm's agitated state.

"It's the drink, my lady. When a man pickles himself in liquor he can't manage without it. I've seen it a few times over the years. I once knew an old soldier who begged and pleaded for a drink until he had fell quite ill—writhing and shaking on the floor, he was. I broke down and bought him a cup of wine. It's like a sickness when the drink takes hold of them like that."

"Will you drink along with him tonight? I'd like to get him deep in his cups and see if we can find out how he came into money recently."

"It's difficult work but I trust myself to rise to the occasion." He said it with such a sober expression that Ela found herself laughing. "I'll match him cup for cup."

~

Sir Anselm, who had been without drink other than fresh spring water and cow's milk for two days—on Ela's orders—put up no argument about joining them in the hall for dinner and a freshly tapped barrel of Burgundy wine.

"I may leave tomorrow at first light?" he asked, as they took their seats at Ela's table.

"If you are inclined to rise from your bed that early, you can indeed," said Ela with a smile. Whether she followed through on that promise depended entirely on what information they might extract from him tonight.

Elsie brought in cups and a jug of wine and filled the cups at the table. Sir Anselm took his with a shaking hand. Even then, he contemplated the shimmering golden surface of his wine before taking a delicate sip of it, like a man sipping a hot toddy.

"Smooth as silk," he exclaimed. He sipped again. "It has a taste of the hills near Auxerre."

Ela blinked. "It's from that region, so you're right. How did you acquire such intimate knowledge of wine?"

"My father had a taste for fine wines and imported them for his table."

"Where did you grow up?"

"We spent the winter season in London and summer at the family estate near Worcester." Rather than slurping down the contents of his cup, Sir Anselm put it gently on the table and took an offered sweetmeat from Elsie's platter. He ate it with knightly grace.

"How did you come to live in Wiltshire?"

"I suppose I drifted here, like dandelion fluff," he said with a smile. He took a rather more eager sip of his wine. "After I spent through my spoils of war, I wandered over here to visit my brother and I saw opportunity amid the rich sheep pastures and prosperous towns of this shire."

Sitting at such close quarters, and listening to the details of his story, Ela realized that Sir Anselm was older than she'd thought—closer to forty than thirty. His hair had almost no gray in it, but up close she could see the beginning of wrinkles around the eyes and mouth of his long, solemn face.

"Have you been married?" she asked casually. It was the politest way she could think of to ask why a man in middle age had no wife or children.

"I'm afraid I'm not that much of a catch." He took the deepest swig yet of his wine. "My noble birth confines me to courting ladies of similar standing, however my lack of wealth and my business in sheep fleeces are sure to frighten any young noblewoman's parents into hiding her from sight when I approach."

"You would not consider courting the daughter of a successful tradesman?" Ela asked out of genuine curiosity. The strictures of social class sometimes fascinated her. She inhabited a very fine sliver of society. As the daughter of a wealthy and powerful earl, she'd been told from a very early age that only members of the very upper echelons of nobility were suitable companions. However, not being royal, she was not considered a suitable bride for royalty—unless her intended spouse was the bastard son of a king. Her marriage to William—one of Henry II's illegitimate—but claimed and even well-loved—heirs, was planned when she was still a young girl and she'd had no say in it one way or the other. "I've heard of more than a few marriages between minor nobles and wealthy merchants."

"I would certainly consider it if such a damsel or her parents would show even the slightest inkling of interest in a proposal from me. My business does not yet generate sufficient profits to support a wife and children in suitable comfort. Thus I'm looking to branch out into buying and selling lambs as well as fleeces."

"Very sensible." Ela found herself warming to Sir Anselm,

even as Bill Talbot topped up both their cups with the smooth white wine. "You'll find that a wife steadies a man and provides comfort such that he no longer needs to find it at the bottom of a wine cup."

Sir Anselm looked down at his cup and she could see she'd embarrassed him. His hands had stopped shaking and his whole face had relaxed considerably with even one cup of wine. "I confess I've become too dependent on wine for solace. I suppose that's because my only friendships occur over a brimming cup at the Three Keys."

Ela decided this was as good a moment as any to question him about Lucas Willow, who was still in the dungeon, despite his wife's angry protests. "Has Lucas Willow ever been to your house?" Were they just casual acquaintances, or was there more to the relationship?

Visibly taken aback, Sir Anselm hesitated. "He's delivered his fleeces to my manor on more than one occasion. I may have given him a cup of ale or a wedge of bread and cheese."

"So the two of you have more than a passing acquaintance."

"I suppose you could say that, but I wouldn't call us friends."

"Do you know his wife?"

"Not at all. Never even met her," he said quickly.

"Did you know Wilf the Younger, the apothecary, who was her father?"

"Can't say I did. Perhaps if I had I'd have found a means to calm my nerves other than drink. A terrible shame for him to be killed in that way."

"When I spoke to people at the Three Keys they wondered if Lucas Willow had killed his father-in-law to take over the shop, but Willow himself says he had no interest in the business and preferred to farm. Which is true?"

"Lucas Willow wouldn't kill his father-in-law. I don't think that for a moment. He's a sturdy and sensible man."

"What about his wife?"

"As I just told you, I don't know her. I dare say she's a good woman as I've never heard different. I hardly think she'd strangle her father, especially when he was very old anyway according to his son-in-law."

Ela resolved to release Lucas Willow from her dungeon in the morning. He'd had no shortage of opportunity to kill his father-in-law but lacked motive.

"Do you have other friends in the vicinity?"

"I'm afraid I'm friendless as a newborn babe, except for those I meet over a cup of ale at the Three Keys. I confess that sometimes I envied my brother his simple life of prayer and quiet companionship within the carved stone halls of Bradenstoke Abbey."

Ela's heart quickened at the mention of his murdered brother. Perhaps he was about to reveal some confidences. "It's a shame that you weren't able to spend more time with him when you lived so near to each other."

"Indeed it was. I often thought the same. But holy brothers have little in common with gruff and hardened men of business like myself." He attempted something along the lines of a wry grin. "So conversation was strained on the rare occasions when we did meet. As you know from dear Sister Alisande's account, my act of contrition at the abbey was quite businesslike despite our filial ties."

"Did you feel any resentment toward him?" asked Ela, with what she hoped was a kind expression. "Because he seemed so happy and well settled in his cloistered life?"

He contemplated this for a moment. "I envied his contentment. And our mother was pleased to see him settled in a respectable life. I'm afraid my path has caused her and my stepfather some grief and consternation."

"What exactly did they object to?" The question was somewhat rhetorical. Ela would be apoplectic if one of her dear children decided to set up in business as a buyer and seller of fleeces or any other trade. Still, she was trying to get a sense of the man, and what motivated him.

"I suppose that I no longer have a taste for fighting, any more than I have a taste for muttered prayers, so I earn my keep as a tradesman. A ride in the countryside on a fine bright day and a deep cup of new wine by a fire are my pleasures."

"Those pleasures are nothing to be ashamed of. I enjoy them myself." Ela found herself feeling almost motherly toward the hapless knight.

They ate a good meal of salmon poached in berries, and peas tossed with mint from the garden. Sir Anselm tossed back cup after cup of wine—Elsie had been tasked with refilling his cup at every opportunity—and poor Bill, already slurring his words, soon abandoned the effort of trying to keep up with him.

As Elsie poured a layer of thick cream over her cherry tart, Ela decided that Sir Anselm was about as drunk as a man could get without becoming incoherent or unconscious, so she resolved to question him about the newfound wealth Farmer Whiting had mentioned. The conversation had been warm and personal, covering topics such as their horses and dogs and which towns had the best markets. But it was time to dig deeper.

"I spoke to some men at the Three Keys who told me that you recently made a good deal of money." She watched his face.

He was lifting his newly filled cup to his lips and it hovered in midair, almost spilling a drop as his hand shook. "I didn't tell anyone about that." He took his sip.

"They noticed your kind generosity. One said you'd done business with a wealthy client."

Anselm stared at her, frozen. Perhaps he was racking his mind for what details could have slipped from his lips when they were too wet with strong drink. "All my clients are wealthier men than myself. That's how they afford my fleeces," he said, barely slurring his words. His cherry tart sat untouched, the cream sliding off it onto the plate.

"Whom did you make this trade with?" She asked as if simply curious.

"That's none of your business." He lowered his gaze and seemed to contemplate the glistening cherries below.

"I'm afraid it is. Perhaps you've forgotten that I'm the sheriff of Wiltshire," she said in a firmer tone.

He glanced up in alarm. "I never meant for anything to happen."

Ela leaned in, smelling blood. "You never meant for your brother to die?"

"Of course not. Why would I want that?"

"But the man who paid you had something to do with your brother's death?" Her whole body jangled with anticipation.

"No," he protested, looking at her with bleary eyes.

He's lying.

CHAPTER 10

"What did he pay you for?" Ela asked, getting as close to Sir Anselm as she could.

"He wanted me to visit my brother." Anselm slurred his words.

He's letting the cat out of the bag. She schooled her features into a casual expression. "For what purpose?"

"He said I should make confession. I told him I had nothing to confess."

"So it wasn't your brother who invited you to make confession. This man told you to go visit the abbey and make one."

Sir Anselm, drunk as he was, seemed to realize that he'd stepped in it. "I didn't say that."

"Yes, you did. Why would this man want you to visit your brother?"

"I don't know."

"You must have asked him," Ela found his half-answers infuriating. "Who was this man who paid you a great sum to visit your brother?"

"I don't know. He didn't tell me his name. Just told me to

go to the abbey to make confession and there'd be more where this came from."

"Did he come back?"

"No." He frowned. "Not yet."

Ela realized she might need to set Sir Anselm free to set a trap for this mysterious visitor. "I don't believe that you have no idea who he is."

"I swear it! I've never seen him before."

"Describe him."

Beads of sweat had formed on Anselm's brow and upper lip. "He wore a hood that covered his face. I couldn't see his eyes or his features."

"Tall or short?"

"Somewhere in between." He frowned. "Carried himself like a soldier."

"How was he dressed?"

"Gray cloak, dark tunic—brown or faded black—brown leather boots. Not a beggar, to be sure."

"And he said he'd be back with more money after you visited your brother?"

He stared at her, blinking. Then shook his head like he had a flea in his ear. He seemed to be retreating inside himself. "I didn't say that."

"Yes, you did."

"I didn't say that. I didn't! I don't know who he was or why he came. I don't know why he wanted me to visit my brother or why my brother fell dead the day after I met him for confession." Tears now formed in his eyes, which made Ela reflect that it was odd she hadn't seen any before. Even a hard-hearted man would be devastated that he'd played a role in his brother's death.

She knew he wasn't telling the full truth, but how much of his account was a lie? And how could she release him to lay a trap for this stranger, when it seemed certain that he had at least some culpability in Father Gilbert's murder?

After considerable effort to extract more information from drunk and hapless Anselm, Ela sent him to bed. She posted a guard outside his room and told them to keep him there despite any amount of protest.

~

THE NEXT MORNING, Ela gave the order for Lucas Willow to be released so he could return to his sheep. Ela summoned Haughton to accompany her to Bradenstoke to ask more questions about Sir Anselm's visit and how someone—anyone—might have gained access to Father Gilbert's cell.

Haughton rode his bay palfrey next to her. "You're quite sure Lucas Willow wasn't involved in dispatching his father-in-law? His wife seems very keen to take over the shop. I spent the day yesterday telling her about the effects of various potions and antidotes and she was both interested and intelligent in her questions. She'd already created a new bound ledger ready to record new profits and purchases and customers. I get the impression she's been waiting her whole life to step into her father's shoes."

"I'm sure some say the same about myself in the role of sheriff," said Ela with a wry smile. "The fact remains that I did not kill my husband or my father to assume the role."

Haughton laughed. "Your point is well taken, my lady. I can only hope she'll be a valued apothecary to the people of Devizes as her father was."

"No one will say a bad word about her husband. He seems a good steward of his flock and even Sir Anselm said that he never missed an opportunity to visit his old father-in-law. I don't suppose he's too happy that he'll have to live above the shop."

"I don't envy him that conversation—or battle—with his wife. She's a strong-willed and determined woman who'd be glad to never look on a sheep again."

"But you don't suspect her of killing her father?"

"Not in the least. I'm a good judge of character."

"She didn't show much emotion over his death."

"She's a dignified woman and not one to weep and wail in public." He turned to look at her. "Much like another woman I know."

"I resent these repeated comparisons of myself to a red-faced farmer's wife turned shopkeeper," said Ela, only half in jest. "I almost think I'd prefer the usual comparisons to Empress Matilda or Eleanor of Aquitaine. I can at least aspire to insults above my birth and breeding."

Haughton laughed again, and they broke into a canter across the countryside, with the phalanx of guards cantering behind at a discreet distance.

Their conversation turned serious as they rode up the lane towards the abbey. "Sir Anselm claims he was paid to visit his brother—presumably while someone else poisoned his prayerbook—but I'm not sure if he was an unwitting participant in his brother's death or some kind of paid assassin who hid his cunning under a facade of drunken buffoonery."

"Did you manage to get him sozzled last night to extract information from him?" She apprised Haughton of her rather reckless but effective scheme.

"He was barely able to speak, but when he did he came right out and said he'd been paid to visit his brother. He insisted that he didn't know who paid him, or why."

"Which seems unlikely!" said Haughton.

"He described the man who paid him but the description was vague enough to be lies. I don't trust him at all. There's something about him that's just...off. I've asked my steward to find out what he can about his military service and his family history. Hopefully, it won't take weeks or months to gather the information."

~

Eventually, they rode into the courtyard outside Bradenstoke and handed their horses to the lay brother serving as groom. Ela addressed another lay brother sweeping the stone floor. "Would you please fetch Brother Michael?" asked Ela. She caught her breath, wondering if she was about to hear that Michael had sickened and died.

"Yes, my lady." The burly lay brother hurried away, lifting his long habit with one hand.

"He's not dead, at least," whispered Ela to Haughton. "Which means we must consider him a suspect as he's the only person who had unfettered access to Father Gilbert's cell." She had a feeling of being watched, perhaps through the tiny crevices in the carved design of the cloister columns, or from the top of a nearby bell tower. The unnatural silence during the height of a weekday morning was eerie and unsettling. Even the bees seemed to be hiding in their skeps.

The lay brother returned with Brother Michael shuffling along behind him. "We got your message to seal the chamber, my lady," said Michael. "I nailed a board across the door so no one can enter."

"How have you been feeling?" asked Ela, watching his expression carefully.

He looked confused. "Sad…we're all very sad about Father Gilbert's passing."

"Naturally, but your health…have you experienced any signs of illness?"

"Right as rain, my lady, I'm happy to say." His pink-cheeked complexion underscored his words.

"Did you enter Father Gilbert's room again, after we left you there?"

"Only to clean it a little," he said brightly. "But I didn't move anything."

Ela glanced at Haughton.

"You wiped up the dust?" Haughton took a step toward Michael, which made him flinch slightly.

"Yes, sir, it's my job to—"

"I don't believe you," said Haughton in a sharp voice.

Michael shuffled. "I…I…Father Gilbert lamented over my lack of cleaning skills."

"Well, you should be rejoicing in it, because if you'd cleaned that room you might well be dead."

The look of shock on Brother Michael's face suggested that he was either innocent or had the acting talent of a professional mummer. Ela waited for him to say something, but he simply looked from her to Giles as if this mysterious pronouncement might become clear.

"Have you heard how Father Gilbert died?"

He hesitated for a moment. "They said something about poison."

"Who did?" Ela wondered how far this news had traveled.

"I'm not sure, my lady. Some of them think he was witched by Sister Alisande, but the rest of us think that he must have been poisoned." That was a reasonable enough assumption to soothe Ela's suspicions momentarily.

"What kind of poison?" she pressed.

"I don't know. I suppose in something he ate or drank. That's how you get poisoned, isn't it?"

Ela turned to Haughton, wondering if they should reveal his discovery about the nature of the dust in Father Gilbert's prayerbook. The method of his murder had already been revealed in the hall of Salisbury Castle and word of it was likely spreading across the county. Had the news not yet journeyed back here to Bradenstoke?

"The dust in Father Gilbert's prayerbook contained the poison," said Haughton quietly. "It was ground from the flesh of a deadly mushroom that can kill a man if he consumes even a tiny amount. If you'd done your job of attending to the cleanliness of the room you'd have got the dust on your hands and mouth and nose and might have sickened and died a day or more ago."

Brother Michael blinked in astonishment. "But you took the prayerbook with you. So why seal the room now the poison is gone?"

"Even the trace amounts left on the floor and the prie-dieu might be harmful when touched and inadvertently eaten, especially to one whose health is already frail."

Michael's eyes widened slightly. "One of us did get sick. Father Augustine took to his bed the day before yesterday and has been refusing food."

"Did he enter this room at any point either before or after Father Gilbert's death?"

"Not to my knowledge, but I was sent to help with the shearing of the abbey's flock the day after Father Gilbert's death, so I'd been in the shed doing that all day and lay flat on my back that evening as I was so exhausted."

"Please take me to Father Augustine," said Ela.

ELA REMEMBERED Father Augustine as the rather prickly abbott who first ordered the newly dead body to be moved and then shoved Sister Alisande forward as the chief suspect in Father Gilbert's death. She'd taken him for a man of sixty or so, but—lying in his bed, pale as the linen-clad pillows and with his skin draping over the bones of his face like a veil, he looked considerably older.

Father Augustine's room over the priory gate was—as the lay brother had observed on her first visit—less austere than Father Gilbert's. It was larger, with one window that provided a view out over the lane leading up to the priory and another that looked onto the cloister quadrangle.

The floor was of smooth wood polished with beeswax, which gave the room a pleasant smell. A shelf, fixed to the wall, contained a neat stack of leather-bound volumes. Under one window stood a large wooden chest, painted with small effigies of the saints arranged like jewels along a belt of gilding. It was a piece extravagant enough for a king's chamber and Ela felt a small shock of surprise on finding it in a priest's cell.

Ela greeted the priest, who could barely manage enough breath for a reply. "Father Augustine, did you enter Father Gilbert's chamber either before or after his death?"

"No." The word fled his lips surprisingly fast considering his weakened state. Ela didn't believe him. Now she was curious to know whether he'd entered before—possibly bearing poison on his person—or after.

"We know Father Gilbert was poisoned as we found the poison in his room."

Father Augustine's wan face barely changed. "I didn't poison him."

His denial, weak as it was and without the provocation of an accusation, deepened Ela's suspicions.

"What are your symptoms?" asked Giles Haughton.

"I'm weak and tired. So tired. I don't think I could get out of bed if I tried."

"Fever?" continued Haughton.

"No. The brothers have felt my forehead countless times but they say I'm cold rather than hot."

"The poison used on Father Gilbert causes organ failure," said Haughton. "It works on the liver and kidneys and limits their function until the body can no longer sustain life."

"I had nothing to do with poisoning Father Gilbert."

Ela admired the amount of energy it must have taken to speak this relatively long sentence in his weakened state. "If you entered his room, and especially if you touched a surface in it, you might have picked up the substance on your fingers and then eaten enough of it to sicken you. The coroner and I both suffered considerable ill effects and find ourselves lucky to have recovered."

"You both look well, praise be to God." Even Father Augustine seemed to be rallying, possibly just from the effort of communication.

"Praise be to God, indeed," said Haughton. "But you may not be so lucky if we're not able to give you the antidote."

"Antidote?" The abbot's words echoed in Ela's mind. Haughton had mentioned no such thing before, despite his illness—and hers.

"The only means to counter the effects of this poison. But of course, there's no point giving it to you if you never entered Father Gilbert's cell."

"I did," said Father Augustine quickly. "I forgot, but now you've reminded me."

Clever Haughton, thought Ela. "Was that before Father Gilbert fell dead at the altar?"

"Of course not! That would make me his poisoner." The abbott's head seemed to sink deeper into his pillow, and his wispy gray hair spread about it like a sad halo. "I did go in later on the day of his death to retrieve his prayer book for the abbey's collection."

"Brother Michael thought you might do that. He said that the abbey has quite a library."

"It's grown since I've been here, I'm proud to say." The

effort of these words seemed to leave him winded, and he gasped for breath. "But Father Gilbert's prayer book wasn't there. Perhaps the poisoner stole it."

"Indeed not, for I removed it myself," said Haughton. "Which is fortunate, since it was dust found in the pages of the prayer book that proved to be the agent of his death."

"Dust?" Father Augustine's brow crumpled. "How could dust kill a hearty young man like Father Gilbert?"

"If it's dust made of powdered death cap mushroom. They say one fresh mushroom contains enough poison to kill twenty men. By drying it and turning it into a fine powder, only a very tiny amount is required to make a man deathly ill."

Ela studied Haughton's face to see if he suspected Father Augustine. The abbott's surprise about the nature of the poison seemed genuine to her, and she now suspected him of avarice—if a love of books can be described so negatively—rather than murder.

"What's the antidote?" asked Father Augustine, lifting his head from the pillow for an instant before falling back into it.

"I'll visit your kitchens and describe the healing tonic to your cook so that she may prepare it at once."

"I'd be most grateful."

"Did you remove anything from Father Gilbert's room?" asked Haughton. "Anything at all, even a comb or a scrap of parchment? Because such a thing might bear a deadly poison lurking right here in your chamber."

"Nothing," said Father Augustine, sounding very tired. "For there was nothing in there. Nothing at all. Though it was dusty, now that I think about it. I meant to have words with Brother Michael about that. Very dusty indeed."

"Were there any visitors to the abbey in the days before Father Gilbert's death?"

"There were a few on Sunday. Parishioners come for Mass and confession."

"Do you remember a tall man called Sir Anselm Allsop?" asked Haughton.

"I've heard the name. I believe he's one of the abbey tenants who holds a farm nearby."

"Yes. Did you see him on the Sunday before Father Gilbert fell dead at the altar?"

He blinked slowly, and his head seemed to sink back into the pillow. "I don't know. There were several local folk. He may have been here. Perhaps one of the brothers can remember better than I."

~

"Is there an antidote?" asked Ela, once she and Haughton were outside Father Augustine's chamber.

"I'm afraid that was rather an exaggeration. If the poison has attacked his organs he'll be dead by the end of the week. But hope is a more potent medicine than despair and since you and I both recovered, perhaps he will, too."

"How can the room be made safe without killing the person who cleans it?" asked Ela. "The longer it's left in that state, the more likely that another hapless individual will enter and ingest the poison."

"Father Augustine may be the poisoner," said Haughton. "In which case the course of justice shall be swift and meted out by the Lord himself."

"That does not protect Sister Alisande from accusations of witchcraft and murder. If it's him I want to see him accused before a jury, ill-to-death or not."

"I suspect you'll have to bring a jury here to Bradenstoke, as he seems too weak to travel. He may not last the night."

"But why would Father Augustine want to kill his fellow

priest?" asked Ela. They'd paused in a quiet corner of the cloister, out of earshot of a lay brother sweeping the stone floor.

"Such an act is hard to fathom, but sometimes petty jealousies can take on outsized proportions in such an insular environment as a monastery. Rivalries and hostilities can even dwarf those at the king's court."

"Let's bring a jury here if we can. We'll return in the morning with two jurors and interview Father Augustine and the third priest and anyone else who seems useful."

CHAPTER 11

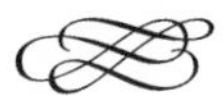

It wasn't easy to convince two of the town's most prominent citizens to give up their day to a long ride across the country to interview a sickly priest. Those such as the baker and the miller had work that couldn't be neglected. The older, less busy jurors were not inclined to endure the punishing journey to Bradenstoke.

Haughton finally managed to convince Stephen Hale the cordwainer and Will Dyer the cooper to leave their apprentices in charge of their workshops and set out for the monastery. They arrived shortly after the bells for Nones and found the priory in an uproar.

"Father Augustine is dead, my lady!" cried Michael, the lay brother who'd first alerted them of Father Gilbert's murder.

"Did he die in the night?" asked Ela softly.

"No, my lady. This very hour." Brother Michael's staring eyes and white lips spoke of shock at the circumstance. "Father Sebastian just gave him last rites."

Ela spotted the third priest—now the only living priest at Bradenstoke—in frenzied conversation with a different lay brother on the far side of the cloister. He fell silent as she approached him, and a frown creased his forehead. "Sister Alisande is behind this! She's witched him!" He spoke to Giles Haughton as if Ela wasn't even there.

"What would make you think that?" replied Haughton.

"He became delirious in his last hours, muttering and mumbling about the devil and the flames of hell."

"I fail to see what those have to do with Sister Alisande," said Ela curtly.

"Right before he breathed his last—I was with him, having performed the duties of extreme unction—he cried out that the anchoress had put a curse on him."

Father Sebastian was a man of about forty with greasy brown hair and a shiny white face. His beady brown eyes peered out from behind heavy lids with long lashes.

Again, Ela had a strong instinct that he was lying.

"Was anyone else a witness to this statement?"

"No, my lady," said Father Sebastian with a simpering expression. "I'd begged for privacy to give him his last rites."

"Then how are we to know that he died naturally and that you didn't press a pillow to his face?" asked Ela, lifting a brow.

Father Sebastian gasped. "Why would I do such a terrible thing?"

"I don't know," said Ela brightly. "Just as we don't know why someone chose to poison Father Gilbert. The poison found in his room was most certainly not sprinkled there by ancient and fragile Sister Alisande who's barely set foot outside her cell in decades. I resent the effort to blame every evil in this monastery on an innocent elderly woman."

"But she did cry out before Father Gilbert fell dead," said Father Sebastian, looking flustered. He probably wasn't used to anyone arguing with him, let alone a woman. "She knew he was about to die. How is that not witchcraft?"

Ela did not deign to answer him. "I wonder what will happen now that you are the only priest at Bradenstoke? Do you wish to be abbot, Father Sebastian?" asked Ela, feigning an air of kind curiosity.

"Why of course it would be a great honor, my lady, to serve the community of Bradenstoke in that capacity."

"What benefits does the abbot enjoy, that an ordinary priest does not?"

"Well, he has reason to go abroad more often, on abbey business. He sometimes dines with the bishop and on more than one occasion has attended the king himself at his court."

"Has he really?" said Ela, glancing at Haughton. "That does sound like an enviable lifestyle."

Father Sebastian suddenly seemed to sniff out the direction of her questions. His shiny cheeks flushed pink. "Are you suggesting I killed both Father Gilbert and Father Augustine to take up the mantle of abbot?"

"I didn't say that, Father Sebastian," said Ela softly. "You did."

"I…I…I would never do such a terrible thing! As a priest, my highest concern is for my immortal soul."

"Your immortal soul?" asked Ela, "Or those of the souls entrusted to your care?"

"Oh, theirs first, to be sure, my lady." Perspiration made his face almost luminous. "But I can assure you that I had no hand in killing either of my fellow men of God. I'm devastated by their loss."

"Have you ever visited the apothecary in Devizes?" asked Ela.

"Never. Why?"

"When were you last in Devizes?" asked Haughton.

"Why, I…" He raised his gaze as if searching around in the reaches of his brain. "Perhaps last month. I was invited to dine at the house of a parishioner who trades in fine cloth and has made some of the vestments for our abbey."

"Do you expect to be made abbot?" asked Ela. "Now that your fellow priests have died?"

His mouth worked and Ela could tell he was giving this matter serious thought, not just pretending to ponder it. "No." His shoulders sagged somewhat. "I'm a simple country priest and not from an important family. Bradenstoke, as you know, is associated with some of the most prominent nobles in the land, including yourself."

Ela nodded. "Can you think of anyone, either within Bradenstoke or without, who might have reason to kill Father Gilbert or Father Augustine?"

His forehead creased slightly and again Ela could tell he was truly pondering her question, not just pretending to. Eventually, he met her gaze. "I can think of no one and no reason. We live a simple, retired life here at Bradenstoke, far from the cares of the world."

"But you do receive occasional visits from the sons and daughters and even the elders of great families, do you not?"

"Well, yes. We have a guesthouse and passing travelers do avail themselves of our hospitality along their travels."

"And do they join you for Mass or take confession?"

"Sometimes."

"Could you provide me with a list of men and women who have visited Bradenstoke within the last year?"

His mouth dropped open. "We don't keep a visitors' book of any sort, I'm afraid."

"A list from your memory might suffice."

"My memory is a feeble and faulty instrument, I'm afraid."

"Does it recall the presence of a Sir Anselm Allsop, who rents a manor from the abbey?" She reasoned that if Father Augustine knew of him, then Father Sebastian should as well.

"I've never heard of such a person, so I wouldn't know him if I saw him." Ela wondered if he was telling the truth.

"I need a list of everyone who entered and left the abbey on the Sunday before Father Gilbert's death. The coroner will move among you and each of you is to give him the name of any man or woman you saw here that day." Ela straightened her shoulders. "We will confirm your recollections with the memory of Sister Alisande, who is currently living in my castle."

Father Sebastian brightened at the mention of Alisande. "Surely she must be tried for her crimes against man and God."

"To my knowledge, she has committed no crimes of any kind, unless great age and a touch of infirmity may be considered crimes. She certainly isn't implicated in the death of Father Augustine, who didn't sicken until after she was gone."

"The evil work of witches knows no bounds in terms of distance or time," said Father Sebastian, suddenly animated. "She could have killed him by waving her hands in the air!"

Ela sighed. "Jurors, do you have questions for Father Sebastian?"

Stephen Hale peered down the length of his nose at the priest. "Why did the monastery harbor a suspected witch in its midst?"

"I...well, Sister Alisande has been here longer than any of us. She's the same age my grandmother would be if she were still alive."

"Are you saying that seniority and advanced age excuse the practice of witchcraft?" asked Hale.

Father Sebastian blinked. "I'm not sure that any of us were aware of her practicing witchcraft. There have been a few—strange—incidents, but she's never been seen conjuring or preparing potions if that's what you mean."

"But you think she's a witch. That's what you said," pressed Hale.

"I can't see any other explanation for why Father Gilbert, a young man in perfect health, fell dead at the altar without any ill omen other than her cry of warning."

"Father Gilbert was killed by a large quantity of poisoned mushroom powder sprinkled within his cell. I do not doubt that his death was a deliberate poisoning by someone who intended him to die from repeated exposure over several days," said Ela. "Father Augustine appears to have died by the same poison, most likely because he simply entered the room to retrieve a prayerbook and had the misfortune to get the dust on his hands and unwittingly consume it. He was older, so less of the toxin was required to kill him. Unless Sister Alisande is an arch poisoner, with access to deadly toxins and the means to spread them without injury to herself, we can eliminate her as a suspect."

"But a witch could cast a spell to protect herself," protested Will Dyer, who'd stood silent and stolid this whole time.

Ela resisted the urge to roll her eyes. Why were two experienced and usually sensible jurors so quick to suspect witchcraft? "Do you intend to blame every crime in Wiltshire on witchcraft and sorcery? Surely it could be used as an excuse for almost every mischief and misfortune in England. It's far more likely that Father Gilbert was deliberately murdered for some reason that we have not yet discovered. Do you agree, Sir Giles?" She looked imploringly at Haughton.

"Indeed I do, my lady. I cannot think of a single case in my long career as coroner where a crime or murder was committed by witchcraft or curses or enchantments of any kind."

Ela breathed a silent prayer of thanks that at least Giles

Haughton was still on her side, and hoped to protect Sister Alisande from these dangerous accusations.

"Did you enter Father Gilbert's cell at any point?" asked Ela of the priest.

"No, my lady."

"Keep it that way. I'll expect a list of visitors to Bradenstoke during this entire twelvemonth to be brought to my castle before dusk on Friday."

~

THE NEXT MORNING, the household was abustle with preparations for the arrival of Ela's mother, which had been announced by a messenger who arrived in the night. Alianore spent a good deal of time in London, at her house not far from Westminster. She had connections in both high and low places, and a keen ear for the latest gossip. Ela could hardly wait to hear the latest intelligence about the king's recent efforts to unseat de Burgh from his self-appointed throne.

Ela almost flew from her dais at the announcement of her mother's name. She asked a page to dismiss the remaining petitioners until the following day. Alianore swept into the hall with her tiny pet dog in her arms. The gleeful expression on her bold features told Ela that she had news so exciting that it might cause a fire between her ears if it didn't soon escape.

"Mother, do come up to my solar and refresh yourself before dinner," exclaimed Ela, before her mother's cloak was even removed.

Alianore laughed. "Goodness, such hospitality. How could I refuse?"

Ela wanted to grab her mother's hand and run with her up the stairs to the privacy of her quiet room. Rumors swirled throughout the land and no one seemed to know quite what to make of them. Furthermore, they were afraid to ask, in case they should somehow get swept up in the dangerous current of unrest sweeping through the halls of power.

Ela closed the door behind her mother. "Stephen Seagrave is now justiciar of England?" She'd received a proclamation to that effect, but no further explanation.

Alianore sat in a chair near the window and arranged her skirts delicately about her knees. A smile spread slowly across her lips. "De Burgh has gone to ground like a common fox!" She clasped her ringed hands together. "I know you've despised him ever since he sent his rosy-cheeked nephew to beg for your hand."

"I disliked him long before that, and have gained no love for him since. Is he truly banished from the king's presence?"

"Not just banished, vanished! He proposed going on a crusade to Jerusalem, but the king forbade it."

While Ela relished the idea of de Burgh coming to a sticky end in the blistering heat of the Holy Land, she preferred to see him face justice here at home. "How is it possible for him to disappear? He's a man whose entire life takes place in the public eye."

"Some are saying he's taken sanctuary in a place of worship."

"Not here in Salisbury, I know that much. He and Bishop Poore were thick as thieves a few years ago but Poore is now in Durham and some say de Burgh had a hand in his removal from Salisbury. I enjoy good relations with the current bishop, Robert de Bingham, and I'm sure I would have heard if de Burgh applied to him for sanctuary here."

"No one knows! We can eliminate any church with an Angevin or Italian bishop, as he stands accused of discriminating against them in favor of English bishops," said Alianore.

"I remember hearing that Bishop le Grante was en route to the Vatican to complain about such treatment, but he died on the way."

Alianore leaned in, eyes wide. "Now they're saying that de Burgh may have poisoned him!"

Ela stared. Was de Burgh some kind of mass poisoner? "Poisoned Bishop Le Grante?"

"I heard it from the very lips of a rather important man in the government of London, but I hesitate to reveal my source."

"I don't need to know your source. But I've heard of other instances where de Burgh is accused of poisoning those who oppose him."

Alianore's face stilled. She looked at Ela for a moment. "There are whispers that he poisoned your dear husband."

Ela blinked rapidly. She'd asked Haughton to spread the rumor for her. Had it reached the lips and ears of those in London from him? Or had it sprung up independently? "Who said this?"

"I've only heard it third hand and not from anyone with authority. Of course, they know to be careful since I am a member of dear William's family. But I never heard this rumor until recently." Alianore peered at her. "Do you countenance it with any truth?"

Yes. Ela gasped, trying to formulate her thoughts. "Naturally it would not be in my interests—or those of my sons—to accuse the second most powerful man in the land of murdering my husband..."

"Indeed not. Discretion is often the sharpest tool in one's armory." Alianore's gaze didn't waver. "But you do believe it. I can see it in your face."

Ela's heart pounded. Did she dare to seek justice for her

husband? "The king said that he'd invite everyone in the land to come forward with their complaints against de Burgh, that they may be weighed in the courts and his fate determined."

Alianore's gaze softened. "No, my dear. Don't even think of it."

"You think I must remain silent?" She'd always counseled herself thus.

"Absolutely. You're perhaps the wealthiest widow in the kingdom, and sheriff of Wiltshire and castellan of the king's garrison to boot. Your power is likely an affront to those who might seize a chance to grasp it from you. Don't give them an opening."

"You think de Burgh may survive this reckoning?"

"I've lived many years on this earth and never met a man more cunning. Sometimes I think he owns half the land in the kingdom! Did you hear he recently took the de Clare boy as a ward so he could lay claim to the earldoms of Hertford and Gloucester? They say he intends to marry the lad to his daughter Megotta."

Ela inhaled slowly "He has so many castles in Wales that I almost believe the story that he conspired with Llywelyn against Henry. I suspect he's capable of almost anything in his lust for money and power."

"What I don't understand is—why now?" asked Alianore. "De Burgh's had Henry wrapped around his little finger for over a decade. What changed his mind?"

Ela wondered how much to reveal about her recent visit to the king. "I visited King Henry myself to warn him that I'd heard a rumor that de Burgh had poisoned William Marshal." She waited to gauge her mother's reaction.

Alianore's eyes widened. "Goodness. You did stick your neck out already."

"Not that far. I couched it as a terrible rumor that the

king might want to quash. But now I can see that I was simply adding another stick of kindling to a fire built by others."

Alianore wove her fingers together. "It's best to tread carefully."

"I agree. But I do wish I knew where de Burgh was. It's not prudent for me to show too much interest."

"Fortunately, I need show no such compunction. I shall write to all my friends and beg them for the latest and most salacious news."

~

"YOU SAID you would let me go," Sir Anselm protested, after yet another night behind a locked door in her castle. "You promised." He'd risen to greet Ela at the door to the chamber where she was keeping him under guard.

"I did." Ela had been going back and forth on what to do about Anselm. While he didn't have any obvious motive for killing his brother or the apothecary, he'd visited the dead priest only days before his death from a slow-acting poison and been in the immediate vicinity of Wilf the Younger's shop the night he died.

She also knew he was a liar and she didn't trust any single thing he'd said. "I'll let you go if you tell me the name of the man who paid the large sum of money to visit your brother."

"I've told you two dozen times...I don't know his name."

"I don't believe you."

"You can stretch me on a rack and I still can't tell you who he was—because I don't know!" Sir Anselm's red-rimmed eyes pleaded with her. She'd kept him deprived of strong drink again, in the hope that she might use it as a bargaining tool.

"You shall have a cask of fine wine from the king's cellars, one that he sent me as a gift, if you can give me even a useful hint as to his identity."

This did seem to focus his attention. "A hint, you say?"

"Anything you can tell me. Did he speak with an accent? Did he walk with a limp? Did he smell of garlic? Did he favor his left hand over his right?" She leaned in. "Anything you can tell me might bring me closer to finding him."

"I had no wish to play a part in my brother's death," he said earnestly. He'd said that at least two dozen times, to the point where she almost believed him. "And I've already told you I couldn't see his face or hair because of his hood."

"A hood similar to the one you wore while getting buckles made in the smithy next to the apothecary's shop?" Ela wanted him to know that he was still under suspicion for the murders himself. "You must admit that it's not the season for hoods. It's warm outside and many a man would leave his cloak at home, not drape it to cover his head. Why did you wear a hood that day?"

Sir Anselm sagged. "Although you find me in diminished circumstances, I was raised in a noble household. A man of my birth would normally send a servant on such small errands as ordering new buckles for his horse's breast collar. I confess I was embarrassed to be seen waiting there like a stable lad sent on an errand. The one man that I keep to serve me was indisposed so I was forced to go myself."

Ela narrowed her eyes and peered at him. "Why did you wait in the shop while he worked? Why not leave the blacksmith to his business and join your friends in the Three Keys?"

Sir Anselm's mouth worked for a moment before he replied. "I wanted to make sure they were made carefully and well. I'd never hired that particular blacksmith before and wasn't sure of the quality of his work."

Doubt gnawed at Ela's insides. "Everyone in Devizes

knows you as a man who trades in wool, not as the scion of a great house. I find it hard to believe you felt a need to conceal your identity with a hood."

"Perhaps it does seem irrational, my lady. I find that navigating my life and its business is a daily battle that sometimes I am equal to, and sometimes not."

"I suspect you'd be very grateful to someone who would provide you with the means to live a life more suited to your birth?"

"Indeed yes, my lady."

"So you might find yourself tempted to do almost any kind of work if it would give you enough money or goods to secure your future?"

He hesitated at this, and she saw his hands tremble. "If you're suggesting that I am desperate enough to kill a man for any sum of money, you are wrong."

"But you're a trained knight. If your king called upon you to kill a man in his name, would you say no?"

Sir Anselm swallowed. "The king himself? I dare say I would follow his bidding. However, this man was certainly not King Henry. He was at least my age or older and King Henry is a youth."

"I did not mean to suggest that the king himself was involved, but how could you tell his age if his face was covered by a hood?"

"I saw his hands and they were sunburned and had sinews visible like a man who's been on the earth at least thirty years."

"What color were the hairs on his hands?"

He hesitated. "I didn't see any."

"Were his nails clean or dirty?"

"Clean and pared, my lady." He spoke quickly. "I noticed that right away."

"But sunburned and callused like the hands of a working man?"

"Sunburned like the hands of a man who rides a horse. I can't say if they were callused as I never saw his palms. He gave me a purse of coins. He said there would be more after I met with my brother."

"You did meet with your brother. Did he come back?"

"No."

"Did you try to contact him?"

"I don't have a way of contacting him."

"How did he reach out to you in the first place?"

"He approached me on the road out of Devizes. I was traveling back to my manor with a cartload of fleeces that I'd bought from a local farmer. He asked for a ride and I gave him one. Somehow the topic of my brother being a priest at Bradenstoke came up."

So the man had stalked and followed Anselm, looking for an opportunity to catch him alone. "Did he bring it up, or you?"

"I suppose he did. I can't think why I would have. He waxed on about the importance of confession and cleansing my soul and insisted that I needed to visit my brother and make my confession."

"What did you say?"

"I told him I preferred not to. I don't claim to live a blameless life but I don't hold with confessing sins that I intend to commit again in the near future."

"Like drinking too much."

"Exactly. I don't cheat my clients or customers. I don't covet another man's wife or gorge myself on victuals. I live a simple life. I trust that the Lord will take me as I am."

"How did he convince you to make a confession?"

"That's when he offered me money."

"How much?"

He hesitated and looked at the floor. "Ten pounds."

"Ten pounds!" Ela could hardly believe her ears. "That's an extraordinary sum. Did it not arouse your suspicions as to his motives?"

He shifted from one foot to the other. "I suppose it did. It was such an odd thing for him to say. Why would he care whether I make a confession or not, let alone wish to pay me for absolving myself of my paltry sins?"

"Did you ask him?"

"No. It seemed rude to ask. And I began to wonder if he was some sort of mystical figure like the Good Samaritan in the Bible sent to set my life on the right course."

Ela resisted the urge to roll her eyes. She couldn't tell how much of this account was lies, but she was confident it wasn't all true. "Where did he take leave of you?"

"I told him I was turning off the road to head to my manor, and he said he had further to go, but he'd be fine on foot. Then he climbed down from the cart and headed off down the road."

"How was he dressed?"

"I did notice that he wore soft shoes like a man expecting to ride rather than walk a great distance. His cloak was of fine wool and his hose had no holes. He didn't look like a poor man, and since he'd just given me a purse with ten pounds in it I knew he wasn't one. The whole experience was strange, and had almost a mystical quality."

Against her better judgment, Ela decided to set Sir Anselm Allsop free, but keep him under close observation. While it seemed that he might have played a role in his brother's death, there was a chance it was unwitting. For one thing, he had no obvious motive. Right now she didn't have enough information to pursue a conviction at the assizes. The best she could hope for was that in giving him liberty she'd bait a trap for the man who paid him. "If he comes back, you must tell me at once."

And she didn't intend to rely on Anselm's cooperation, either. She sent guards to watch the road to his manor and apprehend any strangers with or without bags filled with coins.

CHAPTER 12

Back in the hall, Ela's mother greeted her effusively. "You're not going to believe this, darling!" The tiny white dog in her arms barked for emphasis. "The messenger just delivered a letter from my dear friend Cressida. The king has summoned Hubert de Burgh to Westminster to give a full accounting of his expenditures on behalf of the royal treasuring, going back to the first year of his reign."

"That should be interesting to behold. I daresay that a good deal of the king's gold has gone into de Burgh's coffers."

"Or into his estates. The man owns enough land to start his own sovereign nation."

"When is this to take place?"

"Next week. Do you think we should be there to see it?" Alianore lifted a brow. "Dear Henry is a close relative after all."

"Oh my…" Ela looked around to see if anyone else could hear. "I would so like to see old Hubert wiggling like a worm skewered on a hook."

"There's bound to be tremendous feasting. Nobles are gathering in London like vultures around a carcass."

"Each of them no doubt anxious to rip some of the meat from de Burgh's vast estates and holdings."

"You should join them, my dear. No one ever died from having too many estates at their command."

Ela laughed. "Avarice is a sin, dear Mother. I do not intend to risk my place in God's kingdom grasping for another man's land."

"Or his ox, or his ass," her mother laughed, clearly giddy at the idea of de Burgh being under siege for once. "But the barons of England will have no such compunction. They're probably carving his estates among them like so much plum pudding. You should be there. Not to reach for a fat plum, but simply to observe."

"I suppose a few days away from Salisbury might give me a fresh perspective on these perplexing murders. Sir John Dacus can continue the investigation in my absence. I can still find no sensible reason that poor Father Gilbert was murdered, and I fear for Sister Alisande's future if I can't apprehend the perpetrator and bring him to justice."

"You think they'll insist on a trial by ordeal or some such horror?"

"I certainly don't intend to allow that to happen in my jurisdiction, but I doubt she'll be allowed to quietly fold back into her life of prayer and contemplation. Fear makes men hateful. Every time she so much as sneezes, someone will be quick to blame her for a failed harvest or even a meal that turns the stomach, let alone any illnesses or deaths. We need to find the true killer so she can return home with her innocence beyond doubt." She sighed. "I asked Father Sebastian to prepare a list of all the visitors to Bradenstoke over the last few months. I'm hoping those names will give me a line or two of inquiry to pursue."

"When is he bringing you the list?"

"Friday."

"Perfect, we shall leave for London on Saturday and be at Westminster on Monday to drink good wine and gloat while de Burgh squirms."

~

A MESSENGER ARRIVED at the castle on Friday afternoon, with a neatly lettered parchment containing the names of—supposedly—every visitor to Bradenstoke over the last twelvemonth, and those who had visited on that fateful Sunday before Father Gilbert dropped dead in the chapel.

The first names on the list were merchants and tradesmen who visited regularly. Sir Anselm Allsop was not among them, confirming his insistence that he rarely visited. His name was found further down the list, among those who held manors or farms connected to the abbey and had visited at least once during that year.

The name of the dead herb seller of Devizes was not on the list, and nor was Lucas Willow or his wife Sarah, but Ned Skelton, the blacksmith neighbor, was there. Most of the names were unknown to Ela and each would need to be investigated carefully to determine their reason for visiting the abbey on that day or any other. Ela resolved to set her co-sheriff John Dacus to work on the task.

The list of visiting nobles was fairly short but did include two members of the Marshal family and—to Ela's satisfaction—the name Hubert de Burgh.

~

ALIANORE CONTRIVED to get herself and Ela invited to Westminster on the day of de Burgh's inquisition.

"I still don't know how you do that, mother. You've taught me that if I just turn up it will be too awkward for even the king himself to turn me away. I have found that to be true, but how do you secure yourself an invitation?"

"I simply ask for one, darling. I'm but an elderly woman who enjoys an entertainment and Henry himself has told me he finds my conversation amusing."

"I suppose I should work on sharpening my wit," said Ela, while Elsie arranged an expensive new veil about her shoulders.

"There's no need for that, my dear, when your children are the king's cousins."

Their carriage arrived in the courtyard of the palace at Westminster, where de Burgh had been invited to lay bare his management of the king's accounts. They alighted and were led into a painted hall.

Instead of the anticipated refreshments and festive atmosphere, the table in the middle was bare and pages and servants hurried about like unfed chickens in a barnyard.

"What's amiss?" asked Alianore of the young blond page who'd led them in.

"The king's anticipated visitor has not arrived," said the boy quietly.

Ela could see other nobles gathered in small knots around the edge of the room. She recognized Peter de Roches, once justiciar to King John and now Bishop of Winchester, and Alianore introduced her to Henry's new chief advisors, Peter de Rievaulx, and Peter de Rivallis. Staking his independence from de Burgh, the king had gathered these Poitevins to his court and his bosom. Ela wished they could have been persuaded to have names that didn't sound so alike. On the plus side, she could address them all interchangeably as Sir Peter and thus hide any confusion.

"De Burgh's a no-show," said de Rievaulx. "Won't come

out of hiding to defend himself. Insisted on delaying the proceedings until Exaltation of the Holy Cross in mid-September. What does that say, I ask you?"

"That he's guilty of something," said Alianore quietly. "And needs more time to compound some convincing lies." She glanced at Ela, who had no desire to engage in mere gossip. She held, on her person, the list of visitors to Bradenstoke. She craved the opportunity to ask de Burgh, to his face, if he'd taken confession at Bradenstoke from Father Gilbert.

"That's what everyone's whispering, my lady," said de Rivallis. "He's been the king's right hand since his youth, and now he won't show his face to account for his deeds and failures? His cowardice beggars belief."

"He must be brought here by force," said Alianore with conviction.

"The king is in agreement." De Rivallis gestured at the other well-dressed nobles gathered along the walls of the hall. "But no one knows where he is."

The lack of refreshments was disconcerting. Ela realized she'd arrived hoping to feast amid the corpse of de Burgh's career and was now being disappointed on two fronts.

After a short while Henry III himself appeared, two earnest young Frenchmen at his side. He swept into the room and announced, to all and sundry. "De Burgh's wife Margaret and his daughter Megotta have taken sanctuary at Bury St. Edmunds."

"Perhaps he's with them, Your Grace," said a tall, dark man who Ela knew to be the new justiciar, Steven Seagrave. "I can take a party out at once. If he's not there I'll question his wife as she may know his whereabouts."

"And you think she'll tell you?" asked Henry, curiously.

"I can remind her of her grave duty of obedience to king and country."

"Perhaps you'll find she owes more allegiance to the kingdom of Scotland," said Henry, quite serious.

"I suspect she'll take great pains to prove otherwise," said Seagrave, who looked quite excited at the prospect of harassing de Burgh's lady wife in her abbey hiding place. "I hardly think she'll risk a charge of treason."

Ela blinked. Would de Burgh let his wife be taken prisoner, or would such an outrage draw him out into the open?

She couldn't resist airing her thoughts on his non-appearance. "Your Grace, I am astonished that de Burgh, who has served the kings of this country for many years, is afraid to face justice. Surely the whole point of calling him to account is to provide him with the opportunity to prove that all of his dealings on your behalf, and in your service, were done with scrupulous honesty."

"My sentiments exactly, dear Ela," said Henry warmly. "If he has nothing to hide, he should be here to defend his reputation. As it is, he's taking a shovel to it. I feel thoroughly justified in calling his activities into question."

Ela tried not to gloat, at least not visibly. It wasn't godly to wish for your enemy's downfall. Or was it? The psalms were full of such bitter and vengeful sentiments. Still, she schooled her face into a neutral expression. "I wonder if he's taken sanctuary at Merton," she said quietly, as if to herself.

"Do you know something I don't know, Countess Ela?" asked Henry, suddenly serious.

"Most assuredly not, Your Grace," said Ela quickly. "But he's mentioned to me in passing that he donates money to the priory there and often visited for prayer and confession. Since Merton Priory is only a few miles from London, it may have seemed a convenient place to take immediate refuge."

"He took confession there? No doubt he had a lot to confess," said Henry, in an unusually deep voice. "And he didn't want to spit his guilty words into the ears of my palace clerics. But who does he think he is to refuse my summons and hide from justice?"

Henry's face reddened and she could see that the young king was genuinely furious at this shocking snub by his elder courtier and formerly trusted ally. "Steven, please visit Merton and inquire within. The priests cannot lie to you. They'll know if he's there or not. If he's not at Merton, then travel to Bury St. Edmunds and interview his wife. Even the great Hubert de Burgh, married through scheming to a king's daughter, cannot hide from the king of England!"

SOON LONDON WAS abuzz with the news that Hubert de Burgh had taken Holy sanctuary at Merton Priory, just south of London.

"I did so want to see him sweating before a jury of his peers," said Alianore with a sigh. She and Ela sat on a carved stone bench in the garden of her London house. A fountain trickled nearby and bees and butterflies buzzed around clouds of lavender and sage and mint in the late summer air.

"We shall." Ela felt confident that Hubert de Burgh could not hide from the king's wrath for long. "I suspect that the king's new advisors would gladly take turns running him through with a sword, let alone with sharp words."

"You don't suppose they'll kill him before he has a chance to be held accountable, do you?" asked Alianore. She sipped a cup of chilled wine.

Ela peered into her cup of the sweet Rhenish wine, served with delicate flower petals floating on its surface. "I think not. He's too powerful and was close to Henry for too long. And he has key allies in the church. He's not a man to be trifled with."

"But he's trifling with the king!"

"He is, and I find it astonishing. I wouldn't have thought him so cowardly."

"He must have good reason to be so very afraid," said Alianore with a raised brow. "Do you suspect he's on his knees in fervent prayer at this very moment?"

"I doubt it," said Ela with a sigh. "Knowing de Burgh, he'll have brought servants into sanctuary with him and be living a life of typical luxury—with fresh-cooked meals and fine raiment—within the walls of the priory. He'd hardly be able to do that in some remote and austere chapel, surrounded by dour monks who exist on little more than bread and water."

"I suppose you're right, though I do cherish a vision of him hiding in a lightless crypt, eating bland monkish fare," said Alianore with a mischievous look.

"The problem is, he cannot be legally removed from sanctuary in a holy place."

"Oh, stuff and nonsense. The king's men can remove him from anywhere they please."

"By force? While they could do that, it would be seen as a gross violation of the sanctity of the church."

"I hardly think the pope will excommunicate King Henry III over it."

"Given the shame and disgrace his father King John suffered at the hands of the pope, I doubt Henry will take any risks in that regard. And he doesn't want to endure the wrath of his bishops, either. I suspect he'll choose to wait it out. Holy sanctuary can be maintained for only forty days and forty nights—"

"Like Christ in the wilderness," mused Alianore.

"Not in the least like Christ in the wilderness," retorted Ela. "But Henry can't do anything until then."

"De Burgh is such a cunning fox. I suppose he'll be hoping that Henry cools down. Or he may write wheedling letters trying to win back his favor."

"I would if I were in his shoes," said Ela. "But as you've seen yourself, Henry is furious with him and now feels doubly betrayed by his refusal to face justice."

"No doubt de Burgh is writing to every friend and ally he's ever had, trying to gather a veritable army of supporters to plead his cause."

"Except that he's made more enemies than friends along the way."

"Your husband being one of them," said Alianore softly.

And me being another, thought Ela. "He was so confident in his intimacy with the king, that he wielded power carelessly. He's run roughshod over many good men, seizing their lands and disinheriting their sons. Even if we have to wait forty days, he'll have to face the charges against him eventually. He may even hang for his crimes."

"From your words to God's ears," said Alianore, with a tiny smile.

"Mother! Don't say such things. God has far more urgent matters to concern himself with."

"Don't tell me you prefer to stand back and wait for de Burgh to receive justice on Judgment Day?"

"Well, no. I intend to question him about his visit to Bradenstoke Abbey eight weeks ago. I suspect that he confessed to Father Gilbert, the priest who was poisoned."

Alianore stared at her. "Why would he kill a priest? They can't ever reveal what's told to them in confession but must take it to their grave."

"I don't suspect him of killing the priest with his own hands. He only visited once, well in advance of the murder. But, if he had uttered what he later realized to be...grave indiscretions, I think him quite capable of utterly removing the risk of exposure."

"But a priest? Is de Burgh not a pious man?"

"He claims deep faith, but his life has been almost a deliberate violation of every single one of the Ten Commandments. His avarice alone is legendary. And you know that he's—at least in whispers—now suspected of several other murders."

"Oh, I would like to see him dragged from the abbey in his nightcap and brought here to be poked like a baiting bear."

"All in good time, Mother. All in good time."

"HOW DARE HE?" Young Henry III paced back and forth in the great hall at Westminster Palace. Ela was keen to offer her moral support and guidance to the king, and Alianore was desperate for the latest hot gossip to share with her friends. "After all I've done for him! I put him in charge of every aspect of my finances and entrusted him with all the most important decisions of the kingdom. And now he defies me? He refuses to come face to face with me, and hides behind the skirts of some mewling priests?"

A fine repast was laid out on the table: at least thirty roasted capons steamed on their chargers; wine glittered in silver cups; the rich smell of spiced sauces rose in the air. But it might have been poisoned mushroom dust for all Henry cared. He strode up and down the length of the room, fuming and raging.

Ela had never seen him like this, not even close. It was as if ten years—twenty—of the king's unspoken complaints and muted objections had finally risen over the banks of his good humor and threatened to flood the kingdom.

"He shan't get away with it!" Henry's voice broke, his fury apparent in every word. "Bring him to me at once!"

"But he's taken sanctuary," said Ela softly.

"We can starve him out!" said Henry.

"Not yet," said Ela. "He can be refused food and water but only after forty days."

"Forty days?" shouted Henry. "I don't wish for the man to live that long, let alone to enjoy rich victuals and fine wines in the sanctuary of a richly appointed vestry. Seagrave!" He called for his new justiciar. "Gather your men and bring him here by morning!"

"THE KING'S quite out of his mind," said Alianore, as they traveled back to her house in her carriage. "That beautiful feast sitting there and we couldn't even touch it!"

"All those poor capons. I suppose someone will eat them. He wasn't even in his cups."

"No. At first, I thought he must be, but he was drunk with fury."

"I tried to talk sense into him but I can see he has inherited at least some of his father's legendary temper," said Ela. The carriage jolted along in the dark. "I do hope it doesn't obscure his common sense and ruin his reputation."

"Some of those Poitevins he's gathered around him are spoiling for a fight. That kind of ebullience is better scattered on the tournament ground."

"I agree. I worry about the enmity they'll stir up if they go too far. De Burgh must have some allies left, even if they're staying silent for now. He's been powerful for too long. The king's new courtiers are stoking the king's ego and making him rash. Henry mustn't overestimate his power over the older and surlier men of his kingdom. The last thing we need is another Barons' War."

Ela and her mother were about to head to bed when a messenger arrived with the disturbing news that the king had sent a letter to the mayor of London to gather the inhabitants of the city to ride for Merton. Now, the king's allies were riding across London in the dark, stirring up a mob from all classes of society. Teeth bared, this army of thousands intended to ride south toward Merton and seize Hubert from the priory at dawn.

The entire endeavor gave Ela the chills. "Is King Henry riding with them?"

"No, my lady," said the messenger. "His justiciar prevailed upon him to stay at Westminster."

"Thank goodness," said Ela. "There's no telling what chaos will result from such an unplanned and ill-starred action."

Alianore sent the messenger back to Westminster to wait for more news.

"I thought you were excited to see de Burgh get some comeuppance at last, my dear," said Alianore, nibbling on some fresh raspberries floating in sweet cream.

"Not at the expense of the kingdom being rent asunder. I'd like to see de Burgh be held accountable, not dragged through the streets and turned into a martyr."

"De Burgh seems to have poisoned the entire nation against him. He doesn't have a single friend standing up to plead for him."

"Yes, he does. The clerics at Merton, and there will be others. I'm not fool enough to think he'll face Henry's wrath alone."

"I imagine they'll have him locked up safely in the Tower by Nones tomorrow. Aren't you glad I brought you to London?" Alianore was giddy with all the excitement.

"I'm here because I wish to discuss de Burgh's activities at

Bradenstoke Abbey, where two people now lie dead from the work of one poisoner."

"You don't have to pretend to me, dear. Some guilty pleasure is allowed under the circumstances. You work hard enough."

"I'm not pretending! I need to find the perpetrator or I fear for Sister Alisande. Every time I visit the abbey they're baying for her blood. I don't understand it since I've never met a more meek, mild, and gentle woman. And she's of the Marshal family, so a person of consequence by association. Why do they wish to blame her?"

"It's easy to blame the weak. I suppose a certain kind of bully feels better once he's punished someone for a crime, even if it wasn't the right person."

"But why wouldn't they want to hold out for the right person?"

"Sister Alisande does sound rather odd, you can't argue with that, my dear. It's not normal or healthy to see into the future."

"I sometimes wish I could see into the past," said Ela. "It would be a lot easier than trying to tease it out of people in front of a jury. But I suppose it wouldn't help the course of justice for me to be hanged as a witch."

"No indeed, my dear. And it would tarnish the family name for generations."

Ela pondered this. "You've given me an idea, Maman. I shall approach the Marshal family to see if I can stir up some support for Sister Alisande from that quarter. Perhaps if they would agree to remove her from Bradenstoke and settle her quietly on one of their estates, or in a more remote and obscure abbey, she'd be out of immediate danger."

"It's worth a try, I suppose. I don't know the boys of this generation so well. Their father, of course, was a dear friend.

So sad that his namesake is gone too soon. Do you really think that de Burgh had them both killed?"

"I have no idea. But I'd be very curious to find out."

"Would you come right out and ask him?"

"Absolutely not. Even though he's down right now, de Burgh is like a venomous snake that can lie innocently in the grass, then strike hard and fast when you least expect it."

CHAPTER 13

The next morning Ela awoke to fresh news that Ranulph, Earl of Chester, had pleaded with the king to call off the mob. The old earl was worried that such a great number of men, whipped into a frenzy of vengeance, might get out of control and wreak havoc far beyond their intended purpose. They might even pose a danger to the king himself, or to his estates and authority.

On this advice, the king had changed his mind and asked the mayor of London to recall his men and the crowd they'd assembled, which was done with considerable difficulty since their excitement had been stirred.

"What a disappointment," said Alianore, sipping her morning tisane. "I had so hoped for an exciting day at court today."

"Patience, mother," said Ela. "Haste makes waste. Far better that he should be brought to justice without violating the laws of the church or endangering the king and his courtiers."

"Patience has never been my greatest virtue, my dear, as you well know."

"Nor mine, but with it, I've accomplished feats beyond most men's imagining, so I shall endeavor to show it now."

~

ELA LEARNED THAT RICHARD MARSHAL, Third Earl of Pembroke, had been drawn to London by the excitement around Hubert de Burgh, and she resolved to visit him. Her mother, of course, wanted to come too. She was currently in her chamber, having a fresh veil pinned to her fillet in preparation for a visit. "He's your kin, you know. Your grandfather, Patrick, had a sister called Sybilla, who was the mother of William Marshal. Not the William Marshal who just died but the famous tournament champion."

"That is a blood connection, but several generations back."

"It's enough to prevent your children from marrying any scions of the Marshal line for another generation or two." Genealogical studies had ruined any number of marriage negotiations. In 1215 the fourth Vatican Council had reduced the number of generations of separation required down to four, which was a great relief to many, given the insular world of the Anglo-Norman nobles. "And Richard Marshal's wife is a de Vitre, as I was before my first marriage. Yet another reason to avoid a marital alliance." Alianore's brow lifted. "Which is fine, since I'm told that the entire line is cursed and will die out within two generations."

"I do hope you're joking, mother. The anchoress said the same thing, but you're far too educated and worldly wise to believe in curses."

Alianore gave a mock shudder. "You make me wish I had some salt to throw over my shoulder."

~

The newly minted Earl of Pembroke's London residence was a large freestanding timbered house right on the river with its own dock visible from the approach to the house. A small flag flying from one of the gables indicated that the Earl was in residence—information Alianore had already confirmed from her friends.

Ela and Alianore rode up to the house and dismounted, handing their horses to the guards. "I haven't spoken to Richard Marshal since his dear brother's funeral," whispered Alianore as they waited. A smartly dressed servant answered the door and the guard announced them.

The servant ushered them into a spacious parlor with a marble floor and carved wood paneling on the walls. Just as another servant, a young boy of Moorish appearance, was handing them two silver cups of wine, the Earl appeared.

A tall man, slightly younger than Ela, with dark gold hair and an aristocratic demeanor, the Earl approached Alianore first and kissed her hand graciously, welcoming her to his home. To Ela, he bowed his head slightly and kissed her hand, "Countess Ela, what a pleasant surprise."

"It's good to see you, Sir Richard. Once again, my condolences on the loss of your brother."

"Thank you. It's hard to lose someone so young, but the cut is ten times deeper when you suspect it might have been by foul play."

So true. "Foul play you say? I thought he died of an illness."

"That's what we all thought, at the time. However, given some information that's come to light, we have good reason to suspect that he was poisoned—by the king's former justiciar."

"I heard the same rumor, though I confess I thought it scurrilous gossip. I even heard a rumor that de Burgh killed your father." She wondered if he knew that she'd shared these rumors with the king…and if, in fact, the king was who he'd learned them from. "I told the king that shocking rumors were circulating about his justiciar."

"For that, I must thank you. I confess I shrank from spreading the rumor myself, though I had heard it whispered. Now that Hubert de Burgh is caught in the fowler's snare, he's wiggling and flapping like a helpless bird. What more guilty action could he take than running to hide behind a priest's skirts?"

"I admit I am shocked by his cowardice. It's not like him to run from a fight. Why do you think he's afraid to address the charges against him?"

"Because he's guilty, of course. What clearer confession could there be? Do you know they're also saying that he poisoned your husband?"

She pretended to look surprised. "You've heard someone say this?"

"I have indeed, along with a long list of other crimes that he's suspected of committing against those he considered his rivals."

Ela crossed herself, perhaps as a small penance for stirring the gossip cauldrons of London to advance her cause. "My dear husband died in horrible agony. I thought it was a sickness, but now that you mention poison…" She inhaled, overcome by genuine emotion. Even now, almost six years after her husband's passing, the memory of it sometimes knocked the wind from her. "Do people really believe that de Burgh poisoned him?" She felt a strange rush of energy at speaking the words aloud after years of secret suspicion.

"They say your husband had an argument with de Burgh right before it happened, severe enough that the king had to intervene to mend their friendship for the good of the kingdom. They say that de Burgh invited your husband to his castle and took matters into his own hands by poisoning him during dinner."

"William did indeed sicken as he was returning from de Burgh's home." She'd always considered accusing the justiciar to be a fool's errand. As the king's right-hand man, he was untouchable and above reproach. Had that truly changed? Maybe the time was right to seek justice for her husband's death. A surge of courage—or was it madness?—roused her. "If de Burgh is innocent, he will protest these rumors! That he's not doing so is shocking to me and seems an admission of guilt."

"I agree. A hunger for justice gnaws at me now that I feel it might be a possibility."

Another servant brought in small cakes and Ela took one, mostly to be polite. She had no appetite. "I am here on another matter regarding justice. Your elderly spinster cousin, Alisande, is a nun at Bradenstoke. Are you aware that she stands accused of witchcraft and murder?"

"What?" His genuine shock surprised Ela. "I'm not aware of a cousin called Alisande."

Now it was Ela's turn to be perplexed. Was Alisande a member of the great Marshal family, or had she simply made up the association to win favor with Ela? "She's very ancient, four score years or more. She'd be from the generation before your father's. I think she said her father was a Robert Marshal."

His forehead creased. "At Bradenstoke, you say?"

"She's spent her whole life there as an anchoress. A priest dropped dead at the altar recently and she cried out a warning to him shortly before he fell. Some of those at the abbey have taken against her for this and other similar oddities. At her great age, I suspect her of an addled mind rather than sorcery, so I brought her to my castle to keep her safe from her accusers. The priest was poisoned and unfortunately, we have yet to identify the murderer. Even if she's acquitted during a trial—which is not a certainty by any means—she might be in grave danger if she returned to Bradenstoke."

"If she's a member of the Marshal family she must of course have suitable legal representation to defend her. I'll look into the matter."

"That would be most helpful. And I was hoping that perhaps you could be prevailed upon to find her a suitable home outside Bradenstoke."

The Earl of Pembroke rubbed his chin. "She's a very great age, you say?"

"Yes, quite ancient. She needs a quiet existence away from worldly cares, and also far from those who seek to hang her as a witch."

"Goodness, I can quite see that. Of course, if she is a witch perhaps she can cast a spell to undo the curse that apparently hangs over the Marshal family." Humor lit his light blue eyes.

Ela didn't want to countenance this jest about such a serious matter. "I know you're far too educated and worldly wise to believe in curses and witches."

"Of course I am, dear Ela. I'll have my clerk research the branches of our family tree to ascertain which roots the mysterious Alisande sprang from. If she is indeed a Marshal, you shall hear from me within the week with a plan of action."

"That would be very much appreciated."

"Meanwhile," he sipped his silver cup of wine. "Did you hear that Hubert de Burgh has been stripped of his earldom and that his son John must forfeit all his castles?"

"Truly?" Ela could hardly believe her ears. De Burgh's earldom was his most prized possession and—at least in theory—put him on equal footing with both her and the man standing before her.

Marshal smiled. "He's got the king's back up. Refusing to face his king will go very hard against him. If he has allies in the kingdom I suspect they're afraid to show their faces."

"Why is he refusing to appear?" She truly didn't understand it. "He's not a fool. He has to know it will only make things worse for him."

"I suspect he's buying time, perhaps hoping that the king's temper will cool."

"His obstinacy is having the opposite effect," she replied. "Henry sanctioned the mob that nearly dragged him from sanctuary. "

Richard Marshal shrugged. "Henry asked for a full accounting of his purse from the last few years. De Burgh had responsibility for all the king's expenditures. If he's lined his coffers with the king's money or invested it in castles and manors that should have belonged to the king, he'll hardly be able to defend himself even with the best lawyer in England."

"Do you think he'll hang?"

Marshal stopped to consider this. "It's hard to say. Perhaps the king's heart will soften toward him. But the king's new men will make that difficult as it doesn't serve their interests."

"The Poitevins?"

"Yes, you've no doubt seen them in their gallic finery, prancing about the halls of Westminster. Now, you won't hear a bad word about them from me, fine men for the most part—"

Ela realized he didn't know where her allegiances lay and he'd suddenly thought better of slandering the king's new favorite courtiers. "Yes, they are and excitable and no doubt stirring up the king's ire against the old guard."

"I suppose you and I are the old guard, aren't we?" he asked, a slight smile tilting one side of his mouth.

"I don't see either you or myself as old and we both know —as does the king—that our allegiances lie firmly with him."

"Indeed, yes." He regarded her for a moment.

She had no interest in getting on the wrong side of the king, who was her children's cousin and one of her nearest neighbors for much of the year. He'd been a staunch ally to her on more than one occasion. Without the young king's willingness to listen to her and negotiate, she'd have lost her castle when her husband died. Henry had allowed her to buy a permanent right to both her castle, her earldom, and the role of sheriff of Wiltshire. She was fairly sure he'd gone against the wishes of his justiciar in granting her all those things.

"It will be interesting to see what happens when de Burgh is finally brought to justice," said Marshal, after a pause.

"Will you step forward to accuse him of poisoning your father and brother?" asked Ela, wondering if she was brave enough to do the same.

He inhaled slowly. "I have no concrete evidence pointing directly to him. Nothing but hearsay and happenstance. So I might risk putting my own neck in the noose by accusing a man who may yet rise from the dead like Lazarus."

Ela nodded. "Your caution is noted."

"My caution may look like cowardice." He lifted a wry brow.

"Our great families have remained powerful through the administrations of multiple kings by choosing our fights carefully." Ela regarded him steadily. "It remains to see whether this fight can be won."

"If de Burgh is behind these killings, he's covered his tracks carefully. As sheriff of Wiltshire, you know that the ability to prove guilt is far more important than the guilt itself, at least when it comes to securing a conviction."

"And a man like de Burgh has decades of experience in

currying favor, turning on the charm, promising just the right bribe or reward to secure his aim, no matter how great and how grand."

Pembroke laughed. "Which is how he rose from obscurity to become an earl and husband to a king's daughter, with more castles and land than you or I who are heirs to two of the greatest families in the land."

"If only there was a way to pin even one of these murders on him," mused Ela. "An accusation from someone who sold him the poison, or prepared it, or even administered it. He can't be doing all these things himself. The murder I'm trying to solve may even be his doing."

"The one my supposed family member is accused of?"

"Yes. The priest was poisoned with a deadly mushroom. The dried mushroom powder was purchased at a nearby shop and the apothecary has since been found dead—presumably so he can no longer identify the man who bought the poison."

"Why would de Burgh kill a priest at Bradenstoke?"

"De Burgh visited Bradenstoke some weeks before the killing. It's possible that he made a confession to Father Gilbert, the man who was poisoned."

The earl laughed. "De Burgh is not foolish enough to whisper his crimes in a priest's ear."

"De Burgh is a devout Christian," said Ela. She frowned. "I know it's hard to believe, given his shameless avarice, but I suspect he truly believes that the righteous will ascend to Heaven and receive their just rewards in God's kingdom."

"He's certainly a man who enjoys a reward, just or otherwise."

"Exactly, so he's not likely to risk the bounties of eternal life by failing to confess his misdeeds. Thus, I suspect that if he's committed these crimes, he's also sought absolution for them, knowing that a priest is bound to silence and secrecy."

"But given that last part, why would he kill a priest? Surely that compounds his first sin with a worse one?"

"I've learned that men have a way of justifying acts that are expedient. A knight who kills a man in battle—for example—will not go to hell for the crime of murder. I suspect de Burgh sees these crimes he's committed as if they were noble battles to be fought and won. I wouldn't be surprised if he felt as fresh and clean as a newborn babe after confessing his misdeeds."

Earl Richard looked fascinated. "Do you have any other suspects in the murder of Father Gilbert?"

"Father Gilbert's brother has been questioned. He was at the abbey to take confession the week Father Gilbert died, and was also near the apothecary shop on the night of his death."

"He must be a suspect, then, surely?"

"He admits that someone paid him to go to Bradenstoke that day, but he claims not to know the man who paid him. He has no good reason to kill his brother and seemed distressed that he might have played an unwitting part in his death. They were both younger sons and while they were not close, there seems to be no real enmity between them. I released him from custody so we can watch his movements and study his associates."

"My money would be on him as the killer, perhaps as a proxy for de Burgh."

"But would a man agree to kill his brother? As sheriff, I've learned from experience that when someone is murdered, the culprit is most often a member of their family or a very close associate. Surely a man would have to be a fool to hire himself out as a contract killer for a member of his own family."

Marshal frowned. "But if, as you say, the one brother had no reason to kill the other, he might be seen as being above suspicion. And he would at the very least have good reason for visiting his brother within the walls of Bradenstoke. I presume that an assassin is driven either by a commitment to a cause or by a love of money. Could either of these motivate the man you mention?"

"If there's a cause, I can't see it. Sir Anselm might certainly be driven by a need for money, though. As a younger son, he has no inheritance and has managed to eke out a living buying and selling fleeces."

"A man born into the nobility and forced to stoop to bargaining in the marketplace might well find himself hungry for work that pays enough for him to elevate his life-style to one that fits his station."

Ela inhaled slowly. "While securing his future would certainly provide sufficient motivation, it would require a payment of hundreds of pounds or a manor, at the very least. Who would have the means to pay that much?"

Richard Marshal lifted a brow. "A man who has manors aplenty at his disposal."

Hubert de Burgh. She didn't need to say the name aloud. It was better to be circumspect anyway. She had no way of knowing who listened at the door. Servants always hovered nearby, ready to spring into action if needed. "I suppose many of our peers have an abundance of manors," she said, feeling the need to say something. "You and I, for example."

"But neither you nor I have the motivation to kill a priest at Bradenstoke, or to kill an apothecary to cover our tracks."

"I do have a list of all the visitors to Bradenstoke over these past few months. I don't know how complete it is, since it was compiled at my request. There may well be names missing, but I shall study it for suspects."

Richard Marshal took a quick swig of his wine. "Is de Burgh's name on it?"

"It is."

CHAPTER 14

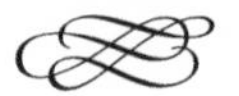

A few days later Ela was preparing for her return to Salisbury when she found herself summoned to appear before the king. "What now?" she protested to her mother, while the messenger waited outside. "I've wasted enough time here in London when there are urgent matters for me to attend to at home."

"You will have to explain that to his majesty," said her mother with a sarcastic smile. "And I don't envy you."

Dressed in a fine robe and with one of her mother's gold chains around her waist, she set out within the hour. The atmosphere at Westminster was rushed and busy, with horses coming and going and serious expressions on all faces. Two pages ushered her into Henry's official viewing room where he sat on his dais.

"Ela, Countess of Salisbury and High Sheriff of Wiltshire," announced a page, as she entered the room. His courtiers, nobles ranging in age and station from beardless boys to the elderly Earl of Chester, sat nearby in silent witness. This gave the meeting the air of a trial.

"Ela my dear, I'm afraid this is not a friendly family visit," said the king, with a serious expression.

Her stomach clenched. How did one respond to this? She half wondered if she was about to be thrown into the Tower. "May God be with you, Your Grace," she said softly. "How may I be of service?"

"Now that my former justiciar's perfidy and treachery have been uncovered, I find myself needing to investigate the accounts of each county in my kingdom. As sheriff, you are charged with collecting the taxes due to the crown and I find myself in need of proof that I've not been cheated in the amount that I am due from your county."

"I can assure you that I've been most careful in both collecting taxes from your subjects and in keeping records of the same. I have detailed ledgers going back to the first year I held the office of sheriff, and I'll be happy to provide you with the originals." She fervently hoped that she'd get them back, but having them copied by scribes would waste time and perhaps introduce errors.

"I'm glad to hear that. I've encountered a surprising amount of resistance from your fellow sheriffs and have had to threaten arrest in one or two cases."

Ela drew in a breath and stood as tall as she could manage. "I can assure you that I endeavor to serve you and England in all my work and shall be most scrupulous in providing all the records you require."

"I'm delighted to hear it. I find myself needing to gather funds as my justiciar's negligence has left the royal treasury far too empty. I am starting with collecting any monies that were due to me but have been forgotten or neglected or misspent in some way."

"I can assure you that every penny of tax collected in Wiltshire is accounted for by my clerks." She hoped this was true. She did oversee their work to a certain extent, but in such a large county she had to delegate most of the responsibilities to a veritable army of tax collectors. Their work was in turn checked by her steward, and any discrepancies were reported to her. She'd removed and punished a few people for either dereliction of duty or misuse of the funds, but the majority had done the work well and carefully—at least she hoped they had.

"My treasurer will examine your records and ensure that we received all the promised funds. My former justiciar wasted a great deal of money by sabotaging my planned expedition to France. What should have been a triumphant return and reconquest of our lost lands, turned into a foolish pilgrimage with no real gains to show for it."

Ela couldn't resist asking. "When will de Burgh stand trial for his misdeeds?"

"He has begged for time to prepare his case," said Henry with a wry expression. "Taking into account his years of service to my father as well as myself, just yesterday I granted him a reprieve until Epiphany."

"That is very generous, Your Grace. Is he still in sanctuary at Merton?"

"He is taking advantage of the reprieve to travel to Bury St Edmunds to meet with his wife."

"Ah." Ela found this rather extraordinary and needed a moment to gather her thoughts. How did de Burgh, so recently saved from a mob twenty thousand strong, feel safe to leave sanctuary and travel the country? His arrogance and self-confidence knew no bounds. Perhaps he was already scheming to somehow turn this whole situation to his advantage and rise from the ashes of his career like a phoenix...burning brighter and more powerful than ever. The thought made her blood run cold.

Then an idea occurred to her. "Your Grace, does it worry

you that in returning to his home and his countrymen, he might attempt to raise an army of supporters to press his case?"

"An army?"

Her words—and now his—stirred his courtiers. One of them, whom Ela recognized as Godfrey de Crowcumbe, rose to his feet. "Your Grace, I did warn you about giving the man his freedom. He is cunning as an ermine and may yet find friends to support his cause."

Henry's entire demeanor had changed. "Surely not. He stands accused of high treason and of emptying the royal treasury to fund his lavish lifestyle."

"He's walked this land for longer than any of us," cut in Peter de Roches. "He may have debts of allegiance to call in at his time of need."

"What do you propose?" asked Henry of his courtiers. Ela tried not to be affronted that he seemed to have forgotten her.

"I propose that we send a party after him and arrest him at once," said de Crowcumbe. "Before he presents a danger to peace in the kingdom."

"If such an idea can take root in our minds then it may yet flourish in his," said the king, now gripping the arms of his ceremonial chair. "Arrest him on the road and put him in the Tower at once. He will await his trial while he is safely under lock and key. Make haste!"

Henry leaped from his throne with youthful athleticism and marched from the room, leaving Ela standing there, astonished at the effect of her words. The other men hurried after him, Godfrey de Crowcumbe already barking orders at the pages and giving other men hurried instructions.

Ela waited until they'd left the room, and only then walked quietly after them.

~

THE NEXT MORNING, Ela was in the middle of a dream where she was fighting—on horseback—to defend Salisbury from an invading enemy. She opened her eyes, breathless, to the sound of her mother's voice.

"De Burgh is in the Tower," crowed Alianore.

Ela, still behind her bed curtains, blinked. "Is it morning?"

"Almost," said her mother. She pulled back Ela's bed curtains and peered in. Alianore wore a brocade dressing gown over her shift and her still thick hair coiled elegantly over one shoulder. "It's nearly light out, and my messenger just brought me the news."

"De Burgh is here in London, right now?"

"That's what they say. Shall we take a carriage over there and find out?"

"No." Ela sat up. "We can't be seen to gloat over him."

"Not until he's good and dead, anyway," said Alianore.

"Don't speak so. It's for the justices or even the king himself to decide if his crimes are punishable by death."

"Oh, stuff and nonsense. This is the most exciting thing to happen in London in years. If you don't get up soon I'll go to Westminster by myself to hear the latest gossip. They say he had already traveled as far as Brentwood in Essex by the time the king's men caught up with him."

"So far?"

"He must have been in a great hurry. And on learning of the men chasing after him, he scurried into the church there and took refuge at the altar."

"Again? So how did the king's men arrest him if he'd taken sanctuary?"

"Godfrey de Crowcumbe would hear none of his protests. He stormed into the chapel and seized de Burgh as he stood naked before the altar, with a sacred host in one hand and a crucifix in the other."

"What?" Ela scrambled from beneath the covers and climbed to her feet on the cold wood floor. "I don't believe it! Why would de Burgh be naked in a church?"

"I have no idea, my darling, I just report the news as I hear it!" Alianore's excitement was infectious, but rather than joy, it stirred alarm in Ela's heart.

"I hope they didn't drag his clothes off or something. Much as I despise the man, I believe in treating such an important prisoner with respect. His arrest and trial must be handled carefully or it may yet backfire and burn down the kingdom. We must go to Westminster at once."

ELA ARRIVED at Westminster midmorning to find Henry III surrounded by his triumphant courtiers. Unlike yesterday's formal proceedings, he had a cup of wine in his hand and a smile on his face.

"Ela my dear, our friend de Burgh is in London awaiting my pleasure," he said cheerfully.

"So I heard," she said cautiously. "Was he taken from the chapel at Brentwood?"

"He was indeed. De Crowcumbe seized him as he pretended to be deep in prayer."

Henry's courtiers were like huntsmen still flushed from the hunt, regaling each other with tales from the previous night's extraordinary ride and the swift return from Essex bearing their prisoner. "We tried to hire a blacksmith to forge irons to bear him back to London, but the poxy man said that de Burgh was a faithful servant of the king and didn't deserve such treatment. He refused to make the restraints! I wanted to have him horsewhipped, but calmer heads prevailed," boasted one ruddy-faced lad.

Ela found herself shocked that they'd felt the need to chain de Burgh. "Was he trying to escape?"

"Well, no. It was more the principle of the thing. I mean, he did evade the king's summons and go into hiding in yet another chapel, so I wouldn't put it past him to dive for some bushes on the way," said another young Frenchman.

"This is an outrage!" A bold voice cut through the air. Ela turned to see a man in cleric's vestments. Not just any robes, but the embroidered finery of the Bishop of London, Roger Niger. Niger marched into King Henry's hall and stood nose to nose with him. "Good morning, Your Grace," he said, with a tiny bow.

Henry stared at him, obviously astonished by his initial statement. "Bishop Niger, what, pray, is the outrage you speak of?"

"Hubert de Burgh, lately justiciar of all England, has been dragged from holy sanctuary by your men! This is an offense against God's holy church and all of those who serve her. He must be released from the Tower at once and returned to our care."

"I'm afraid not, Bishop. He stands accused of crimes against the kingdom and my person. I cannot allow him to travel the land and stir up trouble."

Bishop Niger barely hesitated. "The laws of sanctuary are very particular, Your Grace. They cannot be contravened. To do so is a violation of the compact between crown and cross."

Henry blinked. "Hubert de Burgh is not a man of the cloth. He's lived by the sword and his sharp wit and—quite frankly—rather astonishing avarice. I fail to understand why the church springs so readily to his defense."

"We do not seek to intervene in any business between

yourself and Hubert de Burgh, merely to defend his right to seek sanctuary. Your men tore him away from the altar at Brentwood as he stood there praying."

"He has plenty to pray about," said Henry grimly. "I curse myself for trusting him for so long. He's betrayed my trust and must face justice."

"Of course, Your Grace," said Niger, perhaps reminding himself that he was arguing with the King of England. "And naturally we shall encourage him to put himself forward to address any disputes that you may have with him. But he must be returned to our care at once. Holy sanctuary has been the refuge of kings and queens as well as ordinary men, and must remain inviolate."

"I suppose you do have a point," said Henry. Ela could see his cheerful confidence flagging. He'd been pious and God-fearing since his earliest youth and she could see it went hard with him to argue with a bishop. "I gave him a reprieve until Epiphany but now I realize that was a mistake. He'll use that time to either escape justice or to raise an army of supporters against me."

"He can hardly do that if kept in solitary sanctuary," said Niger.

"What if he just refuses to come out? He must come to London to face trial."

Bishop Niger bowed his head slightly and raised his hands as if in prayer. "Your Grace, sanctuary does not continue indefinitely. After forty days bread and water can be denied to the one seeking refuge, that he can be flushed out from his place of hiding."

"Forty days is a long time," said Henry, his face darkening. "Enough time for him to make considerable mischief. I don't want him to be allowed to return to his home country of East Anglia, or anywhere near it, including Bury St. Edmunds.

Can he go into sanctuary here in London where at least he's close to Westminster?"

Bishop Niger cleared his throat. "From what I hear of the mob that was roused to descend on him, he may feel safer at some distance from the city and the ruffians who were stirred into action against him."

"Is there a place nearby—but not too near—that he could go?"

"Brentwood Abbey in Essex is likely near enough to London but far enough from the rabble to make him feel safe. He can be returned there to the sanctuary he was so rudely dragged from."

"I suppose I could send soldiers to surround the church and ensure that he does not escape and regain his freedom," said Henry, glowering.

"An excellent idea, Your Grace," said Niger, cheering. "I'd be glad to take custody of him myself and convey him safely back to sanctuary." Henry looked at his courtiers, who'd watched this whole exchange in a tense silence. "I have no choice," he explained to them. "Holy sanctuary is the law of the land. The chapel will be guarded by the sheriffs of Essex and Hereford."

"He might tunnel out," said one young courtier, "and escape to freedom!"

"I'll order the sheriffs to dig a great trench all around the chapel so that no one can go in or out. And they shall take away his seal so he can no longer send any formal correspondence. Let him stew in his own juices until he's ready to face me."

Several of the courtiers looked as if they'd like to protest his change of heart, but instead they nodded and muttered about forty days being not so far off and how this evasion would be another charge against the king's wayward quarry.

Finally, Bishop Niger departed for the Tower to escort de Burgh to Brentwood Abbey under guard.

Once Niger had left, the life seemed to drain out of Henry. He put down his wine cup and announced that he was heading to the chapel to pray, and that all of them should join him, for they had indeed committed an outrage against God and His Holy Church.

CHAPTER 15

Finally back in Salisbury, Ela was anxious to learn whether any new information had been gleaned from Sir Anselm. She took Bill into the armory so they could speak without fear of being overheard.

"If we could just identify the man that paid Sir Anselm ten pounds to visit Bradenstoke we'd likely know who killed both priests and the apothecary."

"I've had guards stationed alongside the track to his manor. Not a living soul has entered or left the place except Sir Anselm himself. He has a manservant and a girl living there with him, but they didn't leave the property once. They seem to grow all their food on the property, at least at this time of year."

"You had him followed?"

"Yes. He made a daily journey into Devizes to take a meal and drink at the Three Keys. I'm afraid it's almost impossible to follow someone unobserved along country lanes in such a quiet spot, so I'm confident that he knew he was being watched. He didn't seem to mind, though."

"I wonder if he might have warned his benefactor to stay

away."

"We saw no letters or messengers enter or leave his property or depart from his hands during his visits to Devizes."

"Who did he interact with? Was he watched in the Three Keys?"

"I had a man in there drinking and watching. Though, again, everyone may have suspected that he was there for a purpose, being a stranger in a community where people know each other."

"So anyone watching Sir Anselm would know to steer clear of him."

"I'm afraid so."

Ela let out a sigh. "If we knew more about this mysterious hooded stranger, we could lay a trap for him. As it is, I'm not sure what would motivate him to show himself."

"You have no leads at all as to who might be behind the killings?"

"Well..." Ela reminded herself that Bill was her closest confidant. Still, unlike Giles Haughton, he was at her side on most occasions and might well find himself breaking bread with her chief suspect. Weighing a man down with difficult secrets that he might have to carry for a lifetime, even under the influence of strong drink or extreme provocation, was not something she took lightly. "It may be someone who visited the abbey to confess, then felt the need to cover his tracks by killing his confessor."

"And thus condemning his soul to hell for fresh crimes?"

"As I explained to Richard Marshal, men can find ways to justify their crimes. You've killed a man."

"I'm afraid that I've killed more men than I can count on both hands."

"But on the battlefield, where such an act is one of heroic virtue, not a crime."

Bill frowned. "You're saying that whoever's behind these

murders is a man who fears hell and is justifying his actions by making excuses for them?"

Ela crossed her arms. "So far that's the only pretext I can imagine for a man to kill a priest at Bradenstoke. Father Gilbert lived a quiet and unremarkable life, with no enemies that we can discover. He might, however, be privy to grave confidences in his line of work as a confessor."

"Did Bradenstoke provide a list of visitors to the abbey? The guilty man would surely be on it if your suspicions are correct."

"They did." Again, she hesitated.

Bill watched her face closely. "You have a suspect in mind but you don't wish to speak his name aloud, which tells me exactly who it is."

Shock jolted her. "What? Who do you think it is?"

"If you don't wish to speak the name aloud, my lady, then I don't either. Suffice it to say that this man was both a great friend and a great enemy of your husband."

Ela blinked. "Indeed he was. Bill, your keen intelligence is as welcome as your discretion. Such secrets weigh heavy on my chest and I don't seek to share the burden if I don't have to."

"Your secrets are safe with me, my lady. As safe as if you'd uttered them in a confessional."

"Or not uttered them at all. But the man in question could not possibly have committed these murders himself. He was engaged elsewhere, according to my intelligence."

"So he must have used a proxy—perhaps a professional assassin." Bill frowned. "And this person paid Sir Anselm to visit his brother for confession, so he'd have the opportunity to enter his room and spread the poison."

Ela frowned. "If a man needed a professional killer for some reason, how would he seek to procure one?"

Bill thought for a moment. "The man we speak of is

known to all and his every action is public to some degree. He would only be able to make a secret assignation with someone he already knew and trusted."

Ela considered this. "You think it's someone in his inner circle? His inner circle is the same as the king's."

"To a certain extent. But the man in question has lived a long and multi-faceted life. He has acquaintances and confidantes from before the king was even born. If I were him, I would look back in time and ask myself who owed me a favor."

"Considering all the favors I owe you, I can only pray that you never need a favor that involves taking a life."

Bill's handsome face creased into a smile. "Rest assured that if I find myself wishing to take a life, I shall do the deed myself."

"God forbid."

"Indeed he does forbid it, except under very particular circumstances."

Ela paced around the scarred wooden table at the center of the armory. Rows of polished weapons shone on the wall, ready to be seized and used in time of need. "Who would owe this man a big enough favor to be willing to kill for him, and more than once?"

"Someone whose life he saved? Or someone whose career he saved? He had King John's ear for long enough and those were turbulent times."

She stopped walking and stared at him. "Right now he's trying to save his own life and career. Is that why he had to kill the priest? What could he have confessed that is so damning that he couldn't risk it coming to light?"

"The murder of someone powerful. There are whispers that he had William Marshal the elder killed so he could get closer to the king himself."

"Richard Marshal believes he might have killed the younger William Marshal as well."

"And, I don't wish to shock you too deeply, my lady, but some say that he might have poisoned your dear husband—and my greatest friend in this world."

Ela crossed herself, trying to look surprised. She'd shared her suspicions about this with Haughton, but not with Bill. Bill Talbot was too integral a part of her family and her life. "Please don't breathe a word of this gossip to my children, or anyone else in my household."

"You don't want your sons to impale themselves on a quest for revenge."

"Indeed I do not, and I've seen reversals of fortune sharp enough to snap a man's neck. Things look bad for him now but we must be cautious. And if he has an assassin among us, that man could do his deadly bidding again. None of us is safe until we catch the killer."

She turned and paced around the table again. "I saw no alternative but to lay bait and draw him in by setting Sir Anselm free, and perhaps we can add an enticement for the killer to pay him another visit."

"But how?"

"We can spread the news abroad that Sir Anselm knows who the killer is—he met him after all and heard his voice. When the killer comes to silence Anselm, we'll have him."

"Do you think Anselm will agree?" asked Bill.

"He doesn't have to agree. It will work better if he's unaware of it. He can deny all knowledge and protest that he doesn't know what anyone is talking about, which will seem entirely natural under the circumstances."

"What if the assassin is successful?"

"In killing Sir Anselm? It will be our job to ensure that he doesn't have that opportunity. I'll invite him to the castle again, this time as my guest."

Bill laughed. "I don't imagine he'll be in a rush to take up your invitation."

"I'll offer to pay him for his time and ply him with the finest wines in our cellars."

"This killer moves like a ghost. He entered Bradenstoke and visited Father Gilbert's room unobserved," said Bill.

"Or did he?" said Ela. "Perhaps he's a man who can hide in plain sight."

"You think he's someone who's known to the brothers of Bradenstoke abbey and in the town of Devizes?"

"I think it's possible."

"There is one other possibility that we can't entirely extinguish," said Bill slowly, looking up at a display of axes. "Which is that Sir Anselm himself is the killer."

"He'll be under surveillance night and day. If he is the killer he'll surely reveal it sooner or later."

"I just wonder at the safety of bringing such a man into your castle."

"This castle is the king's garrison," Ela reminded him. "There are trained guards around every corner. If he were inclined to kill, he'll have a much harder time doing it here than anywhere else."

"I suppose that is true," said Bill. "Would you like me to present him with the offer?"

"Please do. And you have full discretion over the promises made."

THE NEXT DAY, Bill returned to Salisbury Castle without Sir Anselm. "He said no."

"How much money did you promise him?" asked Ela. They sat together in a corner of the hall.

"Ten pounds at first. Then I raised it to fifteen!" Bill's

frustration was evident on his usually cheerful face. "I went on about wines and fine cooking and compared the situation at the castle with the dismal aspect of his remote manor. He wouldn't hear any of it."

Ela inhaled slowly. "He cherishes his freedom."

"Or did not enjoy our previous hospitality." Bill shook his head. "I told him that he's not being arrested or compelled in any way and that he's not under suspicion. I even warned him that he might be in danger. He is, after all, the closest thing we have as a witness to his brother's murder."

"And he still said no," said Ela. "Well, this is a setback. I suppose we must continue to watch and follow him as best we can."

"Fifteen pounds is a great sum," said Bill." Probably more than he makes in a year from selling his fleeces in London. It's not a sum that any man would turn down lightly. He also has a military background, which means he's trained to kill a man. Perhaps he was paid the sum to do the deed, not simply act as a decoy."

"We must watch him carefully. I need more evidence to arrest and hold him, especially since he's a noble. If he's the killer, then God willing he'll make a misstep that will ensure his conviction at the assizes."

CHAPTER 16

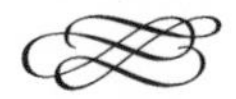

A few days later, Ela received a letter from Richard Marshal that presented another setback in her hopes for justice. She sat in the hall with Petronella, who'd just finished praying with Alisande. "Sir Richard Marshal has consulted his steward, who has checked the records for the family going back some decades, and they can find no trace of Alisande Marshal."

"She's a daughter of Sir Robert Marshal," said Petronella. "Her father died in battle when she was very young."

"I'm afraid they have not identified a Sir Robert Marshal, either."

Petronella stared at her. "What do you mean?"

"That he doesn't exist. Alisande is not a member of the Marshal family."

"Impossible," protested Petronella. "Perhaps you're searching in the wrong Marshal family. It is after all a name associated with a profession. There might be several families with the name of Marshal."

"I'm not aware of another noble family using the name of Marshal. I asked her if Sir William Marshal was a cousin and she said that he was. And she mentioned Richard Marshal, who I met with in London, paying for a Mass to lift a supposed curse on the family. I suppose she overheard him talking to Father Augustine in the chapel. It seems very odd that he doesn't know of her. If they're cousins I would have thought he would visit her in her cell and pay his respects."

"She's very old! Born long before your generation," protested Petronella. "Perhaps she and her father together have been simply forgotten. Let's ask her. I'm sure she can explain it all."

"I certainly hope so. I'm hoping that the Marshal family will protect her from her accusers and provide a secure future for her."

"All she wants is to go back to her cell at Bradenstoke. It's her spiritual home," said Petronella. "She feels like a fish out of water here in the castle."

"I'm trying to save her from being persecuted as a witch."

"She's a holy woman, not a witch. She's been at Bradenstoke longer than any of her accusers."

"I know," said Ela. "I wonder if that's why they resent her. No one seems to know how she came to be there in the first place, amid an order of Augustinian canons. I have to wonder, along with the jury, why she didn't join a nunnery?"

"An anchoress is called to a particular place. Her cell was built next to the chapel so she could hear all the services and take communion from her room, but not interact with the men at all."

"The practice does seem odd—selfish almost—compared to the life of a cloistered nun."

"It sounds so peaceful! She has nothing to do but to pray and feast on the words of the scripture from one day to the next."

"Someone has to bring her meals and wood for her fire and wash her clothes and clean her chamberpot."

"I suppose so," said Petronella. "We haven't discussed it in detail. The Marshal family must be paying for it though, don't you think? Surely the abbey must have records that will prove a link between her and the family."

"I suppose they must. I shall consult the almoner at the abbey."

~

ELA AND PETRONELLA rode to Bradenstoke together to inquire into Alisande's history and ask a few other questions. The almoner was a man in middle age with grizzled stubble on his cheeks. He bowed and fussed and greeted Ela with as much flustered surprise as if she'd woken him from sleep. "Dear sister Alisande, is she well?"

"She is as well as she can be when she's been extirpated from her lifelong home. I'm wondering how she came to be here, in an abbey of men. And who pays for her food and fuel and clothes?"

"Sister Alisande has been here longer than any man in the abbey. I couldn't tell you the circumstances under which she came here. I've asked, but no one knows. Except her, of course."

"Have you asked her?"

"I did once. She said that her family made a sizable donation at the time that she came here. I can find no record of it, but I suppose that's the most likely circumstance. I wonder why she didn't go to the nunnery at Amesbury, or Wilton Abbey, instead. I asked her this, too, and she said she was called to Bradenstoke."

"I understand completely," said Petronella. "It's a sacred place. Sister Alisande spoke of a holy well that was here even before the monastery was built. I would be walled in here myself if my mother would let me. To worship and praise

God in such a spiritual sanctuary would be a blessing indeed." She turned a serene expression toward Ela.

Ela struggled to think of a way to chastise Petronella—if only for making the conversation about herself—in front of the almoner. She wasn't fast enough, so Petronella continued. "My great great grandfather is buried here along with his wife. And my grandfather. My grandmother Alianore will be buried with him when her time arrives."

"This is true," said Ela quickly, to stop her pious daughter waxing on and perhaps attempting to elbow her way into Alisande's now-vacant cell. "If Salisbury cathedral hadn't been erected so close to his time of death, I'm sure my husband would rest here as well. So, it seems that the funds required to support dear Sister Alisande come from the general funds of the abbey, in the absence of any recorded donation?"

"Indeed they do, and it's been quite a princely sum over the years, my lady, since she's of a very great age. I dare say that any donation given when she was a girl your daughter's age has long since been exhausted. If you, or anyone else would care to make an offering..." An expectant half smile lifted the corners of his mouth.

"I suppose that I am contributing to her care by hosting her in my castle for the time being," said Ela sharply. "I didn't find it safe to leave her here, exposed as she was to accusations of witchcraft and sorcery." It occurred to her that there might be a groundswell of opinion on removing Alisande for purely financial reasons. Even in a holy place such as Bradenstoke Abbey, men were not above the temptations of greed or excessive parsimony. "Who was the first person to suggest that Alisande's visions and foresight might be anything other than holy?"

"Why, I don't recall, my lady."

"Have they been going on as long as you've been here?"

"Oh no, I don't remember any whisperings or mutterings about her intentions until quite recently."

"And who first voiced them, that you recall?"

The almoner frowned as if racking his brain. "Perhaps our newest priest, Father Sebastian? Our abbot, Father Augustine, occasionally raised the matter of the ongoing expenditure, but it's only recently that anyone has sowed doubt about Sister Alisande's holiness."

"God rest his soul," said Ela, crossing herself, while doubting Father Augustine's intentions. "Father Augustine was here for more than twenty years. What was the relationship between Sister Alisande and Father Augustine?"

"He didn't approve of her being here due to her being a woman in a house of Augustinian canons. He'd raised the issue of removing her on several occasions. The difficulty was in finding somewhere else that would take her when she has no known means of support."

"Did no one think to contact the Marshal family about the matter?"

"I believe someone did and they claimed to know nothing of her."

"How long ago was this?"

"Oh, a long time ago. Ten years at least."

Ela blinked, more confused than ever. "So, when she was said to have no relationship with the Marshal family, was there discussion about her future?"

The almoner looked a little sheepish. "I believe the discussion tended in a direction of believing that she would soon be quit of this mortal coil, so it was not worth making a big fuss over."

"Yet here she still was, ten years later—alive and in good health."

"Indeed, God be praised." The almoner arranged his face into a peaceful expression.

"It seems as if not everyone was praising God for her good fortune in being long-lived, including Father Sebastian. Who else muttered words against her being here?"

"Oh dear me, I suppose most men in the monastery have felt uncomfortable with a woman in their midst at some time or another. With her cell built up against a window of the church, she can see in at all hours of the day and night and watch all activities both inside and outside the chapel. Some have even muttered that she might overhear the confidences of the confessional."

Ela's ears pricked up. Sister Alisande could indeed hear the secrets of the confessional, as she'd admitted in Ela's hall. "Where exactly do confessions take place?"

"There's a wooden box of sorts in the back of the nave. It is far enough from her cell that she probably doesn't hear much, but she might overhear anything uttered in a loud voice."

"And she can see who is coming and going from the confessional?" At this point, she wanted to confirm Sister Alisande's side of the story.

"I daresay she could if she happened to be looking through her window into the chapel. She spends much time at her prie-dieu which faces another wall. She knows that the men of Bradenstoke don't like being watched or spoken to, so she's learned to keep to herself."

"Well, I suppose that makes sense," said Ela. "Does she speak to anyone at all, on a given day?"

"She used to. Some of the common people even approached her window on the outside for advice."

"What kind of advice?"

He blinked, "Spiritual advice, I presume. I'm not sure what other useful advice she might provide after an entire life spent in the confinement of a single room. But the abbot said it was a distraction and told her to resist the temptation to interact with others."

What an odd life Sister Alisande had chosen for herself. Ela wondered if she'd ever had cause to regret it.

"With Father Augustine and Father Gilbert dead, which priest says Mass?"

"That would be Father Sebastian."

"Please take me to him."

FATHER SEBASTIAN WAS in the vestry. He seemed preoccupied with arranging his vestments and finding a page in his book as the almoner introduced Ela as Countess of Salisbury and High Sheriff of Wiltshire.

This made him look up at her as if she might have two heads. "I'm very busy preparing for the holy service."

"I shall attend the service, and speak with you afterward," she said, schooling her voice to hide her surprise at his rudeness. It was his manner that disturbed her, not the delay. She knew that the commitment to the daily celebration of the hours could not be postponed for secular activities.

Father Sebastian conducted the Nones service in the same brisk and rather fussy manner that he'd displayed in the vestry. He uttered the psalms in clipped tones as if admonishing those present. The readings felt rushed and almost frantic. Rather than feeling refreshed and soothed by the sacred service, Ela felt her nerves jangle as he raced through the familiar texts as if there might be a prize for finishing fast.

As the monks filed out, Ela stayed seated in the chapel, waiting for Father Sebastian to approach her. After some moments, it became clear that she'd need to go find him.

"How extraordinary, Mama," said Petronella. "He seems very nervous."

"He does seem flustered," Ela agreed. "I wonder if my presence here is disturbing to him."

"Because you're a woman?"

"Or because I'm the sheriff."

"And he's guilty of something?"

"It's certainly a possibility to consider."

"Just imagine, if Sister Alisande was here in her cell, she'd have heard the whole service and our conversation, all without rising from her prie-dieu." Petronella turned to gaze at the window that connected the tiny cell to the nave of the chapel.

"I find the arrangement very odd," said Ela. "And I dare say many of the men here do as well. I'd imagine they find it more peaceful not to have a set of very ancient blue eyes gazing at them as they go about their business."

"Or a set of wizened but still sharp ears listening to their conversations," agreed Petronella. "While I envy her solitude, I wouldn't want to be walled up in a place where I wasn't wanted."

Ela and Petronella exited the chapel and stood near Sister Alisande's empty cell. Since Father Sebastian was nowhere to be seen, she sent a guard to find him. Instead of bringing him back to meet them, the guard came back with a sheepish expression and said that the priest was waiting for them in the vestry.

Already irked, but not wishing to create a scene in the abbey, Ela entered the vestry with Petronella and the guards behind her. Father Sebastian looked up from a book as if she'd interrupted him at his reading.

"Father Sebastian, I am here in my capacity as sheriff to investigate two suspicious deaths in this abbey. Perhaps I should have you brought back to my castle where I can interview you in front of a jury."

He closed his book with a look of alarm. "I hardly think that is necessary, my lady."

"I'll decide what's necessary," she said coldly. "How long have you lived at Bradenstoke?"

"Three years."

"Not long at all," said Ela. "What did you think of the anchoress in your midst?"

"Her presence here seemed a singular act of selfishness. Why would a woman choose to live in an order of men if not to sow discord and unease? And now recent events have revealed her to be a witch."

Ela resisted the urge to roll her eyes. "What makes you think she's a witch?"

"She cursed dear Father Gilbert right before he fell."

"From what I've been told, she warned him, rather than cursing him. I've had the good fortune of getting to know Sister Alisande while she's been staying at my castle, and I find her to be kind and good and genuinely devoted to worshipping God. I can't think of a single reason why someone would accuse her of witchcraft or evil. I find it extraordinary that these accusations persist when they seem to be totally unfounded. I'm quite sure she didn't kill Father Gilbert and Father Augustine. Which begs the question of who did?"

She peered at him. He fussed with the book he'd just closed. "If I knew, I would certainly tell you."

"Are you the only priest here now?"

"Yes."

"Father Augustine was the abbot. Do you expect that they will make you the abbot?"

He straightened his shoulders. "That will be up to the bishop."

"I imagine that he will likely bring in an abbot from outside the abbey," she said, watching his reaction closely.

He shifted in his seat. "He might prefer someone from inside the community, who knows it well. But I leave that in his hands and those of God."

"Then I doubt that someone who's been here only three years would be his choice," she said, glad of a little revenge after his rude treatment of her.

Color rose up his neck. "What does this have to do with the deaths?"

"Men have been known to kill a rival for a position that they covet."

"I can assure you that I did not murder my fellow priests," he spluttered, color rising to his face.

"You appear to have more motivation than Sister Alisande," said Ela mildly. "Why would she want Father Gilbert and Father Augustine dead?"

His lips pursed. "I cannot claim to have any insight into the mind of a witch."

Ela inhaled slowly, "You seem deeply opposed to Sister Alisande returning to her cell here in the abbey."

"Indeed I am."

"Would you prefer to see her exiled and excommunicated?" She allowed one of her eyebrows to lift slightly.

He licked his lips, and she could almost hear his thoughts stumbling over each other. "If she's found to be a murderess, then she should meet the fate of one."

"A hanging? Even though she's almost as old as these abbey walls and gentle as a lamb? It seems that your heart is filled with rancor rather than the love of God and compassion for your fellow man."

Father Sebastian now looked like he was about to combust. Ela had found that sometimes pushing a man to the limits of his temper was a good way to get him to reveal things he'd rather keep secret.

"Have you ever heard of a priest revealing a confidence told to him during confession?" she asked.

He blinked rapidly. "We are not permitted to reveal anything said to us during confession."

"Not in public, but surely you share secrets among yourselves?"

"Certainly not, my lady." He spoke sharply, as if scolding her.

"I heard that Father Gilbert might have revealed a confidence." This was not true, at least not as far as she knew, but she hoped to provoke a reaction.

"I don't know anything about that." He spoke so fast that the words ran together.

"Did he ever take confession from a powerful man?"

"Of course. Bradenstoke is frequented by the nobility and even royalty on occasion."

"Do you think it's possible that someone shared sensitive information with him in the confessional and that he may have endangered his life by revealing it?"

"I suppose it's possible, but he would be in breach of his vows if that happened. He's not here to defend himself and I've certainly never known him to breach the sanctity of the confessional."

"Did you know he has a brother who lives locally?"

"I did not."

"He lives on a manor belonging to Bradenstoke Abbey. I'm surprised that you didn't know this."

"We canons don't sit around gossiping like fishwives, my lady. If words are exchanged between us they are more likely to concern the sacred texts than the families we left behind along with our secular lives."

"I see." Ela began to despair of extracting useful information from Father Sebastian. He also didn't have any obvious motive for murder. She thought it unlikely that he'd expect to be chosen as abbot, even in the absence of his fellow priests, given his awkward manner and lack of seniority or pedigree, so it didn't make sense that he'd kill for the role. "I'd like to speak with Brother Oswin. Please take me to him."

CHAPTER 17

Ela was surprised to discover Brother Oswin sitting at a large table with pots of ink and sheets of vellum, engaged in writing a dense page of black and red text with a quill pen.

"My lady," he said, as he rose to his feet, eyes wide with surprise in his moon-round face.

Ela dismissed Father Sebastian and asked Petronella to close the door. "I'm still trying to discover who introduced the poison that killed Father Gilbert and Father Augustine. Do you recall any strangers visiting the abbey in the days before Father Gilbert fell dead at the altar?

Oswin's thin eyebrows rose into his tonsure. "It was a Sunday, my lady. We always have a few parishioners join us on a Sunday."

"Were they all people who come weekly, that you recognized?"

He blinked rapidly, looking rather nervous. "I couldn't say, my lady as they are none of my business. I am a scribe and have no interaction with the parishioners. I've been copying this manuscript for the last twelvemonth. It takes up most of my time."

Ela glanced down at a large book that lay open on the table in front of him. She could see that he was copying the page on the left-hand side. "You have a very neat hand. I can see why the abbey values you as a scribe. But it was Sunday— a day of rest— so I presume that you attended Mass and all of the canonical hours?"

"Yes, my lady. I did. I didn't notice any strangers that I'd never seen before."

It occurred to Ela that if a stranger wanted access to Father Gilbert's chamber, he could safely enter it during any holy service since Father Gilbert would of necessity be in the chapel during that time. Why then would a a would-be assassin need to pay Sir Anselm a great sum of money to keep his brother occupied in the confessional?

She felt fairly certain that Sir Anselm had spun a web of lies to distract her. But the fact remained that no one had seen him go anywhere near Father Gilbert's room, so she couldn't yet directly implicate him in his brother's murder.

"How do you feel about the presence of Sister Alisande here at Bradenstoke?"

"Her presence? Surely you mean her absence. I feel as if the beating heart of the Abbey has been cut out."

"You miss her?" This surprised Ela greatly after all the negative attitudes she'd encountered thus far.

"Oh yes. Her calm and holy nature blessed us all. What a sweet lady, with never a harsh word for anyone."

"I'm glad to find someone who doesn't characterize her as a meddling witch."

He shook his head and tutted. "We lived here happily with her in our midst for many years. Only recently have there been mutterings against her."

"Who started them?"

"I can't be sure. Perhaps Father Sebastian? Or was it Father Augustine? Father Sebastian certainly picked up the thread of discontent and tugged on it. Soon many of the brothers were complaining about a woman living in their midst, being waited on by the lay brothers and eating and drinking up the abbey's funds."

"Why would her presence bother them suddenly, when she's been here her whole life?"

He shook his head. "I don't know. I always valued her peaceful presence. She reminds me of my dear mother who died many years ago. Dear Sister Alisande won't be coming back, will she?"

"I don't think so. I'm sure she'd like to, but I can't recommend that she return to a place where even priests are accusing her of witchcraft. I feel she'd be in danger. Have you ever heard of her getting a glimpse of the future before?"

He hesitated for a moment. "Yes, but I took it as a sign of her holiness. I think it's not unheard of for an anchoress to have sacred visions of the world beyond or events that have not yet happened. I don't believe it has any connection to witchcraft at all."

"I agree, and I'm glad to meet a sensible man at Bradenstoke Abbey, Brother Oswin. Her future would be far safer, though, if I could identify the person who committed the murders. Do you think there is anyone in the abbey who would have the motivation to kill either Father Gilbert or Father Augustine?"

"Certainly not, my lady. We're men of God, whose lives revolve around preparing our souls to meet Our Lord and his Heavenly host in the hereafter. I think we'd be the last people on earth to commit a murder and risk damnation and hell."

"I quite understand. And that suggests that the murderer was a visitor to the abbey. One man who visited the abbey was Father Gilbert's brother, Sir Anselm Allsop. He came not during Mass, or one of the Hours, but in between them. He claims that a man paid him to visit his brother and take confession, so I find myself wondering if you or anyone else saw another man—perhaps an unfamiliar one—on the abbey grounds at around the same time. This person would have entered Father Gilbert's room and sprinkled the deadly mushroom powder in his prayer book."

"My lady, we've talked of little else since Father Gilbert's death. And Father Augustine's death only compounded the loss. None of the lay brothers noticed anyone near Father Gilbert's room, though they each have tasks that take them away from the presbytery during the day."

"Did any of them mention that Father Gilbert's brother had visited him a few days before his death?"

"I admit that they didn't. I suppose they didn't know this man was his brother."

"And Father Gilbert's brother visited a blacksmith's shop in Devizes on the very same night that the apothecary—who sold the killer the mushroom dust—was strangled in his shop."

Brother Oswin frowned. "It certainly sounds as if he's the killer. Do you have him under arrest?"

"I did have him under guard in my castle, but cannot find cause for him to kill any of these people, let alone his brother."

Could the motive be money alone? Did someone pay Sir Anselm ten pounds to kill his brother? He certainly didn't seem to be a hard-hearted assassin who'd kill his brother in cold blood, and even deep in his cups, he'd betrayed no hint that this had happened.

And Sister Alisande had strongly hinted that Hubert de Burgh was responsible. Ela realized she'd latched onto the idea because it appealed to her so much. Was there any truth to it, or was Sister Alisande gathering wool and spinning tall tales with it?

She lifted her chin. "Has Hubert de Burgh, the king's justiciar, ever made confession here at Bradenstoke?"

"Yes, my lady. As has the king himself," he brightened as he spoke. "We consider it a great honor to have the most important men in the kingdom among us."

Ela felt her pulse quicken. "When was the last time either of them was here?" She knew the answer from the list of guests she'd been given. They'd both attended Mass at the abbey for the feast of St John the Baptist in June.

"I certainly remember seeing them both at Mass on St. John the Baptist's day. As you can imagine, all of us here at the abbey feel a sense of awe in the presence of our king." He frowned and broke off. "Is it true that the king is now at odds with his justiciar?"

"I've heard as much." She didn't intend to share gossip with the monk. She certainly wasn't going to mention that Sister Alisande had told her that Hubert de Burgh had killed Father Gilbert. But now that she'd seen Sister Alisande's cell, with its intimate position right up against the chapel and almost within earshot of the confessional, she wondered if Sister Alisande's suspicions were based less in unearthly knowledge and more on an event she'd witnessed or overheard. "But I don't know the details. Thank you, Brother Oswin. If you learn any more about visitors to the abbey during those dark days surrounding the deaths, or if you learn any new information, please send word to me at Salisbury Castle."

"I will indeed, my lady."

~

"Is Sir Anselm Allsop a hired assassin?" asked Ela of Bill that evening as they walked down the colonnaded hallway behind the great hall. She spoke quietly so as not to be overheard.

"He does seem to have been paid a sum of money large enough to buy a murder and to have been in close proximity to the killings. If those are coincidences, they are very unlucky ones."

"He doesn't seem like a killer at all, let alone a professional capable of handling a deadly poison without injury to himself or strangling an old man in cold blood. He's a bumbling drunkard with a trade in sheep fleeces."

"In my experience, professional killers are clever at concealing their profession. I've heard of one who was a court jester who spent his days at his king's elbow but who committed his duties under cover of darkness."

"Do you think his drunkenness is a ruse?" asked Ela.

Bill shrugged. "If he is a hired assassin, then likely it is, though he certainly drank his fill here at your table. Perhaps he felt he had no choice or his deception would be revealed. However, sometimes even the finest warriors have such a weakness but can do their work despite their affliction."

"But why would he kill his brother? That's the part that makes no sense to me."

"What makes you so sure that Sir Anselm really is Father Gilbert's brother?" asked Bill softly. "Do you have any proof other than Sir Anselm telling you?"

Ela froze in mid-step. "You're right. I don't. And no one at the abbey even knew that Father Gilbert had a brother. Have I fallen into a trap?"

"I think it would be prudent to formally arrest Sir Anselm. At the very least he needs to appear before a jury again now that we know he was paid ten pounds by a mysterious stranger to pay a visit to the dead man. There's certainly more to his story than he's admitted. His trade in fleeces could well be a cover for his true profession."

"Have I hosted a killer under my roof and entertained him in my hall?"

"You had him under guard, my lady. Your purpose was to investigate him."

"Yet in my mind, I'd largely exonerated him. If he is guilty then he's clever at concealing his motives and methods. And the most important question is... who hired him and how can we prove it?"

Ela rode along with the party that set out to arrest Sir Anselm. She was curious to see his reaction to the arrest, and she enjoyed a ride early in the day on almost any pretext. The autumn sun warmed the countryside, gilding the sheep as they grazed on the hillsides. Dry weather had bleached the grass, turning the landscape into a tapestry woven with gold threads.

She'd already sent out a summons for a jury to meet after the bells for Nones, so Sir Anselm would be forced to answer questions before he had time to formulate a lot of cunning answers to throw them off the trail.

Bill rode alongside her. "I wonder if he'll make a run for it," he said, as they turned down the lane to Sir Anselm's rented manor. "If he's a professional killer he'll be hard to catch. On the other hand, it's a nice day for a gallop."

"I always enjoy how you see the positive side of any situation," said Ela, as they trotted along the path. She did want to keep the advantage of surprise. They'd had his manor under surveillance, so hopefully if he'd tried to slip away, the guards stationed there would have caught him and held him.

There was no sign of activity as they approached the

well-built stone house set amidst a small orchard of already-harvested apple trees. They approached the door and Ela sent two guards around the back of the house before she commanded another guard to knock.

No one answered. They waited for some time, Ela confident that Sir Anselm wouldn't be able to slip out a back door or a window unobserved. "Where are the servants?" she asked Bill. "He didn't have a household full of them but he mentioned having at least two."

"Open the door," she commanded after the guard had knocked three times without any response. Ela and Bill had dismounted and handed their horses to a guard. As the first guard stepped over the threshold, they followed him and found themselves greeted by a man lying on the floor, trussed up like a pig except with his hands and feet bound behind his back and a rag wadded into his mouth.

Ela stifled a shriek. As sheriff, it did not behoove her to show emotion even under extreme circumstances. She reminded herself that soldiers rode into almost certain death on the battlefield without flinching and she could do the same by mastering her emotions. Still, this sight was so unexpected that she found herself lost for words.

She crossed herself. "This is not Sir Anselm. Is he dead? Untie him at once." The victim was a heavy-set man in a homespun brown garment with dirty bare feet. "And search the rest of the house with great care."

She'd brought fifteen guards with her in total and wished she had more, but she had five of them fan out through the house to search the rooms. One guard cut the bonds tying the man's hands to his feet. He collapsed on the floor.

"I think he's alive," said the guard, tugging the rag from his mouth." The man, limp and almost lifeless, gagged and coughed weakly.

"Fetch him water," said Ela. "He may have been here like

this for hours or even days." A guard rushed out to get a canteen from his horse and poured a narrow stream of water into the man's mouth, which caused him to cough more.

"There's a dead body in here," called a guard from upstairs.

"Don't take your eyes off this man," said Ela. With Bill at her heels and her heart pounding, she climbed the stairs. The second body lay in a bedroom off the upstairs hall, half in and half out of the bed. Blood soaked the floor and the sheets. "It is Sir Anselm," said Ela, with all the breath she could gather. "It looks as if he was killed while trying to rise."

Bill muttered a low curse, then apologized for it. "With him die our chances of learning the truth about him." His sword lay under the bed, in its sheath, as if he kept it there to defend himself from just such an attack.

"Call for the coroner at once," said Ela, now dreading what they'd find in the other rooms. A search of the house found no more bodies, dead or alive, though there were two more beds found to have been recently occupied. One bed downstairs, a pallet on the floor in a small cellar behind the kitchen, seemed to have belonged to the heavy man downstairs since a man's tattered shoes and stockings lay near it. In a small upstairs room, they found a cloak and a pair of women's shoes, also well-worn. Folded nearby lay a clean chemise, rather ragged along the hem.

"A girl slept here," said Ela. "Where is she now?"

"Perhaps she's the killer and made her escape," said Bill softly.

Ela crossed herself again. The unexpected horror of their discovery had scrambled her mind. "Sir Anselm was killed with considerable violence, if the amount of blood is any indication." It was rare—at least in her experience—for a woman to attempt to stab a man who could easily overpower her.

She forced herself to look at Sir Anselm's body. Blood soaked the front of his nightgown and seemed to have run down his face and neck and pooled on the floor. Ela felt nausea rise within her at the gruesome sight. "I'm afraid I must get some air," she gasped, hoping that she wouldn't faint to the floor. She cursed her weakness. Did one ever get used to the sight of a body that had been cruelly murdered? She suspected not.

Bill followed her downstairs despite her protestations. Outside the gaping front doorway she gulped in air, trying to steady herself. "I was almost convinced that Sir Anselm was the killer and now it appears I was wrong about everything."

She hurried back in to question the man found downstairs. He now sat slumped against one plastered wall in the downstairs parlor, legs splayed on the stone floor.

"Who tied you up?" she asked softly.

The man just stared at her blankly. The guards had untied his hands but they lay, limp, in his lap.

"Give him more water," said Ela quickly. She did not want this man to die as well. He was her best hope of unraveling this nightmare. "He's very weak."

The man drank a little more water from a guard's canteen, but it dribbled down his chin and he didn't lift a hand to wipe it.

"Were you overpowered by one man or more?" she asked. His gaze didn't meet hers. He seemed to stare blankly at the other side of the room. Still, he was breathing and swallowing. "Where's the girl? The one who slept upstairs?"

He blinked rapidly a few times, as if he heard her question, but he didn't stir or even attempt to reply.

"What's your name?" Again, no answer.

"We need to find the girl at once," said Ela. "She may be in great danger. Send guards to the Three Keys to learn her identity and that of this man here." Two guards set out at once.

"Weren't there guards stationed here to watch Sir Anselm?" asked Bill.

"There were," said Ela, darkly. "And we must have ridden past them on our way in. Where are they? Please find them and bring them to me."

The guards were found in the woods just off the lane, both fast asleep. At first, she'd thought they seemed dead, but Bill Talbot kicked at them with his feet, and they both stirred.

"For shame!" cried Ela. "To your feet at once!"

One of them rolled over, holding his head. The other one tried to rise but failed in his attempt.

"Are they drunk?" asked Ela, fury boiling her blood. "The man you were supposed to be guarding and observing was killed in his bed! The entire reason you're here is to observe anyone arriving or leaving. He was probably killed by the same man who murdered Father Gilbert and Wilf the Younger, and now the killer has escaped again thanks to your criminal incompetence."

"I think they're drugged, my lady," said Bill. "Their listlessness goes beyond mere sleepiness."

"Or drunk," said Ela, fuming. She leaned in and could indeed smell the familiar whiff of alcohol that rises from someone who's consumed far too much. "Did someone give you a drink?"

One of the men managed to nod.

"Who?"

He seemed to make an effort to speak, but couldn't.

"They're as wordless as the man inside. Put them on the wagon we brought for the arrest. There's no excuse for this dereliction of duty."

CHAPTER 18

It seemed an eternity before Giles Haughton arrived, bringing two jurors to observe the details of the scene. Ela sent them past the still wordless man slumped against the wall downstairs, apparently unable to do more than swallow water, and up to Anselm's bedroom.

Haughton studied Sir Anselm's dead body where it lay, feet and legs still mostly on the bed, torso and head cascading down toward the floor. Blood soaked the chest of the dead man's linen nightshirt. Haughton used his knife to slit the front of the man's garment, then he peeled it back to examine his torso. "This man was killed by a knife wound to the chest. A lucky one, from all appearances, which missed his ribcage and pierced his heart, killing him before he could rise."

"Lucky, or the work of someone who knew how to kill with one blow?" asked Ela.

Haughton studied his hands for defensive wounds and found none. "This man was surprised and didn't have a chance to defend himself. The killer thrust the knife into him while he still lay in bed, though I'd guess he was awake and trying to get up. Haughton pointed to the unstained mattress. "The knife went right through him, just under his ribcage, and there'd be a stain on the mattress if he'd still been lying on it. A knife wound to the heart would have killed him instantly, and he fell dead in the position you found him in."

Haughton observed a line of blood drops on the floor, that Ela hadn't noticed before. "The killer pulled the knife out and walked to the door with it still dripping." They followed the trail of blood drops, which led into the hallway, and down toward the girl's bedroom, where the drops stopped.

Haughton examined the girl's empty bed—a crude, straw-stuffed mattress on the bare floor—and her shoes. "A servant girl likely only has one pair of shoes so she left without them, in a hurry."

"I worry that the assailant abducted her," said Ela.

Haughton approached the window, where a wooden shutter stood open. "Or she escaped out the window when she heard the sound of her master screaming in terror." He leaned out the window and looked down toward the ground. "It's a leap, to be sure, but we must examine the ground downstairs to see if there are signs that she landed down there and made her escape."

"If she did, then where is she now? How long ago do you think the murder happened?"

Back in Anselm's room, Haughton palpated the corpse's arms and legs. "Rigor mortis is fading, so I'd place the death yesterday evening between dusk and midnight."

"Two guards were stationed outside the house," said Ela. "To observe Sir Anselm's movements since he was under suspicion of consorting with the man who murdered his brother—if he was indeed his brother—Father Gilbert. They were both found in the woods, still drunk with liquor or worse."

"Probably fell asleep," grumbled Haughton. "Wouldn't be the first time."

"They smell of drink and I couldn't get a word out of them. At the very least we need to know who gave them the drink. With Sir Anselm dead we need these witnesses to reveal who came to kill him or we'll never learn who killed the others."

"You say that you suspected Anselm of doing business with a killer. Perhaps that person returned to add him to his tally of corpses."

"That does seem likely. We think the apothecary was killed to cover the killer's tracks—so no one could discover who bought the deadly mushroom powder."

"And Anselm was in the smithy next to the apothecary shop on the night of the murder. He could have been hired to do the deed...then was killed when the person who ordered that murder wished to cover his tracks."

"I must search the outside of the house for footprints or other signs that might help lead us to him," said Haughton. "If we can discover how he approached the house, or how he left it, that would be valuable information."

"And the girl," Ela's heart ached with worry for her. "What if he took her as a trophy?"

"If he did, that might make him easier to find."

THEY STUDIED the approach to the front door, which was much trampled by Ela's men and revealed no obvious footprints. Under the girl's window, the soft turf was crushed as if someone had hit the ground hard, scrambling to their feet, and running into the woods, where the trail disappeared.

"These footprints are small," said Ela, as they stood where the last partial footprint led into the leaf litter of the forest. "They're the girl, not the murderer."

"He likely left by the same door he came in," said Haughton.

"It galls me that he entered and left through the front door when I had guards stationed at the house to observe all movement," said Ela, fuming.

"Do you suppose the guards were bribed?" asked Haughton quietly. "Since we know someone was throwing large sums of money around."

"They were certainly bribed with liquor, if nothing else. And they shall regret it until their dying day, which may be soon. We'll question them back at the castle in front of the jury, along with the man found by the front door."

They walked back through the house, hoping for any further sign left by the murderer.

"He'd have been splattered with blood," said Haughton. "Sir Anselm's wound would have gushed when he opened it."

In addition to the blood drips on the dark wood floor of the upstairs hallway and in the girl's room, they found a partial bloody handprint on the wall next to the window, where he must have stopped to peer out. "This gives me hope that the girl escaped," said Ela. "But where is she?"

After they'd examined every inch of the house and most of the grounds, Sir Anselm's body was removed to the mortuary at Salisbury Castle in the hope that careful study of the wounds might reveal more information about the weapon used and the man who wielded it.

Before returning, Ela decided to ride to the Three Keys and see if they could glean any information there. The smoky air, smelling of roasted meat and spilled ale, stung her eyes as they entered. The mistress of the house approached them, wiping her hands on a rag. "Good day, my lady. Would you care for a cup of ale?"

"I'm afraid I must inform you of the death of one of your best customers," said Ela.

"Sir Anselm?" The woman's eyes widened. "What happened?"

"We found him murdered in his bed. Do you happen to know the identity of the man who lived in his house?"

"Oh dear me, yes, that's Teddy Blakely who used to live near the old mill. He's been a widower these last five years and was sorely in need of the work. You say he's dead?"

"He's alive but was left trussed and gagged. Had you seen Sir Anselm here or in Devizes with anyone in the last few days?"

She looked up as if searching the smoke-blackened ceiling for her memories. "No one new. He usually came here by himself. He'd talk to anyone who came in and happened to be sitting near him. Devizes is a big enough town that we do have strangers passing through especially now we have a market here," continued the woman. "Though I can't say I've noticed anyone in particular."

"Do you know the girl who worked for Sir Anselm?"

"Young Kissy, yes, she's Edith's daughter—" She froze. "Is she killed?"

"No, she seems to have escaped. I hope she may have seen the murderer and can help us find him. At the very least I need to locate her to make sure she is safe and not abducted by the killer."

"Saints have mercy. Her family lives in a cottage on the road to Rowde. You can't miss it. The door's painted red and they've a black and white cow in a pen right next to it."

~

Ela, Haughton, and the remaining guards rode at once to the girl's house, which matched the description perfectly. The picturesque cottage was freshly whitewashed. A mound of bright white daisies next to the cow's pen of woven willow stems.

Ela dismounted and approached the door. She could hear sounds within, like someone moving about. She knocked and the sounds stopped.

"Who's there?" asked a woman's voice, with some hesitation.

"It's Ela, Countess of Salisbury and Sheriff of Wiltshire."

After a considerable silence, footsteps approached the door and a woman about Ela's age opened it. Her uncovered hair was falling out of its knot and her eyes had a wild look about them.

"Are you Edith?"

"I am," she said doubtfully.

"Does your daughter work for Sir Anselm Allsop?"

The woman swallowed and glanced over her shoulder. Ela followed her gaze across the dim cottage interior, and it landed on a girl, sitting on the floor, her arms wrapped around her knees, rocking back and forth. "She did, but I think something's happened there so I don't know if she'll be going back."

She looked back at Ela nervously, as if she might be about to blame her for it. Which gave Ela pause. "Is that your daughter?"

"Yes, my lady. I think she ran back here through the woods and fields and it's no short distance, as you know."

"About what time did she arrive home?"

"Not long before dawn. Drenched in sweat she was, face streaked with tears and dust. Hasn't said a word no matter how much I've begged her. I fear he's used her ill, my lady." The woman's emotions were getting the better of her and her eyes reddened.

"Sir Anselm Allsop is dead," said Ela softly.

The woman glanced back at her daughter and Ela saw her start to shake. "She didn't have any blood on her if that's what you think. She's just a mite of a girl and couldn't kill a great big man like that, no matter what he did to her."

"Oh no, mistress, we don't suspect her of killing him. He was murdered with great violence by someone experienced in the taking of a life. We suspect that your daughter's sharp ears and keen instincts prompted her to jump out of her window and make her escape before the killer found her."

The woman let out a whimper. "I don't know why she won't speak."

"Shock, most likely," said Ela. "I've seen it before. It's usually temporary. Do you mind if I try to talk to her?"

Kissy's mother rubbed her hands on her rose-colored homespun gown. "You can try, my lady. I haven't been able to get a single word out of her."

Ela approached the girl, where she sat, still rocking, on the flagstone floor. She crouched down until she was almost eye-level with Kissy, who she could see was about fourteen or fifteen. The girl stopped rocking and stared at her, eyes glassy.

"I know your master is dead, Kissy," said Ela very quietly. "He was murdered in his bed. You were very clever to make your escape and run home. God be praised that you're alive and well."

Tears welled in the girl's eyes.

"You heard the killer enter the house?"

She stared at Ela for a moment, then nodded.

"Did you hear Teddy Blakely cry out after he opened the door?"

The girl shook her head.

"You heard someone climb the stairs?"

She nodded assent.

"And you heard him go into your master's bedroom?"

The girl nodded again, and two fat tears rolled over her rosy, plump cheeks.

"You did the right thing, dear Kissy. Don't blame yourself for anything. You're very lucky to be alive." She swallowed, hating herself for pressing this poor girl who'd had the fright of her life. "Did you happen to hear the killer say anything?"

The girl shook her head.

"Did you happen to get a look at him?"

Again, she mutely shook her head. Ela put her hand on the girl's shoulder. "You're safe now. I'm the sheriff and I'm going to catch the man who killed your master and make him pay for his crimes." She hoped the passage of time wouldn't make her a liar. "If you remember anything at all, even the smallest detail, please come to me at the castle at once."

THE GUARDS who'd fallen asleep on their watch were left to stew in the dungeon overnight. Teddy Blakely, who was not under suspicion, had been left at the manor to tend to the sheep but was summoned to appear before the jury the next day, in the hope that he could describe his attacker.

It would take Teddy some time to travel to Ela's castle from the manor, so first she had the two guards brought up from the dungeon to face the jurors. They were brought into the space between the tables, hands tied behind their backs and shame on their faces.

"Timothy Stoke and Martin Ludlow, you're both charged with dereliction of duty. Your sole task was to closely observe Sir Anselm Allsop and any visitors to or from his manor. Sir Anselm has been murdered on your watch, and we have no idea who killed him. Did you see anyone approach the house?

Martin Ludlow was a man of about forty with a meaty face and thick dark hair. According to the garrison commander, he'd distinguished himself in several battles during a long career as a soldier. "I'm afraid we were both passed out, my lady."

"The reason two guards were stationed there is so that you could take turns sleeping. How do you explain the fact that you were both sleeping at once, at the very time that your close attention to the task at hand was required?" She struggled to keep her tone steady while fury heated her blood.

"Sir Anselm's servant brought us cups of wine, my lady," continued Ludlow. "And I suspect it had something in it that put us into a deep sleep."

"By Sir Anselm's servant, do you mean Teddy Blakely?"

"That's the one."

"How many cups of wine did you drink?" asked Ela, looking at the other guard. Timothy Stoke was in his mid-twenties, with wavy blond hair and a handsome face. "Only one each, my lady. That's why we think it must have contained a sleeping draught."

"Had Sir Anselm's servant given you food or drink before?"

"No, my lady," said Ludlow, hanging his head slightly.

"Weren't you supposed to be hidden so that they didn't see you?" she asked.

"We were hidden in the woods so that anyone approaching wouldn't see us, or that we could observe when someone left, but they certainly knew we were there. There's only one lane in and out and one of us had to go buy our food and drink in the village each day."

"Were you not suspicious of this unexpected generosity?"

Now both men looked at the floor. "The servant joked about knowing he wasn't supposed to see us but that he suspected we were thirsty and his master had a barrel of fine wine that he'd just tapped. We didn't see the harm in it."

Ela was glad to be questioning them before Teddy Blakely arrived. "Had you spoken to this servant before?"

"We had greeted him once or twice. He worked outside a lot, tending the garden and orchards. Seemed like a friendly fellow."

"So you took the drink he offered, drank it, then what is the last thing you remember?"

"I don't even remember finishing the drink, my lady," said Stoke. "It acted that fast. Never seen anything like it."

"So you believe he deliberately gave you a drink that would render you senseless."

"I'm sure of it, my lady," said Ludlow.

"You do realize that this in no way excuses your behavior," said Ela. "Accepting wine from anyone in the household of the man you're guarding was risky and foolish in the extreme, and has had disastrous results for my investigation into who killed two priests and the apothecary."

They both shifted awkwardly. She opened questions up to the jurors, who launched in with questions as if both men might be a part of a murder conspiracy rather than just thirsty buffoons. Haughton grilled them on who had or hadn't passed them at any point either on the lane or off it, and they said that Sir Anselm was the only one who ever came or went while they were stationed there.

Teddy Blakely arrived as the jurors were finishing their questions. Ela had the guards moved to the side of the tables, and Teddy brought into the middle. He looked hot and winded from the journey. “I’m sorry it took so long, my lady. I rode my master’s horse and he’s very slow.”

“We hear that you gave my two guards cups of wine that were laced with a sleeping draught,” said Ela, hoping to catch him off guard. “What substance did you use?”

“What?” Teddy looked shocked and awkward. Guilt? Or genuine confusion. She couldn’t tell. “My master asked me to give them wine.”

“Did you find that strange?”

“I suppose I did. He told me to take some myself as well, so I thought he must be feeling generous.”

“You drank the same wine they did?”

“Yes, it was in an earthenware jug.”

Ela looked at Haughton. “Did you see a jug?”

Haughton shook his head. “It may still be in the house, my lady. I would like to see it and examine the dregs.”

“There won’t be any dregs since I washed it out this morning after I finished scrubbing the floor in my master’s room,” said Teddy Blakely.

Ela sagged slightly. More useful evidence was gone. “Did you feel the effects of the sleeping draught?” asked Ela of Teddy.

“Now that you mention it, I must have. I don’t remember anything that happened after I drank it. I assumed it was because I’m not accustomed to wine. I usually only drink ale. But I don’t remember how I came to be tied up.”

“Your master asked you to drink the wine?”

“Yes. He poured himself a cup as well so I had no reason to believe there was anything wrong with it.”

“Did you see him drink it?”

“I did.”

“What time was this?”

“It was well into the evening, after dark.”

"So he sent you out in the dark, to approach two heavily armed guards and give them each a cup of wine?"

Teddy Blakely tugged at the sleeves of his tunic. "He did, my lady."

Ela sighed. "So all of you were drugged when an unknown assailant came to the house and killed your master with a stab to the chest."

"Young Kissy didn't have any, that I know of."

Ela glanced at Haughton. Could the girl have drugged them all? It was hard to fathom her motive. While Ela knew of at least one situation where a girl had killed the master who abused her repeatedly, the vicious thrust to Sir Anselm's chest was the work of someone far stronger and more experienced with killing than a fourteen-year-old serving maid.

"Do you have reason to believe that Kissy wanted you all asleep?"

"No, my lady. I can't think why she would." Ela now regretted not calling the girl here, so they could hear her side of the story if she'd got her voice back.

"Did she prepare the jug of wine? By that, I mean tapping the barrel and bringing it to you?"

Teddy Blakely frowned. "I don't know, my lady. I didn't see who did it."

"Why not? Surely after dark, you were inside the house with her and Sir Anselm."

He licked his lips nervously. "I was already resting in my bed before Sir Anselm roused me to take the wine out to the guards. I drank my cup after I came back in from serving them."

"So, as far as you know, the jug could have been prepared by Kissy or your master."

"Yes, my lady." Rather than bring the girl to her hall to be grilled by the jurors, Ela resolved to visit her and ask her.

"You were tied up in front of the door. Did you rise to answer the door when the stranger arrived?"

"I have no memory of it at all, my lady. I drank my wine and lay down on my pallet in the kitchen. I don't know how I came to be in front of the door."

Ela looked at Haughton. "Why would a killer tie him up if he was already asleep?"

"So he couldn't wake up and find his master to raise the alarm too soon, perhaps?" said Haughton.

"Did your master entertain visitors at the manor?"

"No, my lady. Not a one that I remember."

"And how long have you served him?"

"I was there almost two years, ever since he rented the manor. He did me a favor hiring me as I was in a bad way having lost my wife and being forced to turn the farm we'd shared over to her younger brother's family, since it belonged to her parents. I had nowhere to go and he gave me a roof over my head and food to eat."

"Did he pay you?"

"Not in money, but with food and a place to sleep. I was content with my life. Growing plants and tending animals is the only thing I've ever been good at and I'm proud to say we ate well from the garden I planted and we had enough provisions stocked away to last right through the winter." He stopped and licked his lips again. "Though I don't suppose I'll be allowed to stay there now, will I?"

"The manor belongs to Bradenstoke Abbey so they will likely rent it to another tenant. Perhaps that person can be persuaded to keep you in their service."

Ela opened questions up to the jury and they asked quite a few about Sir Anselm's habits and proclivities. Ela herself asked about the frequency and intensity of his drinking.

"He drank more than a man should," said Teddy. "It wasn't my place to say anything, of course. He would drink at the Three Keys all afternoon, then come home and drain four more cups of wine or ale."

"Did his mood or mannerisms change when he was in his cups?"

"I can't say they did," said Teddy. "He was a quiet and steady master, not given to fits of temper. He didn't seem to expect much of life except to eat and drink and tend to his business."

"And how would you describe his business?"

"Well, he bought fleeces and stored them in the shed until he had enough to load a cart and take it to a market where he could sell them for a profit."

"From what you could see, did he make a good living at this business?"

Teddy Blakely hesitated. "Well, he seems to have made enough to keep body and soul together, but I've been a sheep man all my life and he didn't always buy the best quality. Didn't have an eye for it. And recently he started buying sheep to breed and didn't make the best choices there, either."

"Did he ask for your help in choosing them?"

"He did ask my opinion, but then he didn't always take my advice. You want to buy ewes with soft, thick fleece, not ones that have pretty faces or an unusual color. He was subject to whims that cost him money, if you ask me."

"Did he have any other source of income?"

"Not that I could see, my lady."

"Did he speak of his brother who was a canon at Bradenstoke?"

"Not that I recall, my lady. I didn't know he had a brother until the priest was dead. Kissy learned about it when she was visiting her parents. She'd go home to them on Sundays with some vegetables from the garden. I offered him condolences but he didn't say anything other than to mutter thanks and dismiss me back to my garden."

"How would you describe his treatment of the girl, Kissy?" asked Ela. "Was he kind to her?"

"I wouldn't say kind, but not too harsh either. She's young and would make mistakes and spill things from time to time. She wasn't the best at scrubbing and laundering, either. But I suppose she was the best he could get for room and board and no pay."

"He didn't pay either of you?"

"No. We were both willing to work for a roof over our heads and food in our bellies—me because I'm old and not worth much as a hired man, and Kissy because she's young and has a lot to learn. I can't say she or I were discontented. Sir Anselm wasn't a difficult master and kept to himself when he wasn't out drinking."

"Did you ever accompany him into Devizes or to the Three Keys?"

"Can't say I did. He would ride there on his horse and there wasn't another horse to ride, and I'm too old and lame to run behind it."

"Is this the horse that kicks?"

"Kicks? Old Midnight? He doesn't have any kick or bite in him, sweet old fellow. I would groom him and get him all saddled up for the master, then rub him down after he returned home. I'd cut him fresh grass and bring him tasty branches from the hedgerows, and fallen apples."

"Sir Anselm told me that his horse was inclined to kick other horses, so he'd asked the groom at Bradenstoke to not tie another horse up near him." Why would Sir Anselm lie about something so innocuous?

"If that's true I know nothing of it. He's a big, slow beast, but doesn't have a mean bone in his body."

"I suppose you must stay and look after him and the

sheep until Sir Anselm's affairs can be settled." She'd attempted to find Father Gilbert's family to return his prayerbook, but so far found no trace of them. Perhaps the animals could be auctioned off to provide alms for old Teddy who might now find himself cast out into the world again. "Did he ever speak of his family or where he came from?"

"Never, my lady. Didn't talk much at all, except to ask for a cup of ale or a plate of meat. Left me entirely to my own ends in the garden. He trusted me, I suppose."

"He seems very lucky to have had such a capable and faithful servant."

The two guards were sent back to the dungeon until Ela had a chance to talk to the girl about them. She'd have to punish them for their laxity but wanted to understand the full extent of what happened before she chose their fate.

As she rode home she wondered why Sir Anselm had lied about his horse kicking when he left it tied up at Bradenstoke. Was he trying to draw attention to his arrival for some reason?

CHAPTER 19

The following day, Ela opened a letter from her mother with news about Hubert de Burgh.

"Darling Ela, I'm sure you'll find it sobering to learn that the king's former justiciar has now been reduced to living the life of a cloistered monk. No longer does he enjoy the company of his servants or the soft touch of fine clothes. His aides have been taken away and he is to receive no more than a half pennyworth of bread per day, to be washed down with a solitary cup of beer! Worse yet, for one so deeply pious, they've taken away his psalter that he should not even enjoy the solace of praying for the salvation of his soul."

Ela could hear the sarcasm dripping from the words. Her mother had even illustrated the margins with hastily inked images of his sad face and a mean loaf of bread. She felt a smile spread across her mouth, then wiped it away. Instead of gloating over her enemy's suffering, she would do better to pray for her own soul.

Still, she was waiting with bated breath for the forty days of sanctuary to end. At that time Hubert would have to choose between starving and facing justice.

Ela cornered Haughton as the jurors dispersed. "Do you have any idea what might have caused the guards and the servant to fall asleep so fast?"

"There are a few different preparations that could cause a man to sleep so fast...henbane, mandrake, and nightshade are all potent."

"Aren't those all deadly poisons?"

"In great enough quantities. In smaller doses, they'll render a man senseless for a while. I used them back when I was a fighting man and had to cut off a soldier's injured limb. They keep the patient quiet and still."

Ela crossed herself at this gruesome image.

"Wild lettuce is a more harmless substance but likely wouldn't knock them out as fast. More rare, but still potent is the juice of the poppy seed."

"Opium?"

He nodded. "It can be used to induce sleep."

"Would these be items that could be bought at an apothecary shop like the one owned by Wilf, the dead man?"

"Indeed they would, my lady. I showed Sarah Willow where they were on the shelves and helped her reorganize them so she might find them more easily."

"If Sir Anselm did indeed kill old Wilf the Younger, as I suspect, then he could have helped himself to whatever substances he wanted. But why would he want all his servants asleep? And why would he drink it himself?"

Haughton shrugged. "I suppose he might have wanted all the others asleep if he was expecting a visitor and didn't want them to see him. Or if he wished to sneak out unobserved."

"But Teddy Blakely says he drank the wine himself, and he doesn't seem to have roused from his bed in time to save his life, which suggests that he was dosed with it as well. I'll visit the girl at once and get her account of what happened."

ELA SET out at once for Kissy's cottage, with Bill beside her. Kissy was outside weeding a patch of cabbage as Ela rode up. She ran inside at the sight of Ela and her party. Her mother came out, squinting in the autumn sun, and asked Ela what she could do for her.

"I need to speak with your daughter about the night her master was killed."

Her mother looked reluctant. "She's skittish as a newborn colt, my lady. I hate to frighten her further."

"I'm afraid we have no choice if we are to catch her master's killer. Please bring her here at once or I'll have to take her back to my castle to speak in front of a jury." She didn't want either of them to think the girl was entirely above suspicion.

The girl came outside again, twisting a lock of mousy hair between her fingers. "Good day, my lady," she said, looking at the ground.

"Did you prepare a jug of wine that Teddy served to the guards?"

"No, my lady."

"Then who did?"

"I don't know, my lady."

"Where did the wine barrel sit inside the house?"

"In the kitchen."

"And where were you at the time it was served?"

"I was upstairs in my room trying to mend a hole in my cloak. I didn't have any extra thread and had to pull some out of the hem to do it."

"So who would have tapped the barrel?"

"Probably Teddy, my lady." This contradicted Teddy's account since he'd also said he didn't know who prepared the jug of wine.

"Did your master ever tap the barrel for himself?"

"Oh yes, often. He stayed up later than any of us and liked to sit drinking into the night."

"Did your master ever take herbs to help him sleep?"

She seemed to think for a moment. "I don't remember him taking herbs. He just used to drink wine until either his head hit the table in front of him or he crawled up to bed."

"Do you remember seeing any herbs in the house?"

"Of course, my lady. We had rosemary, sage, and thyme hanging in the kitchen to use for cooking."

"I mean medicinal herbs. That might be in a bottle or jar or perhaps in a folded piece of cloth or parchment."

"Never seen any, my lady."

Ela resolved to return and search the house for the herbs.

"Did your master ever use you ill or lay a hand on you? Even while saying he was being kind or sweet to you?" She watched the girl's face closely.

"No, my lady, he didn't. My mam told me to watch out for such things and to bite him if he did, but he never even looked at me funny."

"Did anyone offer you a cup of wine from this jug that was poured on that night?"

"Teddy gave me a cup of it and I took it with thanks then poured it out when he wasn't looking. Wine turns my stomach something awful. I don't know how the master drank so much of it."

Ela stared at her for a moment. "Did the master ask Teddy to give it to you?"

"I didn't hear him ask, but I suppose he might have."

Did Teddy give all of them the drink of his own accord? On his master's death he'd lose his home and work that he enjoyed. What reason could he have for wanting Sir Anselm dead?

Ela stopped at Sir Anselm's manor on the way home from Kissy's house. She and her guards and Bill searched every inch of the place, finding quantities of grime and spiderwebs but no trace of any herbs or potions.

She took the opportunity to question Teddy again about who tapped the keg and served the jug of wine. He became a little flustered and at first said that he did, and then that Sir Anselm did. Ela began to wonder if she should arrest him, but that left the problem of what to do about the old horse and the sheep, so she decided to leave him in place for the time being.

Ela arrived home to find a summons from the ecclesiastical authorities for Alisande to appear in front of an ecclesiastical court to face trial on a charge of witchcraft and sorcery.

Petronella stood nearby. "What could happen to her?"

"Well, I suppose the worst-case scenario is that she's convicted of witchcraft."

"Will they kill her?"

"Not for being a witch. Excommunication and possibly exile of some sort would be the usual punishment. But if they decide that her actions—imaginary or otherwise—caused Father Gilbert or Father Augustine's death, they might take her life."

"But that's ridiculous," said Petronella. "Everyone now knows the two priests were poisoned with the deadly mushroom."

"Indeed. Which is why this comes as a surprise. I was hoping the hostility toward Sister Alisande would fade away, but someone must be stirring it." Father Sebastian perhaps. He seemed very keen to rid Bradenstoke of its elderly anchoress, for both spiritual and financial reasons.

"Did Sir Richard Marshal offer to find her a new home? You'd mentioned that he wanted to pay for a lawyer."

"That was before he discovered that there was no traceable link between her and his family. What does she say about her past?"

Petronella knitted her brows. "I've tried to make sense of it but she just says her father was Robert Marshal and she grew up in a castle and came to Bradenstoke as a young girl. Exactly what I told you."

"Let's talk to her now. At the very least I need to warn her about this summons. If the church insists I'll have to give her up to them."

"But you're the sheriff," protested Petronella.

"I have jurisdiction in secular matters, but in ecclesiastical matters they rule supreme. If they take her and try her in their courts there's nothing I can do to protect her."

Petronella looked tearful at the prospect. They climbed the stairs to Sister Alisande's chamber in anxious silence. When they knocked, there was no answer, so Petronella opened the door gently. Sister Alisande was kneeling at her prie-dieu, murmuring prayers under her breath.

Ela cleared her throat. "I'm sorry to disturb you, dear Alisande, but I must ask you some important questions."

Alisande rose from her knees very slowly, and with considerable effort. "Yes, my lady."

"Which castle did you grow up in?" The marshal family had numerous estates. If she could determine which one Alisande had lived in, that could help her narrow down the correct branch of the family.

"Why, it was so long ago that I hardly remember, my lady."

"Please try." If she couldn't get the Marshal family to defend this woman, she had no allies other than Ela, who—as sheriff—was supposed to be impartial. "What was the name of your father's father?"

"I'm afraid I don't know, my lady." Alisande's thin smile reached her pale eyes, which always seemed to beam with peace and goodwill toward all men. "Perhaps I did once, but I've forgotten. It's been many years—a lifetime—since I saw any of them."

"Did any of your family visit you? Perhaps when you were younger?"

"Oh no. The last rites were performed when I entered my cell as an anchoress. I was declared dead to the world. They wouldn't come to visit a dead person." She shone her beatific smile on Ela and Petronella.

Ela blinked, trying to comprehend this. "You never saw any of them again?"

"Not after I took my vows, my lady. I didn't intend to ever leave my cell again and I'm sorry for all this trouble I've caused."

"Which town was your castle near?"

"I don't know, my lady."

"Do you know which county it was in?"

"I don't. I lived a sheltered life." She smiled again.

Ela looked at Petronella. How could she not have any idea of the name of her castle or the vicinity that it sat in?

"Dear Sister Alisande has lived to a very great age," said Petronella softly. "She's filled her head with prayer and praises and no doubt any useless information has fallen by the wayside on her journey to holiness."

Ela nodded. Alisande was certainly old enough to have lost many of her memories even without her solitary existence. “I’m afraid the bishop wants you to appear before an ecclesiastical court on a charge of witchcraft.”

Sister Alisande’s face didn’t flinch. “I shall do my best to answer their questions.”

“I was hoping the Marshal family would provide you with a lawyer to represent you, but they can’t seem to fathom how you’re related to them so I’m afraid they’re shirking the responsibility.”

“I trust my fate to the Lord,” said Sister Alisande softly. “I’ve breathed the air of this earth for long enough and I surrender myself to the bishop and his court to do with me what they will.”

Ela inhaled slowly. She’d trust her fate to the Lord long before she’d rest it in the hands of some of the clerics she’d met. Their motivation was often anything but holy—and she suspected this to be the case in the efforts to expel Alisande from her lifelong home.

“That is brave of you, dear Sister Alisande,” said Ela. “But in the meantime, I shall endeavor to delay their efforts.”

On learning that Haughton was in the mortuary with Anselm’s corpse, Ela decided to pay him a visit. As always the sight of a dead man’s pale and waxy naked flesh gave her a frisson of horror as she entered.

“Good day,” she said, with as much cheer as she could manage. “Have you learned anything new from your examination?”

“Only that he has several healed injuries, one to his left knee, another to his right shoulder, and yet another to the toe of one foot, which must have been crushed at one point.” Haughton still bent over the corpse, peering at his left knee.

“Can you tell how he sustained these injuries?” asked Ela.

"The shoulder injury could have happened during a fall from a horse. I can see that his collarbone has been reset. I suppose the knee injury could be similar, but could also be from a kick or a blow. He was a soldier, didn't you say?"

"Yes, and I've already heard some news back from my steward on his military record."

"Oh yes?" Haughton stood up and wiped his hands on a linen cloth.

"He was never a particularly distinguished warrior but did fight in all the conflicts he mentioned. And he fought alongside Hubert de Burgh, on the side of King John, during the Barons' War."

"I see."

"My husband, of course, fought on the other side out of a sense of conviction. It was one of the many reasons there was bad blood between him and de Burgh even after the conflict was over. And my steward found a small and telling detail amongst the old records." Ela tried to sound less frantic than she felt. "Anselm Allsop was accused of stealing a lady's gold ring during the siege of Windsor Castle. He denied the charge but was found guilty until Hubert de Burgh spoke up in his defense."

"So he owed de Burgh a favor," said Haughton.

"It appears so. But I'm at a loss for how to establish a convincing connection between Allsop and de Burgh, let alone de Burgh and Father Gilbert Berwick. And, according to all accounts, including Sister Alisande's, Allsop didn't go anywhere near Father Gilbert's cell when he visited in the days before his death."

"If de Burgh had Sir Anselm killed, to cover up the fact that he'd hired him to kill the priest to whom he'd confessed confidences, perhaps you can prove the link."

"Except that we have no idea who killed Sir Anselm," said Ela.

"Or do we?" Haughton shot her a mischievous look. "My visit to the apothecary shop proved quite interesting. Sarah Willow said that her husband asked her for a sleeping draught and she gave him some of the powdered mandrake I'd showed her."

"What?" Ela stared at him.

"He procured a sleeping draft the very day that it was given to the guards, Teddy Blakely, and Sir Anselm himself."

Ela steadied herself on the table. "But why? He's a sheep farmer. He has no military service and has probably never even heard of Hubert de Burgh. What would he have to do with any of this?"

"I suspect you should call him before a jury and find out."

CHAPTER 20

Confused by this new and unexpected turn of events, Ela sent guards to arrest Lucas Willow and called for a jury to meet the next morning. She also had guards summon Teddy Blakely to serve as a witness.

Lucas Willow had been placed in the dungeon the night before and was brought into the hall once the jury assembled. His wife Sarah had arrived early, railing against the injustice of his arrest and accusing Ela of harassing innocent people.

"You, too, can be arrested, Mistress Willow," said Ela. "But for now you shall be our first witness." She had the guards place the angry woman in the chair amidst the jury tables. "Sir Giles Haughton informs me that your husband asked for a sleeping draught and you were able to give him a rather dangerous herb to that effect based on knowledge that the coroner shared with you about the substances kept in the shop you recently inherited."

"I told him to be very careful and only use a small amount. He just wanted a good night's sleep, you see."

"Did your husband have trouble sleeping?"

"Not usually, no, but I suppose all the to-do and commotion over me running the shop has upset him. I leave early in the morning to go into Devizes and come back after dark, so all the running of the farm is left to him and I haven't been there to cook and clean as usual. I'm hoping to hire a girl once the business is settled." Mistress Willow looked quite confident in her new role as shopkeeper, despite the apparent inconveniences to her husband.

"Have any other customers asked for a sleeping draught since you took over the shop?"

"No, my lady. And if they did I'd probably advise them to try a posset of milk thistle as it's a good deal safer than mandrake. I only gave my husband the more potent remedy as he complained that milk thistle wouldn't be enough for his wakefulness."

"Did you know that the guards outside Sir Anselm's house and his servant Teddy were given a sleeping draught on the night Sir Anselm was murdered?"

Sarah Willow's stunned silence answered the question for her. "I heard that the master was killed, but nothing about that. What would my Lucas have to do with it?"

"That's what I'm trying to ascertain, Mistress." Whatever it was, Ela was fairly sure that Sarah Willow knew nothing about it. She dismissed the woman but told her to stay in the hall.

Ela then called Lucas Willow into the center of the jurors. The sheep farmer had an uncharacteristically solemn expression as he took his place in the chair.

"Why did you ask your wife for a sleeping draught two days ago?"

"I was having trouble sleeping," he said. He didn't meet her eyes.

"So you took the substance only for yourself?"

"Yes," he mumbled, still looking down.

"It seems an awful coincidence that you happened to acquire a quantity of mandrake on the same day that two of my guards and Teddy Blakely were given a potion that put them to sleep for a long interval while Teddy's master was murdered."

He didn't reply. He sat very still in the chair, feet flat on the floor, as if expecting a blow or perhaps a bolt of lightning from the ceiling.

Ela knew he wasn't telling the whole truth. "I believe that you somehow conspired to put the substance in the cups of wine they drank, but why?"

"I had trouble sleeping." For a moment he screwed up his face, shutting his eyes tight. "As well you might when you discover that a man you thought was your friend had murdered your father-in-law in cold blood." Now he looked up and a fire shone in his pale blue eyes.

Stunned, Ela tried to process this. "You killed Sir Anselm?"

"I did." His wife let out a wail of distress. "My wife knows nothing of it. My dear friend Teddy came to me in a panic because he'd realized his master was a murderer and he was afraid that he'd be the next one killed."

"Teddy Blakely, please come stand before the jurors."

Blakely shuffled forward, a look of utter desperation on his weathered face. "Did you tell Lucas Willow that your master had killed someone?"

He nodded, lips now quivering.

"Who did your master kill?"

Teddy swallowed hard. "He killed old Wilf the apothecary because he'd seen me in there buying the mushroom powder and he didn't want anyone to connect it back to him."

"He told you this?"

"Yes. I'd asked him about the powder because I…I…" He broke off and a strangled sound came from his throat. "I was the one who sprinkled it in Father Gilbert's prayerbook. He had me climb into the presbytery through a window and told me just which room to go in, and I had to wear gloves and a cloth tied over my face which he said was for a disguise. He told me I had just a few moments to do it in while he was in the chapel making his confession and that he'd meet me back in the lane."

"Did you pass anyone on your way to Father Gilbert's room?"

"No, they were all away from their rooms doing other things at that time of day. I suppose he knew that."

"Did you know the powder was poison?"

"I didn't, I swear! He said it was to kill insects that were eating the precious vellum pages and that his brother wouldn't take care of it but preferred to leave such things up to the Lord so he wanted to kill the creatures without him knowing."

"And when did you realize that the dust killed Father Gilbert?"

"I was living very isolated on his manor so it was quite some time before I got the news that Father Gilbert was poisoned. At that time I asked Sir Anselm if the powder I put in his book was what killed him and he said yes but assured me that no one would trace it back to me because old Wilf was dead. At that moment I knew he'd strangled Wilf, especially since Lucas Willow told me he'd been in the blacksmith shop next door on the night he was murdered. I was quite ill myself that night. I suppose I might have swallowed a few grains of the mushroom powder since I didn't know it was deadly."

Teddy Blakely was now shaking like a leaf.

"When did you two speak?" asked Ela of Lucas Willow.

Willow squared his shoulders. "One evening when Sir Anselm was tipping his cup in the Three Keys, I hurried to the manor and asked Teddy about his master. I thought it odd that Anselm was so near the apothecary shop on the night my father in law was killed, and for so long, almost like he was waiting for an opportunity."

"And Teddy told you that he'd had a hand in killing Father Gilbert."

"Yes." Willow looked sad. "He swore up and down that he had no idea it was to kill him. And he said that now Sir Anselm has killed two people, three in fact, one of them to keep him quiet. He was worried that he would be next."

"I suspect that was a legitimate concern," said Ela. "Did you wonder why he hadn't killed you already?"

Teddy rubbed his forehead with a thick hand. "I suppose he depended on me to grow his food and tend to his sheep. He didn't seem to know how to do anything himself and would have starved without me. But I knew I had to tell someone as once the growing season was over and enough store put aside for the winter, I felt my time running short."

"What made you tell Lucas Willow about this?"

"I needed to tell someone. I was afraid for my life. And I wanted him to know that Sir Anselm killed his father-in-law."

"Were you hoping that Lucas Willow would come take revenge and thus save your life while condemning his own?" She asked it as if it was a perfectly normal question.

Teddy Blakely started to blubber with tears. "I don't know, my lady. I don't know what I thought would happen. I didn't expect him to kill anyone."

"I wonder about that," said Ela slowly. "Since he wasn't in the house on the night that the sleeping draught was passed around, was he?"

Blakely shook his head. Then sighed a shuddering sigh. "No, I put the ground mandrake root in the wine. I was careful not to put in too much because Lucas told me it could be dangerous. Just enough to knock them into a deep sleep. I drank it myself."

"And what did you think he was going to do while everyone, including you, was sleeping?"

Blakely swiped at his tears. "I don't know."

Lucas Willow spoke up. "Teddy Blakely never asked me to kill anyone. Even I didn't know for certain what I'd do when I got face to face with the man. I came right out and asked him if he killed my father in law and he said he did."

"He wasn't asleep when you arrived?"

"He was drowsy enough but I woke him up. I didn't want a hardened killer fully awake to slay me in my boots. He woke up enough to fix me with a stare that half froze my blood—looked me right in my eyes and said he'd killed old Wilf and that I'd be next. Then he reached down under the bed. I caught a glimpse of a sword down there and I made my move before he could grab it."

"You stabbed him?" asked Ela, already sure of the answer.

"Aye." Lucas Willow led out a shuddering sigh. "I did it from my anger at him killing my father-in-law who was a good man who helped everyone in the town and for miles around. Wilf was old, but might have lived for many years yet. Now he's dead and my wife is too busy to be my wife and the murderer was questioned then let off scot-free by the sheriff."

Ela stiffened. "He was still under investigation, which is why two guards were stationed by the lane to his property."

"They weren't much use, were they?" asked Willow. "Anyone could have come and gone through the woods on the other side of the house without them being any the wiser. And what kind of guards take wine from the house they're supposed to be guarding?"

"They did neglect their duties," admitted Ela. "But you

should have come to me instead of taking the law into your own hands."

"You already locked me up in your jail," he said with force. "How was I to trust I wouldn't end up in there again while he killed my old friend? And I was afraid that you'd arrest Teddy for killing the priest by sprinkling the powder in his book."

"Teddy himself should have come forward as soon as he realized what he'd done. Instead, he stayed silent while his master killed again."

Teddy sobbed, face in his hands.

"Did the girl, Kissy, know about any of this?" asked Ela.

"Nothing, my lady," said Willow. "Teddy told me he wanted to put her to sleep as well so she wouldn't raise the alarm."

"You didn't want her to be startled awake and possibly foil your plot to kill Sir Anselm Allsop by violence in the middle of the night?" asked Ela, coolly. He'd come armed and ready to kill.

Willow looked down and his shoulders slumped. "I didn't set out to kill him—not until he admitted that he'd killed my father in law. But I didn't want her to get in the way."

"So you and Teddy did plot and plan to have the household asleep to give you a chance to confront Sir Anselm?"

"Yes, my lady," said Lucas Willow very quietly. Blakely still sobbed like a child.

"But why did Teddy Blakely take the sleeping draught himself? He was still asleep when we arrived."

"I told him to. I didn't want him to get scared and he'd have to be tied up so it would look like I overpowered him. It was all my idea, not his."

Ela fixed her gaze on Teddy Blakely. "Just like the plan to kill Father Gilbert was not your idea, but you were the agent of his death?"

Shoulders heaving, Teddy Blakely looked up at her with bloodshot eyes. "Yes, my lady."

Ela glanced at Haughton. This was not at all how she had expected this murder to have unfolded. "As participants in a murder plot, you will both be held in custody until the assizes."

Peter Howard, the baker, raised his hand. "My lady, one could give them credit for ridding Wiltshire of a murderer."

"It is not fitting for ordinary men to take justice into their own hands."

Howard nodded. "You're right, my lady, I just..." he paused. "He was defending himself against a known murderer who'd reached for his sword."

Ela looked at the jury. "Are there any others among you who would like to award Lucas Willow and his henchman the key to Salisbury Castle for his bravery and cunning?"

The jurors sat silent.

"I do have another question, that could find you some leniency if answered carefully and well," she said, after a pause for thought. "Sir Anselm was paid to kill Father Gilbert. Do you know who paid him?"

Lucas Willow looked at Teddy Blakely, who shook his head.

"Did any stranger or strangers come to the house?"

"Never, my lady. Not a one," said Blakely.

Ela sagged, trying to clutch the thin thread of hope that she could find and accuse the true mastermind behind this spate of local killings. With no evidence at all pointing to Hubert de Burgh, she could hardly raise his name at the assizes without endangering herself. "One more question. Was Father Gilbert really Sir Anselm's brother?"

"I don't know, my lady," said Blakely.

"I doubt it," said Willow. "He never mentioned him to anyone and he'd previously told me that all his family was from Warwickshire and he hadn't spoken to any of them in years. Surely he'd have mentioned a brother living locally. I think he just made it up so no one would suspect him of killing him even though he visited him just a few days before he died."

Sarah Willow, now streaming with tears, called out, "How could you, Lucas! I would never have given you the mandrake if you'd told me what you intended to use it for."

"I know, my wife. That's why I didn't tell you." He looked directly at Ela. "My Sarah is a good woman and in time I think she'll be as good an apothecary as her father. She had nothing to do with any of this."

"Now I'll be a widow! And what's to happen to your sheep and the cow? I don't have time to tend to them and run the shop."

"I'll take charge of all the animals left untended by both of you." Ela gave a servant orders to have them brought to her pastures. "And their fate shall be determined at the Assizes."

CHAPTER 21

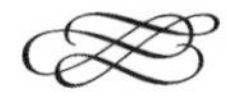

In late October, Ela traveled to Westminster to provide her accounts to the king. Her steward traveled with her to manage the collection of ledgers and scrolls that accounted for every penny in her coffers and every acre and roof and window and chimney of her own estates and holdings as well as those of others in the county.

"Ela, my dear." The king welcomed her into his accounting room, a sort of library where ledgers lined the walls and scribes and clerks sat hunched over tables, scratching at parchment with their quills. "I do hope your accounts will be found to be complete and in order."

"I personally guarantee them, Your Grace," she said, gesturing for her steward and porter to deposit the large trunk of ledgers on the floor for his clerks to inspect. "You will find detailed records of the taxes collected from the king's subjects in Wiltshire in the years since I first had the honor of becoming sheriff."

"I had hoped to see accounts dating back to the years that your husband served as sheriff," said the king, lifting his chin imperiously.

Ela stiffened. "I, too, had hoped for that, Your Grace, but I'm afraid the records were no longer complete. You may recall that a scoundrel named Simon de Hal preceded me in the office, and I can only assume that he had some reason for disposing of them."

Records before her time were patchy and inconsistent. She wasn't about to tarnish her late husband's reputation or endanger her own family by admitting that record-keeping under his tenure might not have been the best.

Simon de Hal had been named sheriff and installed in her castle by Hubert de Burgh after her husband's death. With his reputation for violence and intimidation, de Burgh had no doubt hoped to frighten her away from her ancestral home. How little he knew her.

It had required considerable effort and expense to recover her castle and take the role of sheriff and she didn't feel even an ounce of guilt at blaming the enemy she'd vanquished.

"Naturally I expect you to keep careful records going forward," said the king. "And I'm happy to announce that I'll be collecting a new tax of one-fortieth part of the moveable possessions of each of my free subjects."

Ela's heart sank. "Do you mean the nobles?" She could already picture one-fortieth of her carefully bred sheep and stored apples and carved chairs and casks of wine being loaded onto wagons headed for King Henry's stores. Not to mention one-fortieth of the value of the family's books and jewels and silver cups and other treasures.

"The nobles, to be sure, but every man who owns a pot to piss in—including farmers and freemen—will be charged with sending me one-fortieth of his worldly goods."

"And the sheriff of each county is to collect and account for all these goods and chattels?" said Ela, despite already knowing the answer.

"Indeed, and to provide them to me in their entirety," said Henry cheerfully. "That I may sustain my household and—with God's help—regain our lost possessions on the continent and subdue our enemies in Wales."

"Your wish is my command," muttered Ela woodenly. What an administrative nightmare that would be! And everyone would blame her—Ela of Salisbury—for the pillaging of their fortunes rather than the king himself.

"And I have excellent news regarding my former justiciar, Hubert de Burgh." He beamed. Ela braced herself for the news that Hubert had been forgiven and granted seven new castles to compensate for his suffering. Could this morning get any worse?

"Perhaps you know that he'd been left without aides and attendants and granted only a crust of bread and a cup of ale per day. The forty days of his sanctuary have now run out and the bread and ale have been withheld. He shall now choose whether to face justice or to starve."

"Do you expect him to surrender?" asked Ela, relieved that de Burgh was still on the defensive.

"I confess that I expected him to surrender two months ago when this ordeal started. I offered him the choice of leaving England forever, enduring perpetual imprisonment, or coming to face me in London. I had thought him a man of honor who would stand on his own two feet and face me to account for his crimes. He has proven instead that he is a sniveling coward willing to hide behind the clergy rather than account for his misdeeds."

The king invited Ela to join him for the midday meal, while her steward stayed behind to show his books to the clerks. She sat next to him near the head of the table and they were enjoying a platter of jellied eels when Armand de Périgord, the Grand Master of the Knights Templar, was announced and shown into the king's hall.

After their initial greeting, Henry cleared his throat. "I've been informed that Hubert de Burgh has a great treasure stored with you at your New Temple here in London. Is this true?"

De Périgord, a tall, imposing man with chiseled features and a dark cloak swept back over his shoulders, made a small bow. "You have been informed correctly, Your Grace." Ela expected him to say more, but he simply stood, waiting for the king to speak again.

"Well, then," said Henry, looking eager. "How much money does he have with you? Or is this treasure in jewels and trinkets?"

"I'm afraid I can't say, Your Grace."

Henry stared at him in disbelief. "You won't say? I'm your king. You shall tell me at once."

"I wish I could, Your Grace, but any money or goods deposited with us are locked away in an individual vault and none of us has the right to open it. We are charged with guarding and protecting it for the one who deposited it there."

"The man who deposited funds with you is a traitor and thief who robbed my royal treasury!" growled Henry. "Anything deposited in your temple is mine by right and must be returned to me immediately!"

De Périgord stood calm and steady as a knight tilting toward an opponent at the joust. "As Knights Templar, we are servants of God before we serve any man, Your Grace. I do not wish to offend you—nothing pains me more—but we are bound by our oath to safeguard any treasure unless we have explicit permission from the one who charged us to keep it."

"I dare him to refuse!" cried Henry. Ela didn't think she'd ever seen him angrier. This falling out with his longtime advisor had brought out a darker side of him. "Go to him where he is taking sanctuary and secure permission, for I will have the treasure that he stole from me."

De Périgord bowed again and promised to make haste to the church at once.

Henry was still breathing hard, fury rolling through him, as the knight made his exit. "The arrogance! Those Templars think they're above the laws of my kingdom."

Because they are, thought Ela. Though she very sensibly kept silent. The order had been founded in Jerusalem, not England, and was over a hundred years old. Originally started to protect pilgrims on the routes to the Holy Land, the Templars had become a financial powerhouse throughout Christendom. They probably had more money stashed under lock and key in their New Temple than King Henry III would see in his entire lifetime—and Henry knew it. The king was still expostulating about Hubert's legendary avarice and ill-gotten wealth over a rich pear tart when a messenger appeared with urgent news.

The young man wore royal livery that was considerably splattered with mud and dust, probably from a long ride. "I come directly from the church where your former justiciar has taken refuge, Your Grace. Hubert de Burgh has assented to throw himself upon your mercy and accept whatever fate you choose for him."

The king clapped his hands together. "At last. I did not wish for my former confidant to starve, no matter how ill he has treated me. Have the sheriffs of Hereford and Essex conduct him here—in chains—and secure him in the Tower to await his fate."

The messenger was dismissed with this news, and the king ordered more wine for all to celebrate his former justiciar's surrender.

"I imagine that you've decided his fate already," said Ela

quietly. "Given the length of time that's passed since he was first called to account."

"I find myself torn, dear Ela," said Henry. "Part of me would like to see him hung from the battlements for the liberties that he's taken with the royal coffers and for putting his interests ahead of my own on many occasions. But I don't wish to make a martyr of him, either. So perhaps a life of imprisonment would be preferable to a sentence of death."

"He's a cunning man, Your Grace," said Ela carefully. "Who has decades of experience in turning events to his advantage, no matter how long the odds."

"What you say is true, dear lady," said Henry. He paused, watching her. "And from your words, I surmise that you'd like to see him dead."

Ela swallowed, suddenly sure she'd gone too far. "Oh no, Your Grace. I simply wish to caution you that if he is to be kept as a prisoner it will have to be managed carefully and well." An idea occurred to her. "The castle at Devizes would be an excellent stronghold for him to reside in, should that be your choice. I can personally take responsibility for him being kept secure and safe from rescue or escape."

Henry's young face took on a curious expression. "I had no idea you took such a deep interest in the matter, dear Ela. Why keep him in Devizes and not at Salisbury Castle, secured by the royal garrison?"

Ela had no desire to invite a poisonous adder into her bed-chamber. "I'm sure it would be safer for him to be removed from the administrative center of Wiltshire. My castle has too many powerful men coming and going and too much risk that a friend might gain access to him there. Devizes is more suited to maintaining him in quiet solitude to contemplate the errors and misdeeds of his long life."

"I see what you mean and you make good sense." Henry

stared at his bejeweled wine cup for several long moments. "Or perhaps I'll just hang him."

~

HUBERT DE BURGH'S appearance before the king took place at the king's court in Corn Hill in London. Ela attended, along with earls and barons from all corners of the realm, and many of Hubert's detractors who'd been waiting to see him get his comeuppance after years of arrogant and imperious conduct as the king's trusted advisor.

Hubert's wife, Princess Margaret of Scotland—the bride whom Hubert stood accused of stealing from his royal master—sat among the nobles, swathed in black like a nun or a penitent.

Henry allowed Hubert's enemies to enumerate their accusations against him. Most of them Ela had heard before: he had stolen from the king's treasury; seized estates that by rights belonged to others; that he'd undermined the king's long-awaited expedition to France and allowed the Welsh to run roughshod over English territory. There were the familiar accusations from the Vatican that de Burgh had encouraged the ill-treatment of Italian clergy and the seizure of their goods and property. And, of course, there were the persistent and spreading rumors that de Burgh had poisoned men he considered rivals or impediments to his goals, including her husband.

New charges were added since de Burgh had granted the Templars permission to turn over all his keys and treasure to King Henry to do with as he pleased. Henry had ordered his clerks to empty the vaults and to count the treasure. De Burgh's vaults were found to contain eight thousand pounds in silver coins, a hundred and forty goblets of silver and gold, and a quantity of jewels so valuable as to be worth more than all the other contents combined.

This vast wealth, secreted away from the public eye, flushed out a new round of accusations from Hubert's enemies. There was no shortage of men in the kingdom now willing to wield the sword that would dispatch the former justiciar to meet his final judge.

Ela found herself salivating at the prospect that justice would finally be served to the man who'd taken her husband from her. There would be no need to trace the connection between de Burgh and the murders at Bradenstoke and in Devizes if the man who'd ordered the killings had already descended to hell and was roasting amid the eternal flames. She knew Richard Marshal was eager for the same redress of his family grievances, since he had led the charge against de Burgh in recent weeks.

But Henry demurred. He rose and walked into the middle of the room, where de Burgh sat—looking frail and old and dressed in plain black clothes—in a solitary chair amid the crowds.

"This is not a trial," he said, looking at de Burgh. "Because you have placed your life and your fate in my hands. There shall be no lawyers deliberating and making arguments because I alone—who know you better than any man alive—shall be your judge. There are many here today who will feel satisfaction only if they see you at the end of a rope or meeting the sharp blade of a sword or axe."

Ela watched de Burgh's jaw twitch as the king conjured these gruesome images. She tried not to enjoy it too much. She'd suffered such paroxysms of fury at watching de Burgh roam free while her husband was dead and gone. To finally see him squirming like a salted slug was a sinful pleasure indeed.

"However," continued Henry. "Looking around at the

assembled earls and barons, I am aware that Hubert has faithfully served first my uncle, King Richard, next my father, King John, and—although he has acted badly toward me—he shall not suffer an unjust death at my hands. I would rather be considered a foolish and easy king than a cruel and tyrannical one."

Ela sagged inwardly. Hubert de Burgh would live.

Henry announced that Hubert would not retake any of the royal castles, wardships, or properties that he'd gained during his own rule, but he went on to grant him back all the lands that he had been given by King John and that he had bought for himself, that they should provide the means to support him going forward.

"Hubert de Burgh shall be remanded to the castle at Devizes," he announced, just as Ela began to despair that he'd be punished at all. "Where he shall remain in custody under the control of my brother Earl Richard; William, Earl of Warenne; William, Earl of Ferrers...." Ela listened, praying for her name to be called. Devizes was in Wiltshire—her jurisdiction—and she held an earldom just as the others did. "And Richard Marshal, Earl of Pembroke."

Ela glanced at Richard Marshal, glad that another person whose family had suffered cruel injury at de Burgh's hands would be charged with keeping him under lock and key. Still, she smarted that her name was not among those formally chosen to guard him.

But she would guard him as if her own life depended upon it.

CHAPTER 22

November 1232

Two weeks of severe storms had buffeted the south of England in the wake of Hubert de Burgh's trial. A superstitious person might perhaps have interpreted the tempests as a sign of God's displeasure. Was He angry to find Hubert confined to Devizes castle as a prisoner? Or to be deprived of final judgment of his conduct for a few more years? Either way the recurrent thunder and lightning unsettled everyone. In the storm's wake, tree branches and blown leaves littered every inch of the countryside.

Through this debris came the procession of the traveling judge, now arrived in Salisbury to preside over the Assizes. A tall, thin man of about forty-five, Sir Tristram Beauchamp had thick blond hair liberally mixed with white, giving him a strikingly pale appearance.

Ela wished that Sir Anselm Allsop was on hand to face justice for his crimes, but unfortunately it seemed likely that Teddy Blakely and Lucas Willow would pay the price for them—as well as their own. She did, however, need to explain the role that the dead man had played in drawing these two rather hapless individuals into his evil web.

The justice and his entourage rested a night, feasting in her hall, and the trial began early the next morning. Ela had Elsie arrange for the two prisoners to be washed and combed and dressed in clean tunics so they would have the best chance of a fair trial. While she held them responsible for their own actions, she knew that without Sir Anselm's machinations, none of these murders would have taken place.

She sat next to the judge at the top of the three tables set up for the judge and jury. When the prisoners were brought in, she rose from her chair and walked around to where they were seated between the tables.

"Teddy Blakely was the servant of a man named Sir Anselm Allsop, now deceased," she announced. "From what we've learned, it seems that Allsop was charged by someone —identity unknown—to kill a priest called Father Gilbert. Our best guess is that Father Gilbert had received confidential information from this person during confession and that the mastermind behind these killings decided he'd be safer if Father Gilbert no longer walked the earth."

Sir Tristram cleared his throat. "The notes I received said something about Sir Anselm Allsop being Father Gilbert's brother. Surely a fratricide might stem from personal differences."

"We've since learned that they are not related at all. Father Gilbert's family is from Northumbria, where they still live. Once I discovered this, I was able to return his prayer book to them—carefully cleaned—and express my condolences. Father Gilbert was the younger of two siblings. Both of his parents are still alive and his older brother, who will one day inherit the family estates, lives quietly on a manor not far from Alnwick Castle. His family had no reason to suspect anyone of wanting to kill their son, but we do know that Father Gilbert regularly took confessions from a variety of outsiders, including some of the great men in the kingdom. I can provide you a list of those names if you like."

She had a clerk hand over a carefully edited list of the names of visitors to Bradenstoke during the past year. It included Hubert de Burgh but also several other nobles including the king himself. She did not intend to stick her neck out further to accuse de Burgh, since he was already imprisoned for life and thus no longer represented a danger to the populace. Since she had no solid proof to back up her suspicions, she saw no reason to risk her reputation in the effort.

Alisande was a witness to how Sir Anselm had visited Father Gilbert in the days before his death and had drawn attention to his arrival and departure by making a fuss over his kicking horse, to distract anyone from noticing his servant sneaking into the presbytery from the outside.

Now that Teddy had admitted to wielding the poison, even unwittingly, accusations of witchcraft had dried up and Ela had managed to keep Alisande safely in her castle and away from the ecclesiastical courts.

The judge and the jurors questioned Teddy about what he thought he was doing sprinkling powder in a prayerbook in secret, and Teddy repeated that he'd been sent to save the precious text from the depredations of insects.

"And why did you not come forward at once, when you realized that you were the agent of a priest's death?" asked Beauchamp of Teddy Blakely.

Blakely's chest heaved. "At first I didn't believe it. I thought the death was the work of a witch. I liked my master well enough and was grateful for the roof over my head and work I enjoyed." The beginnings of a sob caught in his throat. "By the time I realized that my master had strangled the apothecary, I knew that I'd killed the priest and I was afraid I'd be blamed for killing him. And for killing the old abbot who died from entering his room."

"So you told your friend Lucas Willow and asked for his help?" asked Beauchamp.

"No!" protested Teddy with a wail. "I asked for his advice. I was afraid to go to the sheriff but I began to worry that my master would kill me to cover his tracks, the same way he killed old Wilf so no one would trace the poison back to me or him."

"Did it not occur to you that your friend, Lucas Willow, would be incensed to learn that your master had killed his father-in-law?"

Teddy Blakely blinked. "I…I suppose I knew he'd be upset. But it never crossed my mind he'd want to k…k…kill him. I've known Lucas Willow all my life and he's the gentlest man you could ever meet."

"But you administered the sleeping drug to the guards, your master, and even yourself, which tells us that you had conspired with him and you knew exactly what he intended to do."

"I knew he wanted to confront my master and ask if he'd killed old Wilf." A sob escaped Blakely's mouth. "I wish I hadn't done it and I'm very sorry. I should have come to the sheriff."

"Indeed you should," said Beauchamp coldly. "We can't have servants and farmers taking justice into their own hands."

Unlike Teddy Blakely, Lucas Willow sat steady as a rock in his chair.

"Lucas Willow!" The judge called his name so loud that Ela jumped. "You are accused of killing a man in a violent and pre-meditated murder. What do you have to say for yourself?"

Willow sat up straighter and cleared his throat. "I apologize for taking matters into my own hands. I shouldn't have done it. But I had done business with him and exchanged words with him almost every day. We even drank together at the Three Keys. You could have knocked me over with a feather when Teddy told me he'd used him to poison the priest and that he'd murdered my father-in-law."

"Why didn't you go to the sheriff?"

"I wasn't inclined to trust the sheriff because I'd already spent time in the dungeon here, accused of killing him myself! I knew I hadn't done that and even though she let me go I was worried I'd somehow end up accused of the crime again."

"So instead you decided to commit the foulest crime a man can perpetrate?" said Beauchamp, looking very unsympathetic.

"I can't entirely say I went there with murder in mind, but I did bring my knife and sharpened it beforehand, so I can't say I didn't. Sir Anselm had been something like a friend to me. I wanted to hear from his own lips whether he did or didn't kill my father in law. When he admitted the killing and threatened my life—then reached for his sword—I thrust my knife in his chest."

Lucas Willow looked down at the flagstone floor of the hall. "Looking back I was more than a fool, but I was furious beyond reckoning. Anselm had already appeared before a jury and been set free. I thought there was a good chance he'd kill Teddy to shut his mouth for good."

Ela cleared her throat. "I must offer regret that I was not yet able to tie Sir Anselm firmly to the murders, despite having suspicion. But Lucas Willow himself knows from his own experience that quite often the first person arrested for a crime is not the actual culprit. I try to be as judicious as possible in choosing who to lock up and for how long. In this case, we had released Sir Anselm partly so we could watch him and see who was coming and going from his house, in the hope that we could find out who hired him to kill the priest."

"What makes you so sure he was hired?" asked Beauchamp. "Could he not have killed the priest on his own accord to keep his confession secret?"

"There is no evidence that Sir Anselm is a godly man. He did not attend services or make any confessions beyond the one made to occupy the priest while his room was poisoned. The person who wanted the priest dead is almost certainly a man who felt the need to unburden himself of the guilt of his sins because he had enough faith to be sure he'd suffer in the hereafter if he didn't."

"Surely piling fresh killing on top of his penance undoes the work of confessing his sins?" said Beauchamp, looking nonplussed.

"I believe that men can often seek and find justification for killings if they try hard enough. Perhaps he confessed this killing to another priest, who now has reason to fear for his life. Or he might have found that the use of a proxy absolved him of guilt."

Sir Tristram paused and stared at Willow for some moments. "If Sir Anselm was indeed the man who planned and ordered the first killing and who strangled the apothecary himself, he deserved to die. Is there any doubt in the minds of the jury about whether he did plan and execute these murders?"

The jurors shifted and muttered and finally their spokesman, Simon Hale the cordwainer, said that they were convinced that Allsop was guilty of murder, based on Teddy Blakely's testimony and the eyewitness evidence that he was lingering at the location of the second murder on the night it was committed, waiting for the opportunity to make his move.

"In that case," said the judge, rather imperiously, "perhaps Farmer Willow should be praised for bringing the swift sword of justice down on Allsop's neck when the sheriff failed to do so."

Ela stiffened. "If Teddy Blakely had come to me with his story, or if Lucas Willow had come to me with Teddy's account, I could have arrested Sir Anselm that day. A lack of eyewitness testimony hampered my investigation from the start." She knew that her desire to catch Sir Anselm's master had caused her to act rashly. She'd been so keen to use him as bait that she had taken an unnecessary risk in releasing him. "As it is I'm glad he did not have the chance to kill Teddy Blakely, as he may well have done eventually."

She didn't mention that accusations of witchcraft had thrown her early investigation off course. The last thing she wanted was to set Alisande up as a target again.

"According to the jurors, Sir Anselm was slain with a single thrust to the heart," said the judge to Lucas Willow. "You seem to be a skilled and capable killer."

"I've dispatched enough lambs and sheep to meet their maker. In this case, it was a lucky cut because he wore a nightshirt that obscured his chest. I knew at once that I'd killed him, though. He fell dead instantly."

"Did you feel guilt at killing a man?"

"Not at that time. All I could think about was getting away. And I heard a noise in the hallway so I worried someone might try to stop me."

"You heard the servant girl, who escaped out the window. Did you give chase to silence her?"

"I most certainly did not," said Willow, indignant. "I had no wish to harm the girl. Even if she'd seen me do it and screamed I wouldn't have harmed a hair on her head."

"You might never have been caught if it wasn't for your wife telling the sheriff that she'd given you the ingredients to make a powerful sleeping draught," said Beauchamp. "Are you angry with her?"

"Oh no. I'd never involve her in anything like this. She's as honest as the day is long and would never have wanted any part in it, even to avenge her own father's death."

"Is Mistress Willow here?" Beauchamp looked out at the crowd of onlookers.

Sarah Willow came forward, her face crimson beneath her kerchief and her lips pressed together.

"How do you feel about your husband's act of revenge?"

"I think he's a fool who's sacrificed his own life in vain," said Sarah, with strong emotion that didn't match her cold words. "He loved my father and visited him almost every day. But I can see why he did it because the sheriff seemed more keen to lock us up for killing his father, so we could take over his business, than to find the true culprit."

"Is this true?" asked Beauchamp of Ela.

Ela inhaled slowly, starting to feel like she was on trial here today. "As you know, family members are often the most likely suspects in any murder and there was some motivation since Mistress Willow was keen to learn the business and her father had kept her from it. Once we interviewed the Willows and confirmed their accounts, they were released and no longer under suspicion of the original crimes."

"Does the jury have anything further to say in the matter of the murder of Sir Anselm Allsop in his bed?"

After some shuffling and muttering, Thomas Pryce the old thatcher got to his feet. "Lucas Willow is a good man and a good friend to all who know him. He meant to help Teddy Blakely, who was afraid for his life. And he said Sir Anselm threatened to kill him next and was reaching for his sword, so you could argue that he stabbed him in self defense." He sat down abruptly.

Peter Howard, the baker, also rose. "Teddy Blakely wouldn't hurt a fly. He's had a very hard go of it these last few years and was happy with his new situation until the murders happened. His mind lacks penetration so he may not have fully understood what Lucas Willow might do once they were all asleep."

Another juror criticized Ela for letting Sir Anselm go prematurely and for not arresting him properly and putting him in the dungeon in the first place because he was of noble birth and not a commoner, like the two men accused.

Yet another pointed out that the two men knew for certain that Sir Anselm was a murderer, and that Lucas Willow had taken pains to obtain a confession before he drew his knife.

Kissy was called as a witness and—her voice now returned—she said she'd been woken from sleep by raised voices and had overheard the exchange between them. She said it was exactly as Lucas Willow had described it—Anselm admitted to murder and threatened another—and the words had struck such fear in her heart that she'd jumped from the window and run through the woods for home.

Finally, Sir Tristram Beauchamp banged his gavel on the table. "That's enough. I shall pronounce my verdict."

Teddy Blakely descended into tears, and Lucas Willow lifted his chin as if readying his neck for the hangman's noose.

"While I do not commend any man for taking matters of justice into his own hands, as the sheriff herself has stated, sometimes a killing is justified by the circumstances at hand. In light of the sheriff's failure to solve these murders and to arrest the perpetrator, your actions had some merit that I cannot reasonably ignore. Sir Anselm Allsop may well have killed again, either Teddy Blakely or some other person he was ordered to kill, and Wiltshire is well rid of him."

The judge stopped speaking and inhaled deeply, staring down the length of his nose at the two prisoners. "Teddy Blakely and Lucas Willow, I sentence you each to forty lashes in the public square. I trust that this trial will serve as a warning to both of you against committing any further crimes, even in the name of justice."

Lucas Willow's mouth fell open. His wife let out a whimper and fell to her knees, and two men rushed forward to support her. Teddy Blakely looked up through his tears. "Am I spared?"

"You are," said the judge, in a grave tone. "And I hope that you will make the rest of your life an example for others to follow." Then he looked at Lucas Willow. "As for you, I hope that you will endeavor to be a good husband to the woman you almost left a widow by your rash act."

Willow murmured that he would.

"This sentence shall be enacted this very afternoon, then the prisoners can return to their lives."

Ela blinked, still stunned as the guards led the two prisoners out of the hall.

She turned to Sir Tristram Beauchamp. "Your act of mercy is to be commended."

"I have no wish to be vilified by the entire county of Wiltshire for hanging two simple sons of the soil who despatched a multiple-murderer to the hereafter." Conviction sparkled in his pale eyes. "We all make mistakes and some men deserve a second chance."

"Indeed," said Ela, wondering if he was talking about her failure to bring the true villain to justice. "And one day we'll meet our final judge, who shall be the true arbiter of whether our deeds were for good or ill."

EPILOGUE

"I'm crying tears of joy, Mama," said Petronella. "I'm so grateful to finally be able to follow my vocation."

Ela held in her tears during her daughter's veiling ceremony at the newly completed monastery at Lacock. Sister Alisande would also find a new home there, as one of the community of Augustinian canonesses. They stood together, dressed in the gray cowled garment of the order, their black linen veils held in place by white fillets pinned with five red droplet-shaped pieces of fabric that commemorated the five wounds of Christ.

Bill Talbot stood next to Ela, ready to steady her if her emotions overcame her. As the new canonesses walked away into their new sanctuary, Ela turned to him and said, "One day I shall take the veil here myself."

"Not too soon, I hope, my lady," replied Bill.

"Not until my youngest is married," said Ela quietly. "I still have work to do in the world."

"Indeed you do, though the turbulent events of this year

have reached a most satisfactory conclusion," said Bill softly. "If you know what I mean."

Ela nodded. Hubert de Burgh was safely contained in the castle at Devizes. He had a servant and a library and decent meals, but not the freedom to govern the kingdom or grasp more of its estates and castles to his bosom.

The apothecary shop in the same town was doing an excellent business under the careful stewardship of Sarah Willow, who had hired young Kissy to help her wait on customers and prepare her potions and possets.

Following his public punishment, Lucas Willow had expanded his business in lambs and fleeces with the help of Teddy Blakely, who now worked for the Willows, taking care of things that Sarah no longer had time for, such as tending the garden and preserving its fruits and meats for the winter.

A new prior and abbot had been installed at Bradenstoke, and one of his first acts was to remove all traces of the former anchoress and turn Sister Alisande's former cell into a storeroom.

No one ever did find out where Alisande hailed from or who her people were. Perhaps she'd stepped out of one life—a bad marriage or an impoverished widowhood perhaps?—and into one that offered respite and peace. What good could come of digging up a long-forgotten past? Instead, Ela offered to cover her expenses as an act of charity. After her long life of prayer and forbearance, she deserved a quiet retirement in this holy sanctuary.

THE END

AUTHOR'S NOTE

I know many readers of this series have been waiting anxiously for Ela's nemesis Hubert de Burgh to get some comeuppance. History obliged by having Hubert de Burgh fall from grace in a most dramatic fashion in 1232. While—as usual—the murder mystery in this book is entirely imaginary, everything that happened to Hubert de Burgh was described by contemporary chroniclers. The accusations against him are taken from historical sources, even the more outlandish ones, such as that he gave Llywelyn of Wales a magical jewel that made him invincible. The tale of de Burgh being dragged from the altar naked—with a crucifix in one hand and a communion wafer in the other—sounds like it might have been embroidered by his enemies...but if a contemporary historian wrote it down then who am I to shrink from including such a striking image in this book? Once again I owe much to Roger of Wendover for his *Flowers of History*, which transforms the events of his own day into a page-turning scandal sheet that has provided much grist for my author's mill.

Hubert de Burgh is not always described or portrayed as

an arch villain. For most of his life he enjoyed the respect of his peers and was considered to be brilliant and loyal as well as avaricious and scheming. To explore the other sides of his character, readers might enjoy *Fixer and Fighter: The Life of Hubert de Burgh, Earl of Kent, 1170 - 1243,* by Brian Harwood, or Edith Pargeter's *Marriage of Megotta,* about de Burgh's daughter whose marriage was secretly arranged during her father's exile from royal favor.

There is no history of an anchoress at Bradenstoke Abbey, but on a 1923 map of the abbey there is a small room marked "? Vestry," nestled on an exterior wall between the nave and a side chapel, and it's there that I imagine Alisande's cell. There were well over 100 anchoresses in England during the Thirteenth century, and the *Ancren Wisse,* written as a sort of lifestyle guide for them, was penned between 1224 and 1235…so during this exact time period.

Fear of witches had not reached the fever pitch of the 1600's, so women accused of witchcraft in Ela's time might be excommunicated and exiled, but were not likely to be hanged or burned at the stake unless they were accused of some greater crime as well.

William Randolph Hearst bought the remains of Bradenstoke Abbey in 1925 and shipped the stones and timbers to the US, where elements were used to adorn his lavish residences. The tithe barn was later resold and is apparently still sitting in crates in San Luis Obispo, California.

Once again, I must give thanks to Rev. William Lisle Bowles for his exhaustive *Annals and Antiquities of Lacock Abbey* (1835), which shares so much information about Ela and her family. It's hard to imagine how much work it must have been to research such a book during the Regency era. I picture the retired vicar traveling through the countryside in a horse-drawn gig to consult crumbling medieval manuscripts, then penning the poems in his study by candlelight.

Bowles' description of a nun under Augustinian rule guided my description of Petronalla's garb at the end of the book. We don't know exactly when Petronella was veiled, but Ela entered Lacock as a nun on Christmas day in 1238 at the age of 51, and in 1240 she became abbess.

If you have questions or comments, please get in touch at jglewis@stoneheartpress.com

SERIES BOOKLIST

CATHEDRAL OF BONES

BREACH OF FAITH

THE LOST CHILD

FOREST OF SOULS

THE BONE CHESS SET

CLOISTER OF WHISPERS

PALACE OF THORNS

A SURFEIT OF MIRACLES

THE D'ALBIAC INHERITANCE

UNHOLY SANCTUARY

AUTHOR BIOGRAPHY

Author Biography

J. G. Lewis grew up in a Regency-era officer's residence in London, England. She spent her childhood visiting nearby museums and riding ponies in Hyde Park. She came to the U.S. to study semiotics at Brown University and stayed for the sunshine and a career as a museum curator in New York City. Over the years she published quite a few novels, two of which hit the USA Today list. She didn't delve into historical fiction until she discovered genealogy and the impressive cast of potential characters in her family history. Once she realized how many fascinating historical figures are all but forgotten, she decided to breathe life into them again by creating stories for them to inhabit. J. G. Lewis currently lives in Florida with her dogs and horses.

For more information visit www.stoneheartpress.com.

Copyright © *2024 by J. G. Lewis*

All Rights Reserved.

Published 2024 by Stoneheart Press

2709 N Hayden Island Drive

Suite 853852

Portland, Oregon, 97217,

USA

Without limiting the rights under copyright above, no part of this publication may be reproduced, stored in or introduced into a retrieval system, or transmitted in any form or by any means (electronic, mechanical, photocopying, recording or otherwise), without prior written permission of the copyright owner and publisher of this book.

The scanning, uploading and distribution of this book via the Internet or via any other means without the permission of the publisher is illegal and punishable by law. Please purchase only authorized electronic editions and do not participate in or encourage electronic piracy of copyrightable materials. Your support of the author's rights is appreciated.

Cover image includes: detail from Codex Manesse, ca. 1300, Heidelberg University Library; decorative detail from Beatus of Liébana, Fecundus Codex of 1047, Biblioteca Nacional de España; detail with Longespée coat of arms from Matthew Parris, Historia Anglorum, ca. 1250, British Museum.

Made in the USA
Middletown, DE
12 October 2024